While hiking in Montana, the author came across a decaying mound of cast-off artifacts at the base of the Rocky Mountains. He surmised that the discarded items were part of the hopes and dreams that early settlers had for their new life in the Oregon Territory. He wondered what must have gone through their minds when they were forced to relinquish these precious treasures, and how much that loss altered their future.

The author's experience in Montana and the memory of his Grandfather's dog, Bones, ultimately led to the story of Billy Bones.

# THE HILL COUNTRY

# THE NORTH WOODS

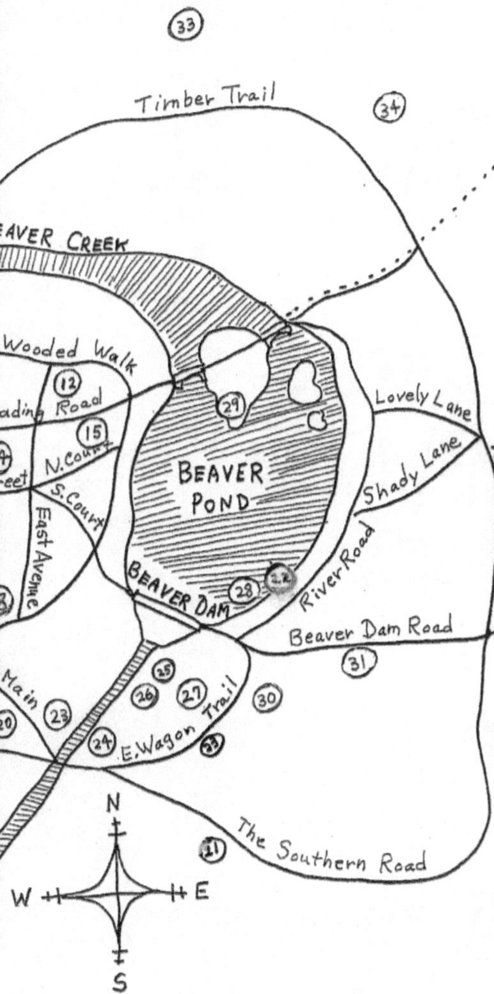


## THE PRAIRIE

1. The lodge
2. Arthur Elk's hut
3. Omar Mountain Goat's cave
4. The store
5. Maurice Rabbit's dugout
6. The Vulture Brothers' hut
7. Lucinda Vulture's hut
8. Deputy Eagle's office
9. Calhoun Coyote's chicken farm
10. Sandy Antelope dugout
11. Cornelius Van Mink's house
12. The Old Meetinghouse
13. Dr. Muskrat's office
14. City Hall
15. Thaddeus Turtle's cottage
16. Elmer Prairie Dog's store
17. Sheriff Lone Wolf's office
18. The boardinghouse
19. The New Meetinghouse
20. Arnold Big Horn's lean-to
21. The new deer's lean-to
22. Georgie Beaver's house
23. Clara Greyhound's cottage

24. Victor Running Deer's lean-to
25. Nosey Coon's tree house
26. Needles Porcupine's hollow
27. Billy Bones' cottage
28. Justin Beaver's house
29. George P. Beaver's castle
30. Gloria Meadowlark's farm
31. Percival Gander's shop
32. The Fortress
33. The Peccary Brother's shed
34. Milton Brown Bear's cave
35. Farmer Jason Crow's farm
36. Winston Wise Owl's tree house
37. Hester Groundhog's tree house

# BILLY BONES

Book Four

## THE GHOST OF CASTLE ROCK

# RON OAKS

Acon Ring Publishing

https://www.aconring.com/

ISBN 978-1-7365940-0-1 Hardcover
ISBN 978-1-7365940-1-8 Paperback
ISBN 978-1-7365940-2-5 eBook

FIRST EDITION

Credits
Cover Painting by Howard Garrett
Illustrations by Ron Oaks

Edited by Anne Ostroff, Louise Carlson, and Laura Oaks
Cover and Interior Design by Delaney-Designs.com
Photography by Sandy Rothberg

To Jan and Laura

# Table of Contents

❧

# PART TWO: THE FINAL CONFLICT

| Chapters | Page |
| --- | --- |

# Illustrations

# Cast of Characters

BOOK FOUR - THE GHOST OF CASTLE ROCK

**HUMANS IN THE NINTEENTH CENTURY**
Warren Nathaniel Stone – schoolmaster taking wagonload of
      books to Oregon Territory
Jimmy Stone – W. N. Stone's grandson

**HUMANS IN THE PRESENT**
William Stuart Sr.  (Will) – purchased land along old wagon trail
William Stuart Jr.  (Bill) – son of William Stuart Sr.
William Stuart III  (Billy) – grandson of William Stuart Sr.
Ben Johnson – Will's neighbor
Danny Red Feather – Billy's friend

**ANIMALS IN THE PRAIRIE:**
Billy Bones (Bones) – Billy Stuart's shepherd dog who entered
      The Enchantment
Victor Running Deer – young buck, deputy in the Prairie
Winston Wise Owl – the gatekeeper, mentor to Billy Bones
Hester Groundhog – Winston's neighbor and confidant
Mayor George P. Beaver – mayor of the Prairie
Constance Beaver – Mayor George P. Beaver's wife
George (Georgie) Beaver – nephew of mayor, entered The
      Enchantment with Billy Bones
Lydia, Little George, and Lucy Beaver – wife and offspring of
      Georgie Beaver
Justin and Gladys Beaver – parents of Georgie Beaver
Cornelius Van Mink – chairman of City Council
Prudence Van Mink – Cornelius Van Mink's wife
Conrad and Priscilla (a changeling) Van Mink – Cornelius Van
      Mink's grandchildren
Thaddeus P. Turtle – spiritual leader of the Old Meetinghouse
Percival (Percy) Gander – tailor and collector of used furniture

Sister Sarah Mourning Dove – spiritual leader of the New
    Meetinghouse
Myrtle Buck – widow of Olen Buck
Melinda Doe – Myrtle Buck's daughter
Calhoun Coyote – father to Lester, Leon, Leroy, and Lenny Coyote;
    has chicken farm
Leonard (Lenny) Coyote – Calhoun Coyote's youngest son
Alvin Muskrat – friend of Billy Bones
Dr. Muskrat – councilor on City Council, Alvin Muskrat's uncle
Nosey Coon and Needles Porcupine – friends of Billy Bones
Johnny Otter – swimming rival of Georgie Beaver
Philip P. Fox – brother of Phineas
Farmer Jason Crow and Gwendolyn Crow – councilor on City
    Council and his wife
Gerard Crow (a changeling) – son of Farmer Jason Crow and
    Gwendolyn Crow
Sterling Buck, Ernest Buck, Patience Doe – three members of the
    new deer herd
Molly Sheepdog – Sheldon Sheepdog's wife
Conan Greyhound – drill instructor of the Prairie
Clara Greyhound – Conan Greyhound's wife
Sandy Antelope, Arnold Big Horn, and Alvin Muskrat – old friends
    of Billy Bones
Elmer Prairie Dog – proprietor of General Store, retired mayor of
    the Prairie
Edwina and Patsy (a changeling) Prairie Dog– wife and daughter of
    Elmer
Whiskers – old cat who had lived on the farm with Billy Bones
    outside The Enchantment
Wendell Red Breast – councilor on City Council, songbird
Hosea Brown Thrasher, Melba Thrush, and Gloria Meadowlark –
    songbirds
Sheriff Walter Lone Wolf – sheriff of the Prairie
Deputy Harold Eagle – deputy of the Prairie and the Hill Country
Sylvester Turtle – councilor on City Council
The Ghost of Castle Rock – enters The Enchantment during last
    summer solstice

## ANIMALS IN THE HILL COUNTRY

Lucinda Vulture – spiritual head of the Hill Country
Festus and Floyd Vulture – sons of Lucinda
Arthur Elk – guard of Tribal Council
Maurice Rabbit – painter on Tribal Council, friend of Billy Bones
Omar Mountain Goat – deceased chief of Tribal Council
Gaylord Cougar, Lucretia Lizard, and Orville Bat – members of
      Tribal Council
Hilda Big Horn – new member of Tribal Council
Big Horn Brothers – two sons of Hilda Big Horn
Two Small Deer – race entries on May Day and Grand Fair

## ANIMALS IN THE NORTH WOODS

Bruno von Shepherd – head of the dog pack
Brigitte von Shepherd – sister of Bruno, Billy Bones' love interest
Angus Wolfhound – second in command of dog pack
Sheldon Sheepdog – cleric of dog pack
Henrietta Collie – love interest of Bruno von Shepherd
Runa Wild Dog – head of pack's banquet hall
Heinz Rottweiler, Neevil Cur, and Fritz Terrier – other male
      dogs in pack
Milton Brown Bear and Bison Bob – retired deputies of the Prairie
Lester, Leon, and Leroy Coyote – sons of Calhoun Coyote
Phineas Fox – moved up from Prairie
Colonel Eddie Crane – on Tribal Council
Zelda Crane – Eddie's wife
Willie Wild Cat – on Tribal Council
Old Ma Peccary – on Tribal Council
The Peccary Brothers – sons of Ma Peccary

# BILLY BONES

Book Four

## THE GHOST OF CASTLE ROCK

At the close of the nineteenth century, a hunting party of young warriors came across an abandoned wagon trail that had been used by pioneers on their way to the Oregon Territory. To their amazement they encountered several miles of discarded trunks, chests, and other such articles that must have been too heavy to carry across the mountains. Later that morning after climbing further up into the foothills, they felt a great disturbance in the earth and saw strange lights coming from the vicinity they had just visited. On their return trip they discovered that all the settlers' treasures had vanished, and the area was strangely still as if all the animals and birds had also disappeared.

# PART ONE

# AN UNEASY TRUCE

# CHAPTER ONE

# THE TRIP TO CITY HALL

The morning of November 2 broke on the cool side, but the sky was clear and the promise of a good day was in the air. The shepherd dog, Billy Bones, had purposely left the east window of his little cottage open so the early rays of the sun would fall on his bunk and awaken him. When he rolled over, he noticed a massive bulge in the bed above him. It took him a few seconds to remember that the ram, Arnold Big Horn, had spent the last four hours in the top bunk.

Immediately the shepherd dog awakened the ram by poking the bulge and barking, "Wake up, Arnold. We need to get over to City Hall for today's practice."

"Are you sure, Billy?" groaned the ram. "We just got to bed a couple hours ago. Can't we skip this one?"

"Nope, I promised Conan Greyhound I'd be there this morning. I'm hopin' he'll be our new instructor, and I've got to be there to arrange it," insisted Billy. "And don't break my top bunk gettin' down. You really make that poor thing squeak and groan! If you're gonna stick around for a while, we'll have to put a mattress on the floor for you."

Arnold Big Horn was staying with Billy because his lean-to west of town needed to be restored. Only the night before, the bighorn and a deer named Sterling Buck had freed Billy after he had been forcibly imprisoned in the North Woods. After liberating Billy, the ram and the young buck had decided to leave the North Woods themselves. They had been contemplating it for some time because of Sandy Antelope's brutal beating by some of Bruno von Shepherd's wild dogs and the unlawful removal of a load of Winston Wise Owl's books.

In addition to Arnold and Sterling's desertion from the North Woods, one of Bruno's most loyal pack members, Conan Greyhound, had also defected on the same day which was a devastating blow to Bruno. It was amazing to Billy, therefore, that all three escapees were planning to attend this morning's drill practice after only a few hours of sleep.

After a few slices of walnut bread from Hester Groundhog's oven and a couple of swallows of water from the collective dipper, the two animals hurried out the Dutch doors and headed north on the East Wagon Trail. Somewhere in the fields to the right of them, they could hear the opulent voice of Gloria Meadowlark as she went about her morning chores. The clear resonant echo of the sound raised their spirits and motivated them to continue onward.

After the two turned west at Beaver Dam Road and headed for the main part of town, they could clearly view the majestic trees surrounding the beaver pond and lining the streams above and below the dam. Billy could not help but recall how ordinary those same trees seemed in the outside world. Even now, as in his first year inside The Enchantment, he was still in awe of the brilliant colors and grandeur of this little world. "It's part of the wonderful gift we've been given after The Great Rift," he thought to himself.

When the dog and the ram neared the dam, they spotted Justin Beaver and Georgie Beaver's two kits playing in the yard east of the pond.

"Has your son left for practice already?" asked Billy.

"You just missed him. He left a few minutes ago!" yelled the older beaver. "And, Arnold, it's good to see you again. I thought you were still up in the North Woods."

"I came down last night with Billy and Sterling Buck. It looks like we'll be around for a while," answered the bighorn.

"Well, have a good practice," returned the carpenter. "I know Georgie'll be happy to see you again."

"Now what's the story with you and Georgie?" inquired Arnold after they crossed the dam. "Didn't he return with you from the outside world last June?"

"Actually, it was Georgie who got us back," explained Billy.

"It was Georgie? I didn't know that!" exclaimed the ram with some surprise.

"Yes, Georgie, you see, his wife and kits accidently stumbled into The Enchantment the year before. When the opening occurred again this year, Georgie was strangely drawn to the same spot between the two trees—you know—the trees at Land's End. I think it had somethin' to do with his great love for his family."

"Well, it's still pretty amazin' if you ask me!" grunted the bighorn.

"And another question, Billy," asked Arnold, as they reached South Court Street. "Who takes part in your drills down here in the Prairie?"

The shepherd dog slowed down for a moment and then turned to the ram. "Well, at this point, just the younger and stronger animals participate. Besides, it's too strenuous for most of our older citizens. And of course, most of the birds don't have the size."

"Then are the drills here like the ones inside The Fortress?"

"Yes, since Sandy Antelope, Alvin Muskrat, and I learned the drills up there," replied Billy, "only we don't use clubs; we use only staffs. In fact, when Conan was still with the North Woods, he came down a month ago and helped us start our practices. That's why I'm hopin' he'll help us again today."

"Bruno von Shepherd's gonna be really mad when he finds out that three members of his extended pack left yesterday. And it's really your fault, Mr. Bones—if you hadn't decided to leave earlier, after just four weeks!" chided Arnold, as he jostled Billy off the path.

"Well, I'll gladly take the blame. Besides, I couldn't stay after Bruno wanted me to swear a blood oath to him. Anyway, we're almost there," grinned the shepherd dog, slapping the bighorn playfully on the back.

When Arnold and Billy reached the area that fronted the City Hall, they discovered that most of the participants had already arrived.

Before joining the group, Arnold asked one last question. "You know, most of us use our animal name for our last name. Where did this 'Bones' come from?"

"'Cause that's what the old man in the outside world called me. And I got the name Billy from his grandson."

"Do you still think about them?" inquired Arnold.

"All the time."

# CHAPTER TWO

# THE OLD MAN'S CONCERN

Will Stuart loved to sit and read by the fireplace on cool November evenings. For the past four months, the retired math professor had allowed a barn cat called Buttons to share his favorite chair with him, either curled up on his lap or coiled affectionately around his shoulder.

When Will's grandson, Billy Stuart III, first lived with him on his small farm adjacent to the great mountains, the only animal allowed in the house had been a shepherd dog called Bones. However, when Bones disappeared a year later, Billy brought a kitten in from the barn. Will fussed about having that "dirty cat" in the house but finally assented, knowing how much the boy missed the dog.

After Bones miraculously returned a year later in the company of a pudgy little beaver, the cat was relegated back to the barn, and for the next two years the dog and the boy were inseparable.

When Billy Stuart's father remarried, he asked his son to come and live with them in Chicago. One month after the boy's departure, Bones inexplicably disappeared again, and almost immediately, Buttons tried to manipulate his way back into the house. After almost closing the squealing cat between the screen door and the back door twice, Will relented and allowed the cat back inside. Before long, Buttons had free reign in spite of Will's previous intentions.

When Billy Stuart III got permission to spend the upcoming summer with his grandfather, Will thought of getting another dog similar to Bones. In an uncanny coincidence, Will's neighbor, Ben Johnson, called him about taking one of his shepherd dog pups. "I tell you, he looks a lot like Bones, and right away I thought of you. He's got those same collie markings—you know, the beautiful tan color and blotches of white on his chest and tail."

"Why don't I come over and take a look?" responded Will, unsure whether his grandson would accept any dog but Bones. "I'll drop by tomorrow morning if that's agreeable."

Bright and early the next day, Will Stuart climbed into his old Dodge pickup. But before he could take off, Buttons scrambled in beside him.

"What would Mr. Johnson say if I brought a cat along with me?" laughed Will, as he tossed Buttons unceremoniously out the door. Not to be undone, Buttons immediately jumped into the back of the pickup with a loud "meow!" before Will could drive off. After trying to remove her a number of times, Will finally succeeded in pitching her into the house and slamming the screen door as quickly as he could.

"Can't take you with me this time, Buttons. I might be bringing back another animal, and there's no way I can handle both of you in the same seat!" shouted Will through the closed door.

When Will Stuart saw the young shepherd dog, he was amazed at his resemblance to Bones. Although the dog was still a pup, he had grown large enough to see that he was indeed a dead ringer for Bones.

"Okay, it's a deal," agreed Will. "I just hope my grandson will accept another dog that looks so much like Bones. He was really fond of him."

"What do you think you'll call him?" asked Ben.

"I suppose I could call him Ringer, since he looks so much like my last dog," replied Will, peering down at the pup wiggling in his arms. "Just look at him!"

Will's immediate problem when he returned home was convincing Buttons to accept the pup. Ringer continually tried to play with her, but the cat would simply whack the dog with one of her paws and climb up in the old man's lap.

"Well, I guess I'll just have to give them time," Will finally decided. "Fortunately, summer's still a long way off, and things will get back to normal when Buttons determines I'm not tossing her back in the barn."

That same evening, Will started worrying again about his grandson's visit. He wondered if he had made the right move—taking on another dog that looked so much like the first.

Bones had been a remarkable animal. Besides being a good companion, he always seemed to know when the boy's bus would arrive after school, and he had saved the boy several times from serious injury. It was almost as if the shepherd dog had psychic gifts—if that was at all possible.

Finally, to help the situation, Will informed Billy's best friend, Danny Red Feather, about the summer visit, and the two boys immediately communicated and looked forward to having a good time together.

On the evenings that followed, Will continued to enjoy his many books neatly stacked on shelves surrounding the fireplace. But from time to time, he would put down whatever book he was reading and wonder how Bones could possibly disappear twice without leaving a trace of any kind.

# CHAPTER THREE

# THE PRACTICE DRILL

"It's about time the two of you showed up. Even Ernest Buck beat you!" laughed the sheriff's deputy, Victor Running Deer.

"I'm sorry, but Arnold and I had sort of a late night," admitted Billy.

"Yes, we heard about it from Sterling Buck," said Sheriff Walter Lone Wolf. "Bruno von Shepherd's gonna be really beside himself today…and, Conan, it was a real surprise to see you this morning."

"Yes, I joined Clara at her cottage yesterday. I'd been thinkin' about it for some time, but when Bruno was gonna change the law and make it difficult to leave again, that sealed it for me!" growled Conan Greyhound.

"I was hopin' Conan would be our instructor," suggested Billy, trying to lighten the mood. "He really did a great job last month, and I think he'd be perfect for the position. What do you say, Conan, are you up for it?"

When Conan Greyhound was mentioned as a possible instructor, all the participants pounded their staffs on the ground in a show of instant support.

"Well, I do have some ideas," began the greyhound. "First, I think we should utilize the talent we have."

"Meaning what?" asked the sheriff.

"Well, here's what I've been thinking. Since we have almost the same number of members from the North Woods as from the Prairie, and since most of us from the North Woods have had at least a year's experience, why don't we just pair up?"

"Pair up? How do you mean?" inquired the wolf again.

"You know, the ones with experience can help the ones who are just startin' out," explained the greyhound. "And Billy, maybe you can help me select partners, since you know everyone in both camps."

"Okay, I'll be glad to, but why don't you start the opening exercises first and let me mull it over for a while," suggested Billy.

"All right, you heard Mr. Bones. So take off your shirts, grab your staffs, and line up!" ordered the greyhound, smiling broadly. "And don't worry about the chilly air. You'll warm up in no time."

For the next fifteen minutes Conan led the eager group in warmup exercises that included various thrusts, parries, and other defensive moves. When it came time for the one-on-one engagements, the greyhound turned to the shepherd dog.

"All right, Billy, how are we gonna pair up these fine citizens?" asked the greyhound.

"Well, let's start with Sterling Buck. Sterling, why don't you take your brother on? I know that's a tough assignment, but I think if anyone can keep Ernest from goofin' off, you can," Billy jested.

"Okay! Okay! Go ahead! Hurt my feelings before we even get started!" cried Ernest Buck good-naturedly.

Billy grinned and quickly turned to the ram. "And now we come to the strong one. Arnold, why don't you work with Victor Running Deer? And don't go easy on him. Since he's the sheriff's deputy, you need to work him as hard as you can." Billy nodded warmly at the deer who had entered The Enchantment with him three years ago, when he blundered into the magical world the first time.

"Now, Alvin Muskrat, it's your turn. Since you've pretty much recovered the use of your arm, why don't you work with Georgie Beaver? He's bigger than you, but there's a lot you can teach him," determined the shepherd dog.

Billy then turned to his new instructor. "As for you, Conan, why don't you work with Sheriff Lone Wolf? You're the best of all of us, and Walter will need all the assistance you can give him, especially with trouble loomin' just over the horizon!"

"Be glad to, Billy," responded the greyhound. "Only The Great Spirit knows what Bruno will do when he finds out that three of us joined you and Alvin and Sandy down here in the Prairie!"

"Speakin' of Sandy Antelope, I guess that means you're next. Why don't you help Philip Fox? I know your leg's somewhat better, but don't get too energetic. And Philip, look after him. He can teach you a lot, but don't let him overdo it," suggested Billy.

"And finally, Lenny Coyote, we come to you, my good friend. Sorry, but I'm afraid you got me. I only had four weeks experience up in The Fortress, but I'll do the best I can," promised the shepherd dog.

"Don't let him fool you," returned Conan. "He's tripped me up a number of times. You're lucky to get him."

After about an hour into the practices, Conan called for a break and made his way over to Billy, who was sitting on a step in front of the great hall. "I've been tryin' to figure out how many are left at The Fortress for their practice today. Let's see. Besides Bruno, there's Angus Wolfhound…."

"Wait. You can't count him," interrupted Billy. "Remember, he's in the Hill Country workin' with a new drill group over there."

"That's right. He stayed with them, didn't he?" remembered Conan. "Let's see, then: there's Heinz Rottweiler, Milton Brown Bear, Bison Bob, Lenny's three brothers, Phineas Fox, and, oh, yes, Neevil Cur and Fritz Terrier. And, of course, we can't forget Sheldon Sheep Dog. Actually, come to think of it, that's one fewer than what we have. I imagine though, when Bruno realizes he's lost three more of his pack, he'll try to talk the four Peccary Brothers into trainin'."

"And that'll be a hopeless task!" laughed Sterling Buck, joining the discussion.

"How about the Hill Country?" inquired Arnold Big Horn, who had moved over to the steps. "If they form a union with the North Woods, that would mean at least six more and would change the odds considerably."

"You talk as if Bruno will actually march on the Prairie, Arnold. I certainly hope it never comes to that!" cried Georgie Beaver, overhearing the conversation.

"You're right. Let's hope that never happens!" warned Billy. "But we have to be prepared, just in case. That's why we started these drill groups like the North Woods in the first place."

"Except for one thing, my friend. Both the North Woods and the Hill Country are working with clubs too," recollected Conan. "I don't see any clubs here!"

"We decided against them, since clubs are dangerous weapons, whereas drilling with staffs is much more like an exercise," returned Billy.

"Yes, we felt that clubs were really weapons of war," added Georgie. "Most of us didn't like how that made us look!"

"Well, I'm afraid you might have to add them if things get worse," warned the greyhound, shaking his head.

"But we don't have clubs, only staffs," said Victor Running Deer, joining the debate.

"Then I would seriously think about makin' some—just in case. If the North Woods has them, Bruno won't hesitate to use them if it comes to an altercation!" cautioned Conan.

"Do you think Bruno would really go that far?" asked Ernest, who for once had a serious tone. "And do you think he believes you'd actually fight against him?"

"Knowing his belief in the loyalty of the original pack, he probably thinks I'll return to the North Woods when I come to my senses," mused Conan. "And of course, I probably would never have left, if it hadn't been for my mate, Clara, and, of course, Molly Sheepdog. They're the ones who had the courage to bolt in the first place, after what happened to Sandy Antelope."

In a more somber atmosphere, the twelve animals continued their practice until almost noon. After deciding that the drill group would meet three mornings a week, Conan Greyhound caught up with Billy Bones and Arnold Big Horn as they were slipping on their shirts and getting ready to leave. Like most males in The Enchantment, they held their trousers up by straps similar to the suspenders that humans wore at the end of the nineteenth century.

"Hey, can I walk with you two, since we're all goin' the same way?" asked the greyhound. "And Billy, Clara and Molly asked me to invite you for lunch. 'Course, they didn't know about Arnold yet, but I'm sure they'd want him to come along."

Billy smiled and put a hand on the greyhound's shoulder. "Thank you, Conan. I think you just made our day!"

# CHAPTER FOUR

# TO CLARA'S COTTAGE

"Wait for me!" called Georgie Beaver, as he noticed Billy Bones, Arnold Big Horn, and Conan Greyhound walking east on South Court Street.

"Well, come on!" shouted the shepherd dog, waving for the beaver to join them, just as several birds popped out of their treehouses to greet the unlikely quartet. Billy took time to introduce Conan to each of the birds, and they in turn welcomed Arnold back to the Prairie. All in all, the salutations gave great warmth to their new camaraderie.

"Well, this is where I get off," said Georgie after the four crossed the beaver dam and came to Justin Beaver's home, sitting out over the water and sparkling in the noonday sun. "Billy, I still need you to help Dad and me build a house for my family. As I said before, we're crowdin' them out of house and home. That is, as soon as you get some of these North Woods issues settled."

"Let's not wait that long, Georgie. Let's start before winter closes in on us," responded the shepherd dog, smiling. "Besides, it'll get my mind off the North Woods for a while," Billy added, clasping his good friend's hand.

"Wow, that's great! I'll tell Dad. Maybe we can start drawin' up plans tomorrow morning!" exclaimed Georgie. "We've already built an underwater foundation out of logs for the part that'll be over the pond."

"I say we make it a lot like your folk's place, except put two rooms off the back instead of one. You know, for your two kits," proposed Billy.

When the trio reached the East Wagon Trail and headed south, Arnold suddenly gave Billy a shove and knocked him off the trail. "If you remember, you said you'd help me with my place first, Mr. Bones!"

"Before you get mad at me, Arnold Big Horn, just hear me out. I was thinkin', why don't you stay with me this winter, and then we can fix your place up in the spring?" suggested Billy, stumbling back onto the trail.

"All right, let's hear more…but it better be good!" warned the ram.

"Well for one thing, my cottage is nice and cozy in the cold months, and I think you'd like it there. And secondly, I could really use your help with Georgie's place." Billy turned away but then turned back and chuckled, "But first, we'll have to get you a mattress that we can lay on the floor. I didn't like the way my upper bunk was creakin' and strainin' last night with your weight on it. Besides, Nosey Coon and Needles Porcupine will be spendin' Sunday nights with us, and that's Nosey's bunk."

"You know, I think I might like that after all," declared Arnold, softening his tone. "It does get lonely out there in the boondocks in the winter. Besides, Sterling and Ernest

Buck want me to practice runnin' with them in preparation for the Spring Race, and this'd be a lot closer. They also mentioned somethin' about their sister, Patience. She wants to enter the race too. I guess Clara Greyhound's responsible for that," determined Arnold, glancing over at Conan.

In the distance they could see Gloria Meadowlark's farm off to the left, and Billy and Clara's cottages with their thatched roofs and Dutch doors on either side of the trail further south. When they reached Billy's cottage, Billy and Arnold stashed their staffs inside the doors, and the three of them continued south to Clara's place.

Clara Greyhound's cottage was much like Billy's except in reverse. It still had a fireplace on the north wall, but the outside door faced west instead of east, and the bed was on the east wall. The main difference was the addition of a room on the south side for Molly Sheepdog. Her room was nice and comfortable and had a small fireplace for the colder months. And for the present, it was a place where she could live until, or even if, Sheldon Sheepdog ever worked up the courage to leave Bruno von Shepherd.

"Make room for one more, Clara!" barked Conan, as the three friends entered the cottage. "It seems Sterling Buck and Arnold here are the newest citizens of the Prairie. They came down with Billy late last night. Sterling's gonna live with his father, but Arnold's stayin' with Billy until they can fix up his old place…so I invited him, too."

"Well I should hope so!" cried Clara and Molly together as they both gave Arnold a welcoming hug. Clara

Greyhound and Molly Sheepdog wore blouses and long patterned skirts like the pioneer women in the late eighteen hundreds—before the occurrence of The Great Rift that created The Enchantment.

"We've plenty of food," the greyhound continued. "And besides, we want to hear about what's happening in the North Woods."

"That reminds me, Clara," said Conan, remembering Bruno von Shepherd. "I forgot to tell you that Bruno's sure you and Molly will come back to The Fortress one day. 'Course, he had no idea that I'd be leavin' as well. He even gave me sort of a compliment for winnin' the Overland Race during the Grand Fair. But then in the next breath, he cussed me out for losin' to you in the Great Medley."

"Well, if he thinks I'm going back, he's out of his mind!" exclaimed Molly, entering the conversation. "But Billy, how did you happen to be in the North Woods last night? I thought you came back with Conan yesterday afternoon."

"What d'ya think?" interrupted Arnold Big Horn, gesturing toward Billy. "This fool walked back up to the North Woods, that's how! In fact, he didn't arrive until after midnight! 'Course, he was lookin' for Brigitte von Shepherd. He wanted her to come back with him 'fore her brother changed the law."

"What law? I don't understand," questioned Molly.

"Well, Bruno was gonna have the council vote again 'bout citizens leavin' without the council's permission—which really means without his permission. But back to Billy, he got caught callin' to Brigitte in the dark, and o' course, they put him in the guest chamber."

"Oh how dreadful!" shouted Clara. "You mean they actually locked him up?"

"That's right," responded Arnold. "That's when Sterling and I decided it was time for us to get out o' there too. So a while later, we busted Billy out. And since Bruno had me guard the guest chamber, it wasn't all that hard. Then we all just skedaddled 'fore anyone was awake and 'fore the vote could take place today that would've curtailed our freedom, too."

"And Brigitte," asked Molly, what happened to her in all this?"

"I'm afraid she wouldn't come," said Billy sadly. "But she did say she'd see me again…or try to…."

"Well…come on then. Let's all sit down and have something to eat. I know the three of you must be starved," said Molly, knowing that the idea of leaving Brigitte with her brother Bruno in the North Woods was a sore subject for Billy Bones.

"Oh, and one more thing that might interest you, Clara," added Arnold. "Patience, Sterling and Ernest's sister, wants to run in the Spring Race on May Day, and I think she wants to speak to you."

Conan turned to his mate as he sat down at the table placed in the center of the large room. "It's like Arnold said earlier, Clara. It looks like you really started something when you entered the Great Medley last summer and ran against me. 'Specially since no female had ever entered a race during the Grand Fair or May Day before."

"Well, I certainly hope I started something," chuckled Clara. "So Patience's thinking of running in the Spring Race. Well, good for her! Good for her!"

# CHAPTER FIVE

# THE GANDER'S SURPRISE

Billy Bones rose early the next morning, hiked down the bluff west of his cottage, and took a cold bath in the little stream that ran below the beaver dam. Feeling refreshed, he reentered his cottage and awakened Arnold Big Horn, now sleeping on a mattress in the southwest corner of the one large room.

"I've got several errands to run this morning, so make yourself at home. There's fruit and bread and jam in the cupboard. I should be home early this afternoon, and hopefully I'll know more about building Georgie's home," whispered Billy. "Oh, and another thing: I've an idea that Sterling and Ernest Buck are comin' by this morning to get you to train with them for the Spring Race. They may even bring Patience with them, so good luck. See you later."

The shepherd dog quietly slipped out the Dutch doors and started north on the East Wagon Trail. When he got to Beaver Dam Road, he turned right and headed for Winston Wise Owl's treehouse at Land's End, where he had entered The Enchantment twice in the last three years. He wanted to let the old gatekeeper know how he escaped from the

North Woods the night before, and how he might have made the return of the owl's books more difficult than ever. But above all, he wanted information about how the wild dogs and the deer fared in their first couple months inside The Enchantment.

The first place Billy came to was Percival Gander's shop. It was designed like a chicken coop, as in the outside world and sat on the right side of the road. Its many windows faced north, so that the clothes inside would not be damaged by direct sunlight. Unfortunately though, every time the dog passed it, it reminded him of the chicken coops on the old man's farm and inevitably of young Billy. Try as he might, he could not help but feel a lump in his throat that hurt when he swallowed.

Percival Gander was not only the Prairie's tailor but also a collector of used furniture. Most of the dog's pieces came from the room below his shop. Billy hoped it was not too early to greet Percy, since he had not seen him since he reentered The Enchantment five months ago. As luck would have it, when Billy drew near, the gander poked his head out of a window close to the entrance and then pulled it back in and then back out again.

"Hello, hello, hello, Billy Bones, how good to see you. Wait 'till I come outside! Yes, come outside!" Percy called.

As the gander waddled down the long ramp that led to his shop, Billy noticed that he still wore his mustard-yellow vest and a measuring tape hung loosely around his shoulders.

"I see you're still wearin' the same shirt that you took

from my shop when you reentered five months ago. Yes, the same shirt!" honked Percy good-naturedly. "I suppose you're on your way to see Mr. Wise Owl. But if you've got a moment, why don't you come into my shop? There's something I want to show you! Yes, something I want to show you!"

Without waiting for a reply, the eccentric goose waggled up the steep ramp and gestured for the dog to follow.

The inside of the shop was still as Billy remembered, with rows of clothing on the left and a large working table and mirror on the right.

"Come with me, Mr. Bones, and see what I have down here at the end of the row. I think it's something you may remember. Yes, something you may remember," repeated Percival.

When Billy reached the end of the row on the left side, he turned back to the gander in astonishment. "Why, that's my blue shirt! But how…?"

"Hester Groundhog found it behind her treehouse the day after you forced Fabian Lynx out of The Enchantment over two years ago. Yes, the day you forced Brother Fabian out!"

"But where…?"

"You hid it under a tarp where she kept some of her tools. Remember? You must have taken all your clothes off before goin' back into the other world. Yes, the other world."

"But how did you…?" Billy sputtered again.

"Hester brought your pants and shirt to me afterwards.

She had no need of them. Yes, no need of them," declared the goose. "Now take off that white shirt and put this old one on. I'll keep the white one and clean it up for you. You can pick it up in a couple of days. Yes, in a couple of days."

The shepherd dog did exactly as he was ordered and removed his white shirt and donned the blue one. After that, he stepped over to the mirror on the other side of the room and looked at himself. He was shocked again at how much older he appeared. Because he had spent two years outside The Enchantment, it aged him at least ten years on the inside. He had departed the magical world an older youth and returned a full-grown adult.

"Seeing yourself differently, eh? You've matured quite a bit. No doubt of that. Yes, no doubt of that," remarked the gander, reading the young dog's mind.

After bidding Percival Gander goodbye and stepping down the steep ramp, Billy Bones continued on to Land's End. The air around him was still chilly, and a cool breeze had risen, allowing him to feel the clean blue shirt flap freely about him.

"Well that was a nice surprise. Percy must have let the seams out. Yes, a nice surprise!" laughed the dog. "And see? That crazy goose has me repeating myself."

After crossing the four-way intersection where Wheat Walk turned north and The Southern Road went south, Billy could see Farmer Jason Crow's farm straight ahead along the fence row on the right. He wondered if Jason's son, Gerard, was about.

Two and a half years ago, Gerard Crow, along with four other animals, had been changed back to the creatures they would have been in the outside world. Brother Fabian Lynx had convinced the City Council to burn five human artifacts that had been left along the Old Wagon

Trail. Unfortunately, these antiquities had been part of the magic of The Great Rift, and their destruction had caused the five to regress to their common animal forms. These "changelings," as they came to be called, also lost their clarity of mind and ability to speak. Gerard, however, like most common crows, still had an amazing awareness and had taken a liking to Billy Bones.

As Billy strode closer to the farmhouse, he looked about for Gerard but could not find him. He would have liked to visit with Jason and his wife but was anxious to see Winston and tell him about his eventful visit to the North Woods. In the distance he could clearly see the two magnificent trees at Land's End that seemed to reach hungrily toward the sky. In back of them and circling north and south was the ever-present mist that marked the edge of The Enchantment.

# CHAPTER SIX

# THE OWL'S STORY

The two splendid trees at Land's End were inhabited by Winston Wise Owl and Hester Groundhog. The entrance to the owl's tree on the left was partway up the trunk and could be reached by a circular staircase. Hester's entrance on the right was a step above ground level. When Billy Bones reached the area between the two trees, Hester opened the top of her Dutch doors and called to him, "Mr. Bones, I see that you're wearing the shirt I found two years ago after you left us."

"Yes, thanks. Percy gave it to me this morning," the dog replied.

"I understand you had quite an interesting meeting with the North Woods and the Hill Country the day before yesterday. It seems we now have open borders. Unfortunately though, I hear Winston didn't have much luck getting his books back," sighed the groundhog.

"That's why I'm here, Miss Groundhog. I want to talk to Mr. Wise Owl about what happened after he left the meeting. Is he up?" asked the shepherd dog.

"Yes, he should be. I invited him over for a midmorning snack. Why don't you join us after you've seen him?" invited Hester.

"I'd like that, but I'll have to keep it short. I've got to meet with Georgie and Justin Beaver later this morning about building a new house for Georgie's family."

"So they're finally thinking about that. I wondered when they'd get around to it," said Hester, nodding her head. "Well, go find Winston, and I'll put the tea on."

When Billy turned toward Winston's treehouse, he thought he saw a young human leaning against the trunk of the tree. It was the same older boy who had smiled down at him each time he entered The Enchantment. Since then, he had conjectured that the boy was Jimmy Stone, grandson of W. N. Stone, whose books had been left in the hollow of Winston's tree. Sadly, after he blinked his eyes and looked a second time, the boy had disappeared.

After climbing the circular staircase, Billy knocked several times before Winston Wise Owl answered the door. He was still wearing his robe over a white shirt and striped pants. The dog noticed the partially-filled bookcases around the one large room. He knew that one-third of his library was still in the Hill Country, and one-third had been confiscated by Bruno von Shepherd's pack in the North Woods.

"I wondered if I'd see you today, Mr. Bones. Please come in and sit down. I take it you must have something new to tell me. Has anything changed concerning our agreements with the other two states?" inquired the old owl.

"Well…yes and no," began Billy. "You see, after you flew away after the meeting, Conan asked me to carry his satchel back to the Prairie. I thought that it was for Clara, but actually his clothes were inside."

During the next few moments, Billy explained to his mentor about the greyhound's exit from the North Woods and how he returned that night to try to convince Brigitte von Shepherd to move down to the Prairie. When the dog got to the part about how he was freed by Arnold Big Horn and Sterling Buck and how they also escaped, the owl interrupted. "But has Bruno tried to retaliate? I mean, that's three of his extended pack members."

"I'm afraid it's four," countermanded the shepherd dog. "You see, Melinda Doe had already left to live with her mother that same afternoon. Apparently she was unhappy with Sterling and the dog who was her roommate."

"My, oh my, oh my!" moaned the old owl. "That makes six, if you include Clara Greyhound and Molly Sheepdog. Oh, and then there's Sandy Antelope and Alvin Muskrat who deserted earlier. That's eight."

"And I guess I could be counted as nine, since Bruno thought I'd stay after the four weeks I spent at The Fortress," added Billy. "And as far as Bruno's concerned, you're right. We have no idea how he'll react. I'm sure the Prairie City Council will meet to discuss the situation before the week is out." After a pause, the shepherd dog continued. "I just wanted you to know that I'm afraid my actions on that night caused a big part of the problem, and it's made the return of your books even more unlikely."

"I see…I see…And how about Brigitte? You didn't mention what happened between you and Miss von Shepherd," wondered Winston.

"She wouldn't come with me, I'm afraid," frowned Billy, hanging his head. "But she did promise to see me again. And that's where it stands."

"Well, that's further along than you were when I last saw you at the meeting, Mr. Bones. At least that's an improvement," concluded the owl. "And for the rest, what's done is done. Come on now. Let's have our morning break with Hester Groundhog, and you can tell me what else is on your mind. I'm sure she's waiting for us."

After a cup of tea and a piece of pecan bread at Hester Groundhog's outside table, Billy asked the owl the question he'd been wanting to ask for some time. "I still don't understand how the pack got separated from the Prairie. Tell me, what was it like when the wild dogs and deer first arrived? Were they angry with each other like Victor Running Deer was with me? I never quite got the story."

"Well, for one thing, there were more dogs than deer. It was really quite unfair. There were twelve in Bruno's pack: five females and seven males, and they were chasing only six deer. I think they were a little ashamed of themselves when they achieved clarity of mind, and besides, they seemed to have trouble finding a place to live."

"Oh, how was that?" asked Billy. "Were there just too many of them?"

"No, I just think Bruno couldn't stand the idea of the pack breaking up. Maybe it was a control thing. Anyway, that's how they ended camping up north."

"All twelve of them were camping out?" inquired Billy again.

"Yes, all twelve of them, and then Justin Beaver finally befriended them. I think maybe it was because of you—since they were all dogs. Anyway, after looking through many of my books left by the humans, Brigitte and Sheldon Sheepdog finally chose the southern style mansion of the Victorian period. After that, with Justin's help they all chipped in and built it."

"Yes, it's very beautiful and large enough for all of them," agreed Billy, thinking of Brigitte again.

"In the meantime, Bruno was becoming more and more disenchanted with the City Council and our *Book of Rules*. And when he heard about how I was almost expelled from The Enchantment and how you were arrested, he had an excuse to separate himself from the Prairie. Finally, Justin got fed up with his attitude and stopped helping after the mansion was finished. After that, Bruno got Milton Brown Bear to help build what is now The Fortress. I think you've seen with your own eyes how that turned out."

"Actually, there was more to it than that," added Hester, who was listening carefully to the story. "I think Bruno discovered he couldn't control the City Council—especially after their experience with Fabian Lynx. I believe he just wanted to run things himself."

"You're probably right there, Hester, but I was giving the kinder version," hooted the owl.

"And how about Sterling and Ernest Buck and the rest

of their family?" asked the shepherd dog, anxious to hear the rest of the story. "Did they hold a grudge, and how did they manage?"

"The deer seemed to adjust remarkably well and quickly made friends in the Prairie. Of course, they had a lot of help from Victor Running Deer. And as you know, they settled south of town on the Southern Road."

"I forgot about Victor. He would befriend them immediately, of course, just like Olen Buck had taken him in," determined Billy.

"Yes, and Olen's mate, Myrtle, and her daughter Melinda invited them over as soon as they got settled," continued the groundhog.

"But Melinda and Sterling, how did that happen? And when did they decide to leave the Prairie?" inquired Billy, thinking how things had been between Victor and Melinda when he left two years ago.

"I think their moving came after an invitation from Bruno von Shepherd. When he saw Sterling run in the Grand Fair, he was very impressed with him," said the owl.

"And…I imagine Melinda maybe wanted to distance herself from Victor," added Hester.

"Yes, I wondered if that might be the case, but I hadn't wanted to ask," Billy admitted.

"I think after Rodney Wild Deer was killed in that fight with Victor, things were never the same between Victor and Melinda. I think Melinda and Sterling's move to the North Woods was probably the expedient thing to do…at the time anyway," imagined the owl. "Well, I guess if you're still planning to see Justin and Georgie this morning, you'd better get moving."

After Billy thanked Hester Groundhog for the refreshments and Winston Wise Owl for the information he had come to hear, the three friends saw a very large bird approaching them from the west.

"Ah, it's Deputy Harold Eagle. I was sort of expecting him after our conversation earlier," remarked Winston. "I think we both know what he's here for!"

The great golden bird, who had jurisdiction in both the Prairie and the Hill Country, landed several yards away and quickly made his way over to the table. He wore a plaid swag across his chest that folded under his great belt.

"Good mornin' to you all," the eagle began in a Scottish brogue. "And Billy, I'm glad you're here. The City Council wants you and Winston to attend a special meetin' they're havin' Saturday mornin', and I'm sure you probably both know what it's all about. And Sheldon Sheepdog and Brigitte von Shepherd are comin' down from the North Woods to discuss the latest defections and how they might affect our mutual relations."

The thought of seeing Brigitte von Shepherd caused Billy's heart to pound harder, and he had to lower his head to mask his true feelings.

"They need you, Billy," Harold continued, "because of your obvious role in the defections. And Mr. Wise Owl, they want you there since it might affect your books. Mr. Sheepdog has particularly asked us not to include the animals that deserted, since they would only complicate the discussion. Well, I must be off, since I've other stops to make. So good day to the three of you!"

After the eagle turned and flew effortlessly off with his powerful wings, the shepherd dog excused himself again and started down the path toward the beaver dam and his meeting with Justin and Georgie Beaver.

# CHAPTER SEVEN

## MEETING AT THE CROSSROADS

When Billy Bones neared Gerard Crow's home, he could see that the changeling was sitting on the roof pulling on an old stalk of corn. When the bird spied the shepherd dog, he dropped the stalk and flew straight for the dog. After circling twice, he joyfully landed on Billy's shoulder.

"Well, my friend, I was wondering when I'd see you again," said Billy, as the crow nuzzled the dog's neck with his beak. "I'm headed for the beaver dam if you'd like to come along."

When the two companions got back to the crossroads, Billy stopped. The view in front of them never failed to amaze him. In the distance, the mountains against the misty edge of The Enchantment shone especially clear in the brisk autumn air. Closer in, the two meetinghouse steeples and the clock tower at City Hall gleamed brightly above the trees, already changed to their fall colors. His mind also went back to the several mishaps that had occurred at that same corner with Victor Running Deer. As he was picturing the deer in his mind, he noticed several runners coming up from the south. "You don't suppose?" he muttered to himself.

As fate would have it, Sterling and Ernest Buck were leading three other runners. When they got closer, Billy realized that one of them was his new housemate, Arnold Big Horn, and close behind him were Victor Running Deer and Patience Doe. The males were shirtless, of course, but the doe wore trousers and a short sleeve blouse, just as Clara Greyhound had worn during her race at the Grand Fair.

When the deer and the ram got to the intersection, they stopped to greet the shepherd dog and the crow on his shoulder.

"Hello there," greeted Sterling Buck.

"Hello yourself," called Billy in return. "I'm glad you're startin' early for the Spring Race on May Day. And I'm happy you included Victor. I'm sure he's out of shape with all that deputizing."

"And Patience too," laughed Ernest. "But she's holdin' her own, and for some reason, she likes to run with Victor!"

"Yeah, I notice that too," chuckled Sterling, "but to each his own."

"Don't pay any attention to those two," interrupted Patience. "If the truth be told, we're just trying to keep up. After all, they jog all the time."

"Well, don't be too hard on Victor. I'm just happy to see him runnin'," said Billy, putting a hand on his old friend's shoulder.

"And I'm glad we ran into you, so we could stop and

take a break," responded Victor, breathing heavily. "Sterling and Ernest show no mercy!"

"And Patience, I'm pleased to see you take up where Clara left off," encouraged the dog. "I'm thinkin' maybe the two of you have really started something."

"I hope so. But we'll have to wait 'til summer to run together, since the Spring Race is mostly for hooved animals. I have an idea that I'm it for now—if I can get into shape, that is," determined Patience.

"It looks like that's the new thing, Billy—the females runnin' along with the males," observed Ernest.

"Well, some of us can be just as good, just as fast… some of us even faster," stated Patience.

"Like Clara!" inserted Ernest.

"Yes," everyone else laughed, "like Clara."

"Well, nice talkin' to you, Billy, but I have to keep this group movin'!" said Sterling, as he turned and led the five animals north on Wheat Walk.

"See you tomorrow morning at drill practice!" yelled Ernest over his shoulder, as he caught up with his older brother.

When Gerard Crow saw the runners heading north, he automatically took to the air and started zigzagging over their heads. When he finally realized that Billy was not joining them, he circled back and returned to the dog's shoulder.

# CHAPTER EIGHT

# THE BEAVER'S PLANS

When Billy and Gerard finally reached the dam, the dog marveled again at how the trees around the beaver pond reached such incredible heights and how most of them housed birds or small animals. Just north of the dam on the east side stood Justin Beaver's place, its white-washed sides already gleaming in the late morning sun.

Billy had to cross a small land bridge to reach the house, built completely over the water. When Billy knocked on the door, Gerard took his cue and flew up to one of the great trees that stood in the space before the little bridge.

"Why, Mr. Bones, come in, come in," greeted Justin's wife Gladys. They're already over at the table working on the plans for the new house. They've been expecting you."

Gladys Beaver, like Molly Sheepdog and Clara Greyhound, wore a large apron over a long patterned skirt that almost reached the floor. Her mate, Justin Beaver, dressed like most of the other males inside The Enchantment, except for a brown carpenter's apron, which he always wore over his other clothes.

Justin and Gladys's home was one oversized room with a large stone fireplace on the east wall. A small room used by Georgie when he was younger was in the back. Like the outside, all the rough-hewn timber walls were whitewashed and gave a nice shine to the room. Small windows on both sides added even more light, but a low ceiling just high enough for Billy to stand in took away some of the brightness.

"Where are Lydia and the young ones?" asked Billy, as he moved to the table.

"Lydia took Little Georgie and Lucy for a walk. I'm afraid if they'd have stayed, we'd never've gotten anything done," chuckled Justin.

"Yeah, they like to join in everything. That'll be great when they're older, but now it's a real pain!" laughed Georgie. "But here, look at what we've done. We took your suggestion and drew the new house to look a lot like Dad's."

"I think that's a good plan," agreed Billy, "'specially since the two houses will be next to each other. I was thinking on my way over that I'm always in awe at the way your home catches the sunlight with its whitewashed timbers.

"Originally I was thinkin' of a place more like yours," admitted Georgie, "but now I think you're right. However, I do like the idea of makin' our ceilings higher, 'specially for animals like Victor Running Dear and Sterling Buck. I hate to have them waitin' outside 'cause they can't stand up in here!"

"You have to remember that when my father first built

this place, most of the animals that visited us were prairie dogs and such," recalled Justin.

"The other thing, Billy, is that we're gonna make ours mostly on land with just the back part over the water," explained Georgie. "That way we need only a log foundation for the last two rooms, which we've already done. In fact, Johnny Otter and Alvin Muskrat have been helpin' us get it ready for the last four weeks, since the work's mostly underwater."

"Yep, we need those rooms to be over the pond so Little George and Lucy can have an underwater entrance just like Georgie's room," expounded the older beaver. "Georgie, of course, wants two rooms instead of one—so each kit will eventually have a separate place. Now the thing we really need is muscle to put up the roughhewn boards over the subfloors that we already laid out."

"That I think I can handle," assured Billy. "Arnold Big Horn has promised to help, and I'm pretty sure I can get Victor Running Deer and Sterling Buck and his brother Ernest to lend a hand."

"Except we can't work on Monday, Wednesday, and Friday mornings," warned Georgie. "We have drill practice on those days, and with things lookin' the way they are, we can't forfeit those times."

"I think you're right, son. I'm afraid they come before everything else right now," agreed Justin.


After another half hour of work on the plans, Lydia

returned with the kits, and Gladys served them all fish and corn, fresh off the cob. Then, to top it off, she added hot cross buns for dessert. Before Billy took his leave, he played with the kits and renewed his good relations with the adult beavers.

"This will be a good time for you and Georgie," remarked Lydia, as Billy was preparing to go. "He missed you those four weeks you were up in the North Woods. I'm glad you're back to stay!"

When Billy left the beaver's home, he looked around for Gerard, but he had already flown away. As he started jogging down Beaver Dam Road, however, the crow reappeared and started circling above him. Finally he landed on Billy's shoulder again and stayed there until they reached the dog's cottage.

# CHAPTER NINE

# THE SPECIAL MEETING

Winston Wise Owl thought of himself as a night owl and always found it hard to rise early. On Saturday morning, he had to attend the special meeting at City Hall concerning the four latest defections from the North Woods. As he donned his sleeveless tailcoat over a white shirt and striped pants, he heard the tall clock on the landing strike eight.

"Hester Groundhog said she'd have a bite for me before I left. I hope she hasn't forgotten," mumbled the old owl. He always depended a lot on his good neighbor and confidant, and in return tried to keep her abreast of the latest news. As he climbed down the circular staircase outside his treehouse, he saw that she had already placed the teapot and two cups on the table between the two trees and was bringing out a loaf of freshly baked bread.

"You better hurry, Mr. Wise Owl, if you're going to make your meeting by nine. I'll slice you a piece of bread, if you pour the tea. There's jam on the table," the old groundhog said.

"Since I'm flying, I feel I can spare twenty minutes,"

replied Winston.

"So you think Brigitte will actually come. I could see that Billy was visibly moved when Deputy Eagle mentioned her name," observed Hester. "I hope for his sake they have a chance to talk."

"Well, we'll see, won't we," answered the owl agreeably. "Whatever happens, I'll fill you in on it."

"Yes, please do…and I want to know everything!" concluded Hester, as she finished slicing the bread and set it in front of him.

The city council members were just taking their seats when Winston entered the east wing of the entrance hall. When the special session was not open to the public, the east wing with its large oak table was used. As usual, Chairman Cornelius Van Mink sat in the center on the north side of the table surrounded by councilors Wendell Red Breast, Farmer Jason Crow, Sylvester Turtle, and Doctor Muskrat. The councilors were all in their frock coats except for Jason Crow, who never dressed formally for anyone.

Before Winston could move to the table, Mayor George P. Beaver entered the room, followed by Sheriff Lone Wolf and Deputy Harold Eagle.

"Good morning, Winston. Why don't you sit with me by the window?" offered the mayor. "We'll let the sheriff and his deputy sit across from the council members, and we'll leave the two seats on the west side for our guests.

Shortly after everyone present was situated, Victor Running Dear and Billy Bones arrived and took the remaining seats on the south side of the table.

"That puts Billy next to Brigitte and Sheldon. I wonder if that's wise?" thought Winston, as Cornelius rose to start the meeting.

"Good morning. And thank you for coming. Our guests should be arriving in about half an hour. That will give us time to have an illuminating discussion before they get here. That's why I invited the sheriff and his deputies and Mr. Bones. We need to know exactly what happened that caused the four recent defections and how it will affect our relations with The North Woods…and if we should prepare for trouble."

"Shouldn't the four animals that deserted be present to tell their story?" asked Doctor Muskrat. "It seems to me…."

"Sheldon Sheepdog has specifically asked us not to invite them," interrupted Cornelius. "Since the desertions were done in secret and there were unknown factors involved, he thought it better to meet without them."

"Now by 'illuminatin' do you mean to get to the bottom of what's goin' on, or are you testin' our vocabulary, councilor?" asked Farmer Jason Crow, turning to Cornelius with a smart- aleck look.

"Most of us know the meaning of the word, Jason," huffed the mink. "Now may we please continue? Sheriff, what can you tell us?"

"I just know what Sterling Buck told me on Wednesday. Apparently he and Arnold Big Horn decided to come back with Billy Bones in the wee hours of that morning, and Conan decided to come down and live with Clara on Tuesday after our three-state meeting."

"I think there's probably more to it than that," disputed Sylvester Turtle. "What really happened…I mean, why did they leave in secret and at the same time?"

"You'll have to ask Mr. Bones," answered the sheriff. "I'm afraid he's the only one who knows the real reason."

"Well, Mr. Bones. Will you elucidate?" asked Cornelius, turning and smiling at Jason Crow.

When Winston observed the look on Billy's face, he realized how difficult the question was for him to answer, since it involved his feelings for Brigitte von Shepherd.

Billy began, "When I first visited the North Woods, there was a law that forbid Bruno's extended pack from leavin' the North Woods without his permission. It was connected to the blood oath they were required to take when they joined. However, before I left, their new council changed the ruling, and their citizens were free to leave if they were unhappy. And then…on Tuesday, word got out that Bruno wanted the law reinstated, at least for the extended pack. In fact, he planned to reintroduce it to the North Woods Council the next day."

"And what did that have to do with the defections?" asked Sylvester Turtle after Billy paused for a moment.

"Well, as I understand it, Conan Greyhound and Sterling Buck and Arnold Big Horn had all thought about leaving for different reasons," continued Billy. "But when they heard the present law was going to be reversed on Wednesday, they all decided to leave immediately. And of course, if they were going to be successful, they couldn't tell anyone."

"Different reasons? Like what? I don't understand," said Cornelius.

"Well, Arnold and Sterling had been upset about Sandy Antelope's beating after he left the North Woods, and of course, they were against appropriating Mr. Wise Owl's books," explained the shepherd dog, nodding to the old owl. "And then, Conan, of course, had been wishing for some time to join Clara at her new cottage."

"And how about Melinda Doe? You ain't mentioned her." asked the crow.

"Well, I don't know firsthand, but I was informed that she was unhappy with her roommate and wanted to come back and live with her mother," answered Billy simply.

"But what I don't understand, Mr. Bones, is what in tarnation were you doin' up there in the middle of the night in the first place?" asked Jason Crow.

"Yes, Mr. Bones, that's a good question. Why were you up there? And after midnight at that!" probed Cornelius van Mink.

Billy stood silently and motionless for some time. Winston, of course, knew why the dog was uncomfortable and finally decided to intervene. "With your permission, Mr. Bones, may I answer that question?"

Billy turned to his old mentor and simply nodded.

"You see, Mr. Bones was concerned about Bruno von Shepherd's sister, Brigitte, who will join us later this morning. He was hoping that perhaps she would come down to the Prairie also, before the law went into effect," said Winston graciously. "As I understand it, she had expressed some desire to leave but didn't want to upset her brother."

"Does that sound about right, Mr. Bones?" questioned Cornelius again.

"Yes, that's about right," agreed the shepherd dog, as he quietly took his seat.

"And now we need to get to the nitty-gritty," intervened Mayor Beaver. "Sheriff Lone Wolf, are we at all prepared if the North Woods wants to retaliate for these defections? And is that the reason for the drill sessions?"

"For one thing, after the desertions, they have considerably fewer animals in their drill group, so I don't think they'll try anything for a while," stated the sheriff. "But I believe Bruno is still making overtures to the Hill Country, and if they unite, that would certainly change the odds."

"But we have no plans to do that at this time!" barked Sheldon Sheepdog, who had just stepped into the entrance hall with Brigitte von Shepherd. Sheldon had donned a dark coat over his tan vest, and Brigitte wore a gray vest and long skirt over her blue and white striped blouse with puffed sleeves. Sheriff Lone Wolf immediately hurried over and ushered them to the west side of the table, while the others stood until their guests were seated.

"We were just discussing possible repercussions for the last four desertions from the North Woods," explained Chairman van Mink.

"Yes, we heard," answered Sheldon.

"And before we start, we want you to know that no one in the Prairie coerced them into coming," remarked the chairman adamantly.

"Well, it was a shock anyway," continued Sheldon, "and Bruno von Shepherd was terribly upset, especially when Conan left us. He just never expected that."

"You know, of course, that his mate Clara has been with us for some time. It's only natural that Conan would like to be with her," reasoned Dr. Muskrat.

"Yes, I know that only too well, since my mate stays with Clara. But I think Bruno believed they would eventually return to the pack. We all came into The Enchantment together, you know. I think Bruno thought there was a loyalty there," said Sheldon, speaking for his leader.

"Well, what's done is done, Mr. Sheepdog, and there ain't no turnin' back," cawed Jason Crow. "What we need to know is will Bruno and his pack retaliate?" The crow quickly glanced over at Cornelius. "See, I can use some of them fancy words too."

"Good citizens of the Prairie," began Brigitte suddenly standing at her seat. "What we've come to tell you is that no one in the North Woods has any intention of doing harm to anyone inside the Prairie, although my brother and his fellow pack members were terribly hurt by the four defections and would invite them to return at any time."

Just as Brigitte was finishing her remarks, Heinz Rottweiler suddenly burst into the hall and darted over to the table. He had a wild look in his eye as he pushed his way between Sheldon and Billy.

"Sorry I'm late. But I have something to say!" shouted the distraught Rottweiler.

Sheldon Sheepdog immediately rose from his chair.

"Heinz, what are you doing here? I didn't know you were coming."

"When Bruno told me what you were up to, I asked if I might attend also," answered Heinz, placing his hands firmly on the table.

"In that case, is there something you wish to add?" queried Cornelius Van Mink, standing at his place. "I wasn't aware that you were coming, either."

"As you all probably know, the animals that deserted all took an oath of loyalty to our pack!" commenced Heinz, his body shaking with anger. "No matter what laws were changed, I believe those vows take precedence over a stupid ruling by the North Woods Council!"

"So what are you sayin', Mr. Rottweiler? Just spit it out!" cried Jason Crow, standing on the seat of his chair.

"I'm saying that if this council wants good relations with the North Woods, they had better deport Conan Greyhound, Sterling Buck, and Arnold Big Horn immediately from your state—'specially Conan, who was a member of the original pack!"

"Mr. Rottweiler," began Mayor Beaver, "unlike the North Woods, there are no loyalty oaths here. Everyone's free to come and go as they please. Why, we might just as well expel Clara Greyhound and Molly Sheepdog too!"

"Yes, they're guilty as well. But they would've returned to their mates eventually," responded Heinz.

"Is that true, Mr. Sheepdog? And does this dog speak for you and Miss von Shepherd?" asked Cornelius adamantly.

No one spoke for a few tense moments. Finally Sheldon got to his feet and faced the Rottweiler. "Heinz, if you please. Why don't you let Brigitte and me handle this? I think perhaps it's time for you to leave."

"Ha! I'll report this to Bruno and the others, Sheldon. Have you no loyalty? Have you no shame?" growled the Rottweiler as he stomped out of the room.

"Sorry about that interruption, but Heinz does not speak for us," said Sheldon calmly.

"I understand, Mr. Sheepdog. I'm sure he's distressed about losing his friends," concluded Cornelius.

"Yes, especially Conan. They were very close," sighed Sheldon, sitting back down.

After more discussion concerning the well-being of both states, Sheldon introduced another subject. "The council wished me to advance one other matter. It has to do with the Spring Race on May Day. Since most of the best runners now reside inside the Prairie, they were thinking of adding a contest concerning staffs. Inasmuch as all three states are now practicing drills, it might be something that would make it more interesting for everyone. We would have to set up a special committee, of course, which I would gladly do."

"Wouldn't a contest like that be dangerous?" questioned Dr. Muskrat. "Someone could really get hurt."

"Not if we make strict rules and use only staffs," said Sheldon. "And it might even renew old friendships."

After much debate, the City Council agreed to at least form a committee, including Sheldon, Billy Bones, Sheriff

Lone Wolf, and someone from the Hill Country. Before the meeting ended, Winston noticed that Billy approached Brigitte and Sheldon. He could not hear what they were saying, but Brigitte was smiling as the three left the hall together.

# CHAPTER TEN

# BRIGITTE'S ADMISSION

Billy Bones held one of the City Hall's heavy wooden doors open so that Brigitte von Shepherd and Sheldon Sheepdog could move out into the fresh autumn air. "I told Molly and Clara that I'd be seeing you this morning, and they invited you both for lunch. I hope you can come. I know Molly's especially anxious to see Sheldon."

"Yes, and I'm anxious to see her too," said Sheldon enthusiastically.

"And Brigitte, I was hopin' that we'd get a chance to talk," added Billy, feeling his heart pound rapidly in his chest again.

"Well, I think Bruno expects us to return and report to him…especially after Heinz's uproar," answered Brigitte hesitantly.

"I think maybe Bruno can wait this once, Brigitte… especially after Heinz's uproar," disputed Sheldon. "Besides, I think we both have things to discuss with Molly…and Billy."

"Well, I guess…," Brigitte began.

"Then it's settled. I know the Greyhounds and Molly are looking forward to seeing you both," declared the shepherd dog as they stepped down onto Court Street.

On the walk back to Clara's cottage, Sheldon and Billy talked earnestly about the possible contest using staffs and the North Wood's diminished team. When the three reached the East Wagon Trail and turned south, Billy casually reached over and took Brigitte's hand. When she did not resist, he felt a joy in his heart he had not felt since he left The Fortress more than three months ago.

As Billy, Brigitte, and Sheldon neared Clara's cottage, they saw Molly Sheepdog coming down the path toward them. Sheldon quickly ran to meet her, and they embraced

warmly. Billy knew at that moment that despite the conflict between the two states, the two sheepdogs still had great affection for one another. When Molly broke free, she hurried over to the German shepherd. "Brigitte, I'm so glad you came. We've missed you."

After taking Brigitte's hand and reaching for Billy's as well, Molly continued, "Come, our lunch is prepared, and we've been looking forward to seeing you all morning. We have much to talk about."

When the four dogs entered Clara's cottage, Clara and Conan greeted them just as enthusiastically. Billy could see that Brigitte was slightly uncomfortable, but she soon succumbed to Molly and the Greyhounds' sincere welcome.

"Conan hiked over to Calhoun Coyote's farm this morning so we could have chicken for our lunch, and Hester brought over several loaves of her freshly baked bread. So you see, we've been anxiously awaiting you," announced Clara. "Now sit down and eat while everything's nice and hot."

During the first part of the lunch, the five dogs indulged in only light conversation. But after the last slices of bread and pieces of chicken were consumed, Molly introduced the subject they all knew had to be discussed. "Sheldon, how did the meeting go today? I hope Bruno's not planning to retaliate."

"No, just the opposite; he's quite devastated. I'm afraid he can't understand why Arnold and Sterling and Conan deserted—especially you, Conan," answered Sheldon. "In fact, after he asked Brigitte and me to contact the Prairie

City Council, he retired to his room."

"But that brazen entrance by Heinz Rottweiler—how can you explain that?" inquired Billy.

"I'm afraid that was probably Heinz's doing. I don't think my brother was involved," responded Brigitte, entering the conversation for the first time. "Conan is the first male dog to leave the original pack. You must remember, they were very close and fought many battles together. I think all the dogs were upset, but especially Heinz and my brother."

"But we all fought those same battles, Brigitte. That was another time, before we received heightened clarity of mind," declared Molly.

"Nevertheless, there was an unspoken bond formed," continued Brigitte. "And that's why my brother initiated the blood oath—to keep that bond unbroken."

"But then he used that bond to gain power for himself, Brigitte," insisted Clara. "That's where everything went wrong."

"Yes, at first when he invited many of the animals from the Prairie to join what he called his 'extended pack.' He said he wanted freedom from *The Great Book of Rules*. But once he got them there, he used his loyalty oath to curtail their freedom, and he crossed the line," continued Conan.

"And when he had several of his pack of dogs injure Sandy Antelope, the loyalty to the blood oath ended, I'm afraid," determined Molly. "And of course, the hijacking of Winston Wise Owl's books and the capture of Billy Bones here was further evidence of his grasp for power."

"Now his liaison with the Hill Country is even more suspect," suggested Conan. "Surely this must be clear to you, Brigitte—even if he is your brother."

After these last statements, neither Brigitte nor Sheldon spoke for a few moments. Finally Sheldon responded for both of them. "Both Brigitte and I are aware of these failings in Bruno. But for now, you must also understand that we're the only ones of his close associates who can influence him. I'm afraid if we both left, things would certainly become worse, and there would be no stopping him."

"Then you must also understand, Sheldon, why I can't go back with you. There's no way my conscience would allow that," concluded Molly.

"And you must understand, Molly, there is no way I can leave him, if we can stave off any conflict between our two states," retorted Sheldon.

"Enough!" demanded Clara, laughingly. "This is supposed to be a friendly gathering!"

"In that case, allow me to show Miss von Shepherd my cottage before they go," requested Billy, smiling and lightening the mood. "And Brigitte, you'll be perfectly safe because Arnold Big Horn is staying with me until his place is finished."

"Yes, go with him, Brigitte. It'll give me a chance to spend some time with Molly," implored Sheldon. "Come, Molly, show me the rest of this house."

With Sheldon's encouragement, Brigitte and Billy walked over to Billy's cottage. When Arnold saw them enter, he simply grunted and started for the door. "I'll just sit out by the table and give you two some room. Oh…and it's good to see you again, Brigitte. I just hadn't expected it'd be so soon."

The inside of Billy's cottage was much like Clara's, since her place was inspired by his. Brigitte really liked the hutch cupboard next to the fireplace and the bunk bed on the west wall. But most of all, she was impressed by the corner cupboard that Justin Beaver had built in the south-west corner.

"It's a copy of Alvin Muskrat's grandmother's cupboard that was left along the Old Wagon Trail when the human pioneers came through," explained Billy. "The original is up in Maurice Rabbit's home in the Hill Country. We sneaked it up there when Brother Fabian Lynx and his lieutenants threatened to destroy all the human artifacts."

"Billy, you do understand why I must stay with my brother, don't you?" Brigitte asked, suddenly changing the subject and sitting down at the pine table in the middle of the room.

"I'm trying to," Billy answered, turning away.

"It's not only that he's my brother and that he saved me several times when we were in the old world," Brigitte began.

"I know that, but so much has changed…."

"Let me finish. And it's not that Sheldon and I feel we can keep him from doing something drastic to achieve his goals," the German shepherd continued.

"But what else is there?" asked Billy, sitting by her at the table and taking her hands in his.

"It's because of you, Billy. He thinks you want to displace him as leader of the pack! He thinks that Sandy and Arnold and Sterling and the rest are coming to the Prairie because of you! I finally realized that he thought that from the beginning, and that's why he wanted you to be his second in command. It was to keep you under his control."

"But I have no desires that way. Surely you must know…."

"Yes, I know. But Bruno doesn't think that way. He only knows how popular you are in the Prairie and even in the North Woods. And you can imagine if I left…."

"In the name of The Great Spirit, it never occurred to me that I was that big a threat to him," conceded Billy. "Is there no way of changing his mind?"

"I've tried, but as I said, his mind doesn't work that way. Now you see why Sheldon and I are so necessary in the North Woods," Brigitte concluded, as she stood to leave.

After the two dogs returned to Clara's cottage and picked up Sheldon, the three of them walked to the Beaver Creek Bridge which separated the two states. Before Brigitte and Sheldon departed, Brigitte turned and gave Billy a warm hug.

"It probably isn't safe for you to visit the North Woods right now, Billy, but I'll find a way to see you again," Brigitte whispered as she turned and followed Sheldon across the bridge and up the path toward The Fortress and the uncertain future.

# CHAPTER ELEVEN

## THE BIGHORN'S STORY

On Sunday evening Billy Bones and Arnold Big Horn heard a gentle tapping at their cottage door. They had just finished their evening meal and were still sitting at the table.

"That'll be Nosey and Needles, Arnold. As I told you earlier, they spend every Sunday night with me. You better be ready for some fireworks," warned the shepherd dog.

When Billy opened the door for Nosey Coon and Needles Porcupine, they entered as usual and started for the table. Nosey had on what appeared to be a red union-suit top and patched pants held up by a piece of rope. Needles, on the other hand, wore no shirt because of his needle-covered back, and his patched trousers were held up by two straps.

When the two rascals saw Arnold sitting at one of the kitchen chairs, they stopped short, and Nosey immediately inquired, "What's he doin' here?"

"Arnold's my guest over the winter. He'll be goin' to his own home in the spring after we fix it up."

"But I thought he was still up in the North Woods,"

remarked Needles, putting his bedroll down on the chair where he usually sat.

"No, he's back now," explained the dog. "He decided he doesn't want to live up there anymore."

"But where's he gonna sleep, Billy? Is he gonna take my bunk above you?" whined the raccoon, gesturing at his usual spot.

"No, it's okay, Nosey, he'll be sleeping on that mattress over there," grinned Billy, pointing to the southwest corner of the room. "I told him that top bunk was yours every Sunday night."

"Well, does he snore?" asked Nosey, clearly perturbed by the change of routine.

"No more than you, Nosey, 'cept maybe a little louder because of his size," laughed Billy again. "It'll be all right, I promise you."

"But will you still tell us stories, Billy?" asked Needles shyly.

"Of course, and maybe we'll get Arnold to tell us one," said Billy. "How about it, Arnold? You up for it?"

"Maybe, unless they keep whinin' about me bein' here," snorted the ram.

"Well, let's all get ready for bed, and I'll start the stories," decided the shepherd dog.

After Needles placed his bedroll in front of the corner cupboard, and Nosey climbed up into his bunk, Billy set two chairs in the middle of the room where the raccoon and the porcupine could easily hear. After the shepherd dog told a story about Billy Stuart and the old man fishing and skipping stones on the beaver pond, he turned to the bighorn ram. "Okay, it's your turn, Arnold."

"But I don't know any stories about the other world since I ain't never been there," stated Arnold.

"Well, how about when you were younger in the Hill Country? You've never told me about that," suggested the shepherd dog. "Why did you come down to the Prairie in the first place?"

Arnold suddenly turned away. "I don't know if you'd wanna hear 'bout that. It ain't a pretty story."

"If you'd rather not—I don't mean to pry," said Billy, realizing the ram may have had a good reason for never talking about it.

"No, it's weighed on my mind for some time, and it might help me to get it off my chest," decided Arnold.

"Only if you want to," answered Billy.

"Well okay, here goes," began the ram. "When I was growin' up, I was the oldest of four ram lambs."

"I thought you only had two brothers," said Nosey, poking his head over the railing of his bunk.

"Well, I have only two now, but that's part o' the story," explained Arnold. "Anyway, my youngest brother's name was Frank, but we always called him Franky. And I guess you could say he was a bit shy, but he had a really good heart."

"A little like Needles, huh?" added Nosey.

"Well, not exactly. You see, bighorn rams are supposed to butt heads and jump big crevices and climb around on rocks. But unfortunately, Franky didn't like to do that stuff and always made up excuses not to join my Dad and me and my brothers when we went up into the foothills. Anyway, Dad finally caught on and started forcin' him to come along, even though some of the jumps were pretty dangerous. When it was Franky's turn, he'd only jump the smaller ravines, and Dad'd get mad and try to force him to go over the bigger ones too. And since I was always lookin' out for Franky, I'd step in and try to protect him. Then Dad and me'd get into a fight, and Franky'd take off."

"Well, how about your Ma, Hilda? Didn't she try to reason with your Dad?" asked Needles.

"No, she felt the same way my Dad did. They kept sayin' they didn't want a sissy for a son! …'Scuse me a moment." At that point Arnold stood up and got a drink from the water pail.

"If you don't want to continue, it's okay," said Billy.

"No, I wanna finish," insisted Arnold. "It's just that I get so mad thinkin' about it….So this one day when I wasn't there, Dad took Franky out and tried to get him to jump an especially wide ravine. After goadin' him on for some time, Dad finally convinced him to try and even gave him a push." Arnold stopped again and sat back down on his chair. "Anyway, Franky didn't make it, and it killed him o' course….I'm afraid I never forgave my Dad—or my Ma—either, for that matter—and I packed up my things and came down to the Prairie. Thankfully, Sandy Antelope and Olen Buck and some other good citizens of the Prairie helped me fix up an old lean-to on Rocky Route. And that's how I got down here."

"And you never went back?" asked Nosey, peeking between the two bars of the railing.

"Well, my Dad passed on several years ago, and I went back for that. But I've never been back since," stated the ram.

"And your two other brothers?" asked Needles, sitting up on his bedroll.

"Well, they come to see me once in a while. And 'course we see each other durin' the Grand Fair and on May Day. We get along okay. But Ma, she could o' done somethin' but chose not to. And I'll never forgive her for that! I'm not sure she even cared! I think Franky was an embarrassment to her!"

Soon after Arnold's poignant story, when all his guests were in bed, Billy blew out the candles and crawled into his lower bunk. Before going to sleep he started thinking about Arnold's story and about Arnold himself. Although the ram showed a rough exterior, there was a compassionate side to him that he did not often show.

# CHAPTER TWELVE

# THE WINTER SOLSTICE

For the next six weeks, Billy Bones delivered on his promise. Every afternoon during the week, Victor Running Deer, Arnold Big Horn, and Sterling and Ernest Buck and even Conan Greyhound showed up to work on Georgie Beaver's new home. Mornings, of course, were filled with drill practices or roadwork for the Spring Race on May Day. Remarkably, Patience Doe continued to run with the three bucks and the ram, and it soon became obvious that there was a blossoming relationship between Patience and Victor Running Deer.

When the exterior of Georgie's house was finally finished, Gladys and Lydia Beaver, Clara Greyhound, and Molly Sheepdog prepared a banquet for the workers. The big spread was laid out on two long tables in front of the new house so that the outside work could be admired. Even Alvin Muskrat and Johnny Otter, who had helped with the underwater foundation, and Georgie's aunt and uncle, Constance Beaver and Mayor George P. Beaver, came to celebrate.

The walls in the new house were a little higher than the older one, and it was built mostly on land, but the two homes together were indeed a handsome addition to the east side of the pond. The choice of rough-hewn lumber that had been whitewashed also turned out to be the right choice, and the two places glistened in the noonday sun. Mayor Beaver's home on the south edge of the large island in the center of the pond gave an even more majestic look to the overall surroundings. The mayor's home was made of the same materials as the other two, but it had turrets on either side, giving it a castle-like appearance.

"I say welcome, and fine work, Georgie," began the older George Beaver when he walked over to greet his nephew and the shepherd dog. "And Mr. Bones, I understand that you're the one who convinced most of these workers to come and help Georgie and Lydia with their fine new home."

"They were only too happy to do it, I can assure you, since we all love Georgie," responded Billy, putting a hand on his friend's shoulder.

"Not to change the subject, Mr. Bones, but I hope you're planning to attend the Tribal Council Meeting during the winter solstice," remarked the mayor soberly. "We're very concerned about their new chief and his close ties with the North Woods."

"You mean Gaylord Cougar?" asked the shepherd dog. "Yes, I've been worried about that too. But I was hopin' for some peace and quiet—especially now that Georgie's house is finished."

"I understand how you feel," returned the mayor. "And I hate to say this, but I think you're really needed up there.

You don't know who might appear and talk up this union idea between the North Woods and the Hill Country."

"But they agreed to do nothing until at least the next three-state meeting on May second," responded Billy.

"I'm well aware of that, Mr. Bones, but I have an idea that the last four defections have changed the playing field. I'm afraid Bruno von Shepherd might try something rash," cautioned Mayor Beaver.

"Well, it's coming up in a couple of days. I guess I'd better prepare myself," sighed Billy regretfully.

Billy Bones rose early on December 21 so he could hike up to the Hill Country and talk to his good friend Maurice Rabbit before the festivities commenced. He knew there would be a program in the afternoon celebrating the coming of the solstice and the renewal of light, and then a concert that evening. Lucinda Vulture had again invited Melba Thrush, Gloria Meadowlark, Hosea Brown Thrasher, and Wendell Red Breast from the Prairie to sing. He wondered if the tradition would continue if a union was formed with the North Woods.

When the shepherd dog reached the Hill Country, he crossed the bridge at Winding Walk and took the path up to Maurice's place. The rabbit had given him a standing invitation to stay with him during all Tribal Council events. Maurice's home was built into the south side of a mountain with large windows in front. Because he was a painter, he needed as much natural light as he could get.

"Come in! Come in! And get out o' the cold!" cried

the jackrabbit, opening his front door to the dog. "I've been waitin' for you. Throw your bedding on your mattress while I finish putting some greens and bread and honey on the table. Then we'll sit down and have a bite to eat. I've missed you."

After the two animals ate and made some small talk, Billy initiated a more serious discussion. "How is everything, Maurice? Do you hear anything more about uniting with the North Woods?"

"Not much is said openly," answered the rabbit, "but there's a strong undercurrent of mistrust. When Omar Mountain Goat was alive, everyone seemed always happy and content. Now with Gaylord...."

"How about the drill sessions with Angus Wolfhound? Have many citizens joined in?" inquired Billy.

"There are a few, like Gaylord himself and Hilda Big Horn's two sons and a few deer and Arthur Elk. But that's about the extent of it. I went a couple of times, but the others were all so much bigger than me that I felt out of place."

"Yes, size is a problem. I think if it came to an actual confrontation, it would be between the larger animals," agreed the dog. "However, we're thinkin' of a type of tournament during May Day using only staffs and different weight groups. Actually it was Sheldon Sheepdog's idea. He believes that if staffs were used for competition rather than aggression, the states would eventually forget their differences."

"I don't know. It could get out of hand," warned Maurice.

"Not if it was closely regulated and everyone played by the rules," answered Billy. "At least that's Sheldon's thinking. And of course, clubs would be off limits."

Since the winter solstice was greatly anticipated, the old log lodge was packed with onlookers for the afternoon program and evening concert. For these festive events, the room was decorated with pine boughs and other greenery, and the two massive fireplaces on the north and south walls were resplendent with holly berries and brightly-colored ribbons.

Billy Bones thought the songbirds sang gloriously in their concert, and he was happy they were received so enthusiastically, knowing that some councilors had been distancing themselves from the Prairie.

Only residents with grievances attended on the second day. They were called in, one by one, by Arthur Elk, who guarded the heavy doors at the east entrance. The councilors who met them inside were in a semicircle facing the doors. The new chief, Gaylord Cougar, dressed in his golden robe, sat in the center, and Lucretia Lizard and Hilda Big Horn sat on his left in their robes of green and brown. Beyond them was any empty chair for Orville Bat, who was taking a sabbatical and acting as spiritual adviser for the North Woods. To Gaylord's right, the Hill Country's spiritual councilor, Lucinda Vulture, was dressed all in black. At the end of the right side were Billy Bones in his blue robe of truth and Maurice Rabbit in his multicolored robe.

For much of the day the council heard complaints from various citizens. Billy noticed that Gaylord Cougar did not exhibit the same patience that Omar Mountain Goat had and often interrupted their grievances. Fortunately, the other five councilors acted as a jury. This meant that Billy and Lucinda and Maurice could catch his misjudgments and outvote Lucretia and Hilda, who almost always sided with the cougar.

"Tomorrow morning we'll have a drill practice with Angus Wolfhound," announced Gaylord at the end of the session. "Mr. Bones and Maurice, we'd be happy if you'd join us. I'm sure Angus could give you both a few pointers—especially you, Maurice, since you've been missing a number of our drills lately. And then tomorrow afternoon we'll have our quarterly meeting. I'm happy to announce that we'll have a special guest—so please be prompt!"

# CHAPTER THIRTEEN

# THE SPECIAL GUEST

Maurice Rabbit decided to accept the invitation and attend practice the next morning with Billy Bones. The jackrabbit preferred to not participate but did not want the dog to go by himself. Even though Billy was well liked in the community, he did not know how Angus would react, since the three deserters were all his friends. He was relieved when Angus Wolfhound rushed over to him as soon as he arrived at the practice area in front of the sacred lodge.

"A friend of ours will be joinin' us shortly," the wolfhound began. "I'll try to hold it together, but be on your guard. He's really angry! If you'd like to leave, you're welcome to do so."

"Who are you talkin' about?" asked Billy. "You don't mean Bruno?"

"I'm afraid so. He was comin' for the meeting this afternoon but decided to arrive early when he heard you might be here."

"Thanks for tellin' me, Angus. I know you can't be too happy about Conan and Sterling and Arnold yourself," said Billy.

"No, I'm furious. But this is my practice, and I don't wanna see it get out o' hand!" frowned the wolfhound. "In fact, because of the temperature I thought of takin' it inside the lodge. But they've got it all decorated, and I don't wanna mess things up. We'll just have to put up with the cold."

Soon after Angus voiced his concern, Arnold's two brothers and two deer from back in the hills arrived. Shortly after that Arthur Elk walked over from his hut adjacent to the drill area. Finally, Bruno von Shepherd and Gaylord Cougar showed up together. Billy was shocked at how companionable the two leaders appeared to be.

"Mr. Billy Bones and Maurice Rabbit, I see you worked up the courage to join us. I brought a mutual friend along. I hope you don't mind," laughed Gaylord, testing his staff.

Before Billy could respond, Bruno immediately confronted him. "Well, Mr. Bones, we meet again. It's been a while. But I see you've been busy coercing four more of my pack members away from me. That's a low blow even for you!"

"I'm sorry, Mr. von Shepherd, but I'm afraid they came on their own volition," retorted Billy.

"Ha! So they just happened to leave after you made two trips to The Fortress," growled Bruno. "And then two of them left with you.... Come, Mr. Bones, I don't know what you promised them, but I can't believe it was just your sparkling personality."

"It had very little to do with me, Bruno. I think you need to search your own heart for that answer," responded

Billy, walking away from the angry German shepherd.

"Okay, let's get started here!" shouted Angus Wolfhound, trying to avoid a conflict. "Let's begin the opening exercises with just the staff. Since we have guests here today, we won't be using clubs. Now everyone form a line facing me."

Sometime later when the one-on-one drills began, Billy and Maurice immediately paired up, as did the two deer. After that, one of the Big Horn brothers went with the elk and the other decided to work with the cougar, leaving Angus and Bruno together. Finally, when Angus called for partners to switch, Billy and Maurice started to change with the two deer, but Bruno moved instantly between them. "Not so fast, Mr. Bones. Why don't we see if you've improved any since you left our company?"

On seeing the possible danger, Angus immediately intruded. "This may not be a good idea, Bruno. How about workin' with Gaylord?"

At that moment Billy knew he should walk away but could not make himself back down. "It's all right. I'll be glad to work with Mr. von Shepherd."

As Billy and Bruno began trading blows and parries, the contest got more and more competitive. "I think I'll just referee, if you don't mind," said Angus, as the other participants stopped what they were doing and circled the two shepherd dogs.

At first Billy held his own, but eventually Bruno's terrible anger started to push Billy back toward Arthur's hut. "I offered you more than anyone in the pack, and you turned your back on me!" snarled Bruno.

"I didn't turn my back on you! I told you why I couldn't stay, but you weren't listening," returned Billy, fighting off the German shepherd's blows.

"And now you repay me by stealing my pack members from me!" continued Bruno. "Well, this is what I have for you!" cried Bruno, forcing Billy against the wall of participants with a series of well-aimed blows.

Unfortunately, Gaylord's staff was extended into Billy's path as he was forced backwards through the drill group, causing him to trip, fall back, and lose control of his staff. Bruno, losing all restraint, raised his staff to strike Billy on the head. Fortunately, Angus reacted with lightning speed and knocked Bruno's staff out of his hand.

"No, that's against the rules, Bruno. You can't hit another animal when he's down!" yelled Angus, embarrassed by his leader's attempt to hurt Billy. Bruno glared at Angus for a moment but then seemed to regain his composure.

"Well, I guess that's enough for today. As cold as it is, I think we can make this a short one," continued the wolfhound, defusing the situation.

As Billy and Maurice headed back to the rabbit's abode, Billy said apologetically, "I shouldn't have let him goad me into fighting. I should have been strong enough to walk away."

"It wasn't your fault, Billy. But I think it'll affect this afternoon's meeting," responded the jackrabbit. "I believe the direction of the wind has changed and that Bruno von

Shepherd will not be a threat to anyone today. And as unbelievable as it might seem, it was his second in command that blew that wind away!"

Billy knew that Angus Wolfhound had probably been involved in the attack on Sandy Antelope and was certainly loyal to Bruno von Shepherd. However, Billy also reasoned that the wolfhound prided himself on maintaining discipline during his drill instructions, and Bruno's attack on Billy bothered Angus immensely.

True to Maurice's prediction, Bruno was subdued during the afternoon session, and instead of talking about a union, spent most of his time praising Gaylord Cougar for becoming the Hill Country chief. He did, however, give Billy Bones one parting insult.

"I understand, Mr. Cougar, that Mr. Bones wanted to be chief after Omar Mountain Goat died. I'm glad this council had the courage to pick the right councilor," smirked Bruno at the end of the session. "And thanks for letting me meet with you this afternoon."

"Excuse me a moment, Mr. Cougar, but I can't let that stand," interjected Lucinda Vulture, speaking for the first time. "It was my idea that Mr. Bones would make a good chief, not his. And I still believe he would have been an excellent choice."

"Thank you, Lucinda, for that clarification," said Gaylord sarcastically. "And thank you, Mr. von Shepherd, for your kind words. But before we leave, may I remind you that our next meeting will be on March 21 during the spring equinox. At that time I'm hoping that Orville Bat can finally make an appearance, so we can be assured of his wise council. And of course, the three-state meeting on May 2 follows soon after that, and we need to be thinking about what kind of relationship we want with the North Woods."

# CHAPTER FOURTEEN

## SHELDON'S MEETING

Because of the winter snows, a number of the Prairie drill practices had to be cancelled, but by the middle of February they started again enthusiastically. Because of Conan's concerns, the group also started using clubs from time to time. Unlike the staffs, the training with clubs was more combative, but the greyhound carefully taught those skills as well. On the last practice in February, Sheriff Lone Wolf took Conan and Billy Bones aside.

"Sheldon Sheepdog would like to meet with the three of us and Angus Wolfhound on the morning of March 1. He's still pushing for a competition using staffs during the May Day celebrations. He's scheduled to meet with the Prairie City Council in the afternoon and would like us all to be in agreement before then," suggested the sheriff.

"And he still thinks that's a good idea?" inquired Billy. "I told you about my pairing with Bruno von Shepherd during the winter solstice. That didn't go so well."

"I'm sure Sheldon knows, but I think we still owe him the courtesy to listen. I know he's tryin' his best to avoid any kind of conflict between the three states," returned Walter.

"I believe you're right there. Where does he want to meet?" asked the shepherd dog.

"Here at City Hall where the council will convene later," answered the wolf. "And Conan, he'd like you to be on the oranizing committee, if that's all right with you. I know this will be the first time you've seen Angus since you left the North Woods."

"Well, I have to meet up with him sooner or later. It might as well be in a neutral place," decided the greyhound. "Besides, it's his problem, not mine!"

The five committee members arrived at City Hall at almost the same time on the morning of March 1. They decided to assemble in the west wing of the entrance hall where the council would later congregate. When Conan and Angus met, they were cool to each other but not outright hostile. Since Billy had encountered the wolfhound last, he took the seat next to him.

"I think you all know what I have in mind," began the sheepdog. "As I explained to you earlier, both Mr. Cougar and Mr. von Shepherd are concerned that the May Day Race will involve only runners from the Prairie and the Hill Country. They thought that since the race is attended by citizens from all three states, another type of competition should be added. And since all three states are practicin' drill sessions with the staff, I thought the five of us could come up with a contest that would satisfy their expectations."

"The main argument against that, Sheldon, is the

possibility of someone gettin' hurt, especially if participants got angry or held a grudge," reminded Sheriff Lone Wolf.

"Yes, like what almost happened to Billy up in the Hill Country," continued Conan.

"But I was there to referee," answered Angus. "Besides, I don't think most animals would get as angry as Bruno did."

"Yes, I think that if we made the rules rigid enough and had referees like Angus, the contest could be very exciting," determined Sheldon.

"Then I suggest we don't pit states against each other but have open drawings," suggested Billy. "And we need to have separate categories for different weights and sizes."

"You mean maybe I won't get to fight Conan?" growled Angus, glancing at the greyhound.

"Frankly, I think you and Conan should be referees, since you're both instructors," said Billy. That way you could see trouble brewing and stop a contest if necessary. And of course, you'd have to make peace with each other."

"I'll work with him, but I won't necessarily like it!" barked Angus again.

"It will be no bed of roses for me either, Mr. Wolfhound!" snarled the greyhound in return.

"I think both of you need to bury your grievances if this is going to work," scolded Sheldon. "We have a lot at stake here."

"Well, I wasn't the one to jump ship," returned Angus. "But I'll try if he will!"

"And I'll not back out either," agreed Conan finally.

"And speaking of differences, we should make sure that Bruno and Billy don't get paired together," proposed the wolf. "No reason askin' for trouble."

"Well, if we divide into weight classes, their group would be one of the largest," declared Sheldon. "They wouldn't meet unless they're both in the finals, fighting for the championship."

"Yes, how exactly would that work—I mean, to make it fair for everyone?" asked the sheriff.

"As I see it, there would be four weight classes," suggested Sheldon. "For instance, the elk and the bison and the bear would be the heaviest group; then the deer, the antelope, and the bighorns; and after that the wolf, the larger dogs, the cougar, the foxes, and the coyotes. And last, of course, would be the smaller animals."

"And the members of the different teams would only sign up if they wanted to," suggested Walter Lone Wolf. "But how would we choose a winner?"

"Easy," said Angus. "The one who knocks the other member's staff out of their hands or knocks them off their feet would be declared the winner."

"And what would be off limits?" asked Billy.

"Striking someone when they're down, like Bruno tried to do to you, or hitting someone on the head," returned Angus. "And of course, if a fighter was purposely hurting his opponent, we'd have to stop the bout."

"That sounds fair and reasonable," returned Sheldon. "Now when can we meet again?"

"I say we meet in the Hill Country on the second

morning of the spring equinox. We can make any final decisions then," suggested Angus.

"Do you have to pass this by Gaylord Cougar first?" inquired Sheldon.

"No, in fact it was his idea," stated the wolfhound.

"Then can I tell the Prairie City Council that we're planning a contest using staffs that will be safe but enjoyable?" asked Sheldon.

All the members of the committee nodded in agreement, but Billy still had reservations. "What if someone loses his temper?" he thought. "The whole thing could backfire."


Before Conan and Billy left the hall, Angus confronted Conan one last time. "I still don't see how you could be so disloyal to Bruno, Conan. I thought better of you."

"You know that Clara left before me, Angus. We both believe that Bruno wanted to control us and curtail our freedoms. It was the one thing he said we were creating a new state to avoid. You can surely see that!" countered the greyhound.

"All I know is we wouldn't have survived in the other world without Bruno's leadership," contended the wolfhound. "That's why Sheldon and I are still with him. We haven't forgotten!" Angus glanced once more at Billy. "Nor has his sister, Brigitte, as you know only too well, Mr. Billy Bones!"

"But things are different now," rebutted Conan. "We're no longer fighting just to survive anymore!"

After Billy and Conan left the great hall, they walked silently for some time toward the beaver dam. Finally the shepherd dog stopped and turned to the greyhound. "I think Angus will be okay, Conan. I've seen him work with the Hill Country's drill group, and he's very good with them. And you must remember—he saved me from gettin' hurt during the winter solstice."

"But why's he so hostile to me? He surely knows what Bruno's doin'," mused Conan, gazing down at the ground.

"I think he feels guilty for one thing, and he's probably angry with himself."

"Why's that?"

"I think it has to do with Sandy Antelope. He knows that we know he was one of the dogs who attacked Sandy just before the Grand Fair. I'm sure Bruno got him to do it, but that doesn't assuage his guilt."

# CHAPTER FIFTEEN

# THE SPRING EQUINOX

By the time the spring equinox rolled around, Billy Bones and Arnold Big Horn had finished renovating the ram's lean-to on Rocky Route. As with Georgie's house, Victor Running Deer, Sterling Buck, Ernest Buck, and even Sandy Antelope helped from time to time. Together they succeeded in enlarging the building, adding a second window, and restoring the fireplace, which had been falling apart.

On the day before the equinox, Billy invited Nosey Coon and Needles Porcupine to stay the night even though it was not Sunday. The two rascals had become quite fond of Arnold in spite of his rough ways and hated to see him go.

"And who's gonna see that you behave when I'm gone?" asked the ram, picking the raccoon up and throwing him on the shepherd dog's bunk. "Billy's much too nice to you."

"At least we won't have to put up with your snorin', Mr. Smarty Big Horn," giggled Nosey, jumping up from the bed and trying to ram the bighorn with his head.

"Oh, no you don't!" snorted Arnold, tossing Nosey up on the top bunk. "There. Try your shenanigans from up there!"

"Could Arnold visit us again some Sunday and stay the night?" inquired Needles, tugging at the shepherd's arm.

"Do yah think I'd actually come here and put up with you two on purpose?" laughed Arnold, pretending to hit the porcupine with his fist. "You're out of your mind!"

"Yeah, I think that would be great too," grinned Billy, "if I could just get the three of you to act your age!"

When Billy Bones and Arnold Big Horn prepared to leave the next morning, they said goodbye to Nosey and Needles and started north to Beaver Dam Road. After they crossed the dam, they merged onto South Court Street and then onto Court Street until they reached Main Street with its brightly-colored shops. After crossing Main Street, they continued on past the prairie dog town, where only doors and windows showed above ground. Then they moved on to Rocky Route, which eventually led to Arnold's lean-to on the north side of the road.

"Well, here's where I leave you, Arnold. Good luck with your new place. I really enjoyed havin' you around these last few months!" admitted the shepherd dog.

"I've enjoyed it too, even though yah got me to work on two places. Anyway, we'll see yah at drill practices," bleated Arnold as he turned and entered his newly refurbished home.

Just before the dog started up into the foothills, Gerard Crow flew out of the east and landed on his shoulder. "I haven't seen you for a while, my friend. I guess you didn't like the idea of Arnold stayin' with me. Well, I'm back to livin' by myself now, so that should please you."

Soon after the two companions crossed into the Hill Country, the pathway became steeper and more rugged. When they got to Echo Canyon, Billy crossed the creek called Spirit Moves and proceeded toward Maurice Rabbit's dugout. When they reached the jackrabbit's home and knocked on the door, Gerard flew off the dog's shoulder and headed back toward his father's farm.

Upon entering, Billy discovered that Maurice was not alone. Lucinda Vulture was sitting at the table in the center of the room. As usual she was dressed in her long black robe. Billy Bones was in complete awe of the old vulture and felt the two of them had a spiritual connection he did not fully understand—but knew it was an ever-present phenomenon.

"Ah, Mr. Bones, I was hoping you'd arrive early. We have something to discuss before going to the meeting this afternoon," she began. "Here, sit at the table with Maurice and me. As you both know, Orville Bat spends most of his time in the North Woods, and that has changed the complexion of things in our council."

"But I thought Orville was going to be at the meeting today!" exclaimed Billy, taking his seat at the table.

"Yes he is, and that's one of the problems. Fortunately, though, Sheldon Sheepdog will represent the North Woods today and not Bruno himself. And even though the subject of union with the North Woods will raise its ugly head, we may at least have a chance to postpone it. It is my hope that we can stave off the actual vote until after the three-state meeting on May 2."

"Do you think that's possible?" asked Maurice. "With Orville present, they could outvote us four to three."

"That's true, unless we can come up with some sort of plan," sighed the old vulture. "I understand that Gaylord Cougar secretly met with Bruno von Shepherd several times, and I'm afraid Bruno's won him over. I'm hoping that with Sheldon here, we can talk about the May Day competitions and not get too serious about uniting. But if we do...."

"I have an idea that might be worth tryin'," suggested Billy, "if you'd care to hear it."

"I was hoping you would," confessed Lucinda. "Maurice and I have seen a steady deterioration of the council. And I don't think Gaylord fully comprehends what we'd be giving up, once we're under Bruno's thumb."

"Well, that's where my idea begins—with Gaylord Cougar himself," stated Billy determinedly.

For the next few moments, Billy discussed his plan with Lucinda and Maurice, and the three decided to attempt it during the meeting, especially since Bruno would not be physically present.

As it was the spring equinox, Lucinda Vulture, Orville Bat, and Lucretia Lizard began the session by reading from *The Vulture's Appendix* about the change of seasons, the longer days of sunlight, and filling the time with good works and steadfastness of purpose. When Gaylord Cougar stood to start the business meeting, he asked Arthur Elk to empty the sacred lodge of all citizens except the members of the Tribal Council and their guest, Sheldon Sheepdog.

"Mr. Sheepdog, would you please come before the council and share your ideas concerning the Prairie's May Day celebration?" requested Gaylord. "I understand that you already presented your plans before the other councils, and they've each favored your proposal."

"Thank you, Mr. Cougar. Both you and Mr. von Shepherd expressed concerns about the Spring Race, since most of the best runners are now in the Prairie," explained the sheepdog. "Therefore I formed a committee, and they decided that a competition using staffs might be added, since all three states have been practicing drills using staffs."

"And who's on that committee, Mr. Sheepdog?" asked Hilda Big Horn.

"Well, let's see: our own Angus Wolfhound and Billy Bones, and then there's Sheriff Lone Wolf, Conan Greyhound, and myself," stated Sheldon. "In fact, we're meeting tomorrow morning if your council agrees to go ahead with our proposal."

After much discussion, the council decided to go along with the competitions and allow the committee to come up with the details. When Gaylord finally broached the subject of a union with the North Woods, Lucinda immediately launched the idea that she and Billy and Maurice had conceived. "There's only one problem that I see, Mr. Cougar. Who would be the leader of this union—you or Bruno von Shepherd?"

"What do you mean by that, Ms. Vulture? Naturally we'd both be in charge of our own states," answered the cougar.

"But if we were united with them, whose council would make the decisions, ours or theirs?" continued Maurice.

"I understand that the two councils would meet as one and make decisions together," said Gaylord, starting to rethink the situation.

"Yes, but who would have the final say? Who would be the chief?" asked Billy, looking around at the other councilors. "Mr. Sheepdog, have you any ideas about this?"

"Well, as I understand it, Bruno would still be head of the pack at The Fortress. As far as the rest of the Hill Country and the Big Woods is concerned, I'm not sure...."

"Would Bruno ever concede to be second in command," continued Billy. "I hardly think so. I guess Mr. Cougar would have to fill that role."

"But we voted Mr. Cougar as our chief. That's hardly fair!" bleated Hilda Big Horn. "Orville, you've been spending time with Bruno von Shepherd, What's your opinion?"

"Yes, Orville, you know Mr. von Shepherd pretty well by now," stated Lucinda Vulture. "Do you think he'd accept being second in command?"

"Yes, Orville," hissed Lucretia Lizard. "Or would Bruno relegate our chief to second place?"

Orville Bat reacted by drawing his powerfully-clawed feet under him and closing his eyes as tightly as he could.

"Well, Orville, are you going to answer?" demanded Gaylord, entering the discussion.

"I don't know! I don't know!" squeaked the bat, lowering his head.

"Yes, you do," insisted the vulture, realizing that Billy's idea was beginning to work.

"All right, No! Definitely not! Bruno would never accept being second in command. He has to be in charge of everything! Everyone in the North Woods knows that!" squealed Orville as loudly as he could.

"Before we discuss this any further, I think we should all agree on one thing," declared Lucinda Vulture. "We elected Gaylord Cougar to be our chief—not Bruno von Shepherd!"

Billy could see by Gaylord's confusion that he had not thought of what the consequences of union would mean for him personally, and he did not relish the idea of being second in command.

"I think maybe this conversation has gone far enough and we need to continue it after the three-state meeting on May 2," concluded Gaylord uneasily. "This session is adjourned!"

The contest committee met the following morning and decided the rules for the competitions. There would be four classes of contenders, and each class would draw names to see who they would compete against. The winner of each bout would fight the winner of another bout until a champion was chosen in each class. Angus Wolfhound and Conan Greyhound would act as referees and would stay out of the contests. Finally it was concluded that the event should be convened after the Spring Race, in case one of the runners was accidently injured in some way.

"And how about you, Billy?" asked Conan before the committee broke up. "Maybe you should join Angus and me and excuse yourself. A replay of what happened between you and Bruno would not be good."

"I say we let Billy think that possibility over. He can give us an answer on the day of the tournament," decided the sheepdog. "And you can all help me with organizing this event once we get there. It will be something new for all of us, but I believe it will be a good thing…if we can pull it off!"

Billy dropped by Maurice Rabbit's dugout to say good-bye and then started down the path toward Rocky Route. He knew he should have refused to compete in the staff contests, but something in him would not let him back out. He was somewhat ashamed of himself. He was glad, however, that the ploy he had used against Gaylord Cougar had been successful, and that for the moment, the idea of the Hill Country and the North Woods uniting was on the back burner.

Just as Billy Bones started down the steepest part of the path, he saw Gerard Crow flying toward him. After circling twice, the crow landed on his shoulder and stayed there until he got back to his cottage on the East Wagon Trail.

"You might as well stay the night, Gerard. I could use your company."

# CHAPTER SIXTEEN

## THE SPRING RACE

Winston Wise Owl loved the smells that emanated from the booths up and down Main Street on the day of the Spring Race. He liked to get to City Hall early so he could confer with the other judges—Justin Beaver, Jason Crow, and Deputy Harold Eagle, as soon as they came. The owl knew that Sandy Antelope would not be running, so the race would probably be very close between the three deer from the Prairie.

When the other three judges arrived, Winston assigned the handling of the start and finish lines to the beaver and the crow, as usual. After that it would his job to survey the first part of the race that went south around the pond and the eagle's responsibility to oversee the second part until it returned to Court Street.

"We'll have the hardest job, Harold, since we'll be flying over so many low-hanging trees. But do your best. Fortunately, most of the entrants are friends, so there shouldn't be any foul play," reasoned Winston. "Also, it's a beautiful day and not much breeze, so that bodes well for a clean race."

Winston was pleased that the crowds were just as heavy as the year before, since all the runners were either from the Prairie or the Hill Country. Because both the start and finish lines were in front of City Hall, most of the spectators lined up along Court Street. The owl noticed that Billy Bones was standing with Conan and Clara Greyhound in front of the great hall.

When Billy saw Winston, he stepped down from his spot and called, "Mr. Wise Owl, watch out for Sterling and Ernest. They're really at the top of their game!"

"But how about Victor? Isn't he the favorite?" the owl yelled back.

"He was, but I'm not so sure now! His interest may lie elsewhere!" answered Billy, as he grinned and returned to his place by the greyhounds.

At that moment Winston noticed that Melinda Doe and her mother, Myrtle, were also near the finish line. "I wonder who she's rooting for today, Sterling or Victor? Or does she have someone else in mind?" he pondered and then reproached himself for thinking poorly of the doe.

The two brothers, Sterling and Ernest Buck, and their sister, Patience Doe, arrived first. Since Clara Greyhound ran in last year's Great Medley during the Grand Fair and wore pants and a short-sleeved blouse, the sight of Patience in the same attire raised little concern. Arnold Big Horn, accompanied by Sandy Antelope and the two deer from the Hill Country arrived next, followed closely by Victor Running Deer and Arnold's two brothers.

After all the runners had a chance to stretch and the

males removed their shirts, Sandy wished them all good luck and took his place among the spectators. When Jason Crow called the competitors to the starting line, Winston and Harold flew up to the roof of City Hall where it would be easier for them to take off once the race commenced.

"Remember, you ain't allowed to use your hands or trip anyone or bump anyone off the track. If you get caught, you'll be disqualified," warned Jason Crow. "All right, on your mark…get set…go!"

Since all the participants were congenial, the race began without incident. At the same moment, Winston was remembering the rivalry between Victor Running Deer and the ne'er-do-well, Rodney Wild Deer. Because they both had strong feelings for Melinda Doe, a dramatic confrontation always preceded their several races.

True to his concerns, the owl could not see much while the runners were on South Court Street. When they reached the dam, he noticed that Sterling and Ernest had taken a slight lead, closely followed by the rest of the field, who were tightly packed together. An unfortunate disaster struck when one of Arnold's brothers tried to pass Patience Doe on the far side of the pond and accidentally stepped on her foot. This caused the doe to lose her balance and fall to the ground. Most of the other runners ran around or jumped over her, but Victor stopped and helped her to her feet.

By the time Victor and Patience rejoined the race, they had lost considerable ground. Winston noticed that after much urging, Victor finally ran ahead of Patience and tried to work his way back through the pack.

After the runners crossed the two bridges that connected the pond to North Court, Victor made one last valiant effort to catch Sterling and Ernest, but their lead was insurmountable. In the end, Sterling managed to just edge out his brother at the finish line, and a little deer from the Hill Country came in third. For his part, Victor placed a respectable fourth, but it was the first time he would not receive a blue, red, or white ribbon in the Spring Race. Patience ran well considering her fall but only finished toward the end with Arnold's two brothers.

When Winston observed Victor afterwards, he noticed that the buck was worried that Patience might have hurt herself and was examining her foot.

"I think Victor may have strong feelings for Patience, and I believe it's overriding his concern about placing out of the ribbons," the owl thought to himself. "Well, good for him. He's come a long ways."

Shortly after Winston congratulated Sterling and Ernest, he noticed that Melinda had also approached Sterling. The young buck stood and talked to her for a short time, and the conversation appeared to be pleasant enough. Finally he nodded goodbye to her and left with Ernest, Victor, and Patience. Winston was aware that Sterling had to get ready for the competition with staffs that afternoon, but he also knew that there was time for the young buck to renew his relationship with Melinda if he so desired.

# CHAPTER SEVENTEEN

## COMPETITION WITH STAFFS

Sheldon's five-member committee for the competition with staffs met shortly before the participants were scheduled to show up. The sheepdog had already placed the signup table before the steps of the City Hall. The event itself would be held in the field just south of the great hall where the Prairie's team practiced three times a week.

After Sheldon called the members to the table, he addressed Billy Bones. "Well, Mr. Bones, are you going to take part in today's competitions or are you going to help me?"

"I've decided to help you," grinned the shepherd dog.

"Wise decision, Mr. Bones, although I think Mr. von Shepherd will be disappointed. He was looking forward to beating you," said the sheepdog, smiling back at his friend.

"Yes, I'm relieved too," remarked Conan Greyhound. "We'll have enough to do without watching you and Bruno settling your old grudges with a staff."

"Then may we get started?" requested Sheldon. "Sheriff

Lone Wolf, I take it you'll participate. I think we'll need you in your weight bracket."

"Let's wait and see who signs up. If I'm needed, I'll gladly take part," agreed the wolf.

"I think you should, Walter," said Conan enthusiastically. "You've become one of our best contenders. It'd be a shame to lose you."

"Well, let's see how it goes," suggested Sheldon. "Conan and Angus, I think you both should referee every event in case there's trouble. And Billy, why don't you sit behind the table with me? The competitors should start showing up at any moment."

"Shall we just tell them what division they're in? How does that work?" asked Billy, taking his seat.

"Yes, we'll follow the criteria I laid out at our first meeting, except for the foxes—they should go with the smallest group. If you recall, we placed contestants in four groups, from the heaviest to the lightest. Remember, we started with Arthur Elk and Bison Bob and Milton Brown Bear in the heaviest group, but I don't think Milton's interested.

"Yes, I remember the grouping," assured Billy. "The second and third groups should have the most contestants."

"Probably, if most of them show up," agreed the sheepdog.

As it happened, most drill members did sign up, but a few decided not to, as in Billy's case. Surprisingly, by including Sheriff Lone Wolf, there were equal numbers of competitors in all four categories.

Billy was concerned that some North Woods contestants

would be belligerent towards him. Most of them were hospitable, though, with the exception of Neevil Cur, Lenny's brothers, and Bruno von Shepherd.

"I understand you're afraid to face me," growled Bruno after signing up.

"Yes, that's it!" answered Billy, as good-naturedly as he could. "How did you guess?"

After looking at the count and before starting, Sheldon met with the committee. "Since there are only two in the heaviest category, they'll automatically go to the final round. The lightest group has four, after we added the two foxes. The other two groups have eight in each section, so we'll start with them. Then we'll go with the lightest group."

The crowds had already encircled the playing area, and it seemed to Billy that every inhabitant of the little world was there. At one o'clock Sheldon announced the opening of the first tournament with staffs in the history of The Enchantment. "Citizens of The Enchantment, welcome to our first event with staffs. We plan to keep it very simple. If a contestant has his staff knocked away or if he trips and falls, he's eliminated. It's that simple. However, hitting an opponent on the head or when he's down will call for a disqualification."

The excitement started to run especially high when the four pairs in the second group walked on the field. Coincidentally, each entry from the Prairie had drawn a competitor from the Hill Country. Billy knew that this did not bode well for the Hill Country, since Victor, Sterling, and Ernest all showed a real aptitude for the sport, and

Arnold was extremely strong and experienced. In fact, besides Sheriff Lone Wolf, they were the best competitors the Prairie had to offer.

When the first round was completed and the air cleared, the four Prairie competitors had completely dominated the two deer and the two rams from the Hill Country and won all their matches. Afterwards they put on their shirts and waited on the sidelines to draw for their next matches.

The second round featured the third weight group, and the story was much the same. As it happened, Bruno von Shepherd, Heinz Rottweiler, Gaylord Cougar, and Sheriff Lone Wolf had all drawn one of the four coyote brothers. During the four bouts, the coyotes were quite easily defeated. Billy felt sorry for his friend Lenny Coyote but was relieved that Lenny did not have to go against one of his brothers.

The pairings for the next bout were more interesting. The two fox brothers were first on the docket, and Fritz Terrier and Neevil Cur would finish the round. Georgie Beaver, Alvin Muskrat, and Maurice Rabbit had all decided to skip the tournament. Georgie and Maurice were not interested, and Alvin did not like the idea of fighting Neevil Cur after his unfortunate experience in the North Woods when the cur purposely broke his arm.

Although Philip P. Fox tried desperately to use his new skill, he could not match the experience of his brother Phineas from the Hill Country and was tripped up after a few minutes. When it came to the two smaller dogs, Fritz Terrier could not match Neevil Cur's ferocity and lost his staff early in the match.

At this point in the tournament Sheldon called for a short break, and many in attendance hurried off to the refreshment booths. During that time, the competitors drew again for their second rounds. Victor drew Sterling, and Arnold got Sterling's brother, Ernest. Billy felt that the bout between Victor and Sterling should have been the championship round, since both deer were extremely quick and agile, but he knew that drawings were still the fairest way.

When the crowd returned, Sheldon announced the second part of the competition. True to Billy's predictions, Victor and Sterling's match was a thing of beauty. One deer would get the upper hand for a while, and then the other deer would regain his footing and drive the other back with a series of quick blows and parries. Finally Victor caught Sterling a little off guard and sent his staff flying so far into the air that it landed on the steps of City Hall, just missing Hilda Big Horn.

Ernest's bout against Arnold was a different story. Arnold's powerful blows and years of experience finally overcame the faster more agile deer. After several minutes Ernest was knocked off his feet, and the bout ended with a bang, placing Arnold in the championship round against Victor Running Deer.

In the third division Heinz Rottweiler drew Walter Lone Wolf, leaving Bruno von Shepherd and Gaylord Cougar to finish the round. Billy Bones wondered if Sheriff Lone Wolf was as good as Conan thought he was. He knew that Bruno, for his part, was confident that the North Woods would easily dominate both matches.

In the match between Heinz and Walter, the Rottweiler was shocked by the wolf's skill and strength. Conan had taught him well. After backing the sheriff into the crowd, Heinz's confidence made him careless, and Walter knocked the staff out of Heinz's hands with a quick upper thrust. Afterwards the Rottweiler simply shook his head in disbelief and offered his hand to the victorious wolf.

As far as the second bout was concerned, Gaylord Cougar did not have the skill or experience to go up against Bruno von Shepherd. However, Bruno was very magnanimous and made the cougar look more skilled than he was. After several minutes longer than the bout needed to continue, Bruno clipped the staff out of Gaylord's grasp, and the bout was over. This victory meant that Bruno and the Prairie sheriff would meet in the final match.

After the second round competitions, Sheldon Sheepdog announced that there would be another short break before the championship matches. Billy was pleased that up until then, Angus and Conan had kept complete control of the various contests, and nothing unforeseen had happened to jeopardize the event. During the break Billy Bones also took the time to talk with Brigitte von Shepherd, who was dressed in a white blouse and a long blue skirt.

"I was hoping to see you today. I'm sorry I haven't spoken to you sooner, but I promised Sheldon I would help him with the drawings and other duties," began Billy.

"I was wondering what you would be doing today.

Even though Bruno wanted to compete with you in the worst way, I was hoping you'd find a way to avoid it. I thank you for that," replied Brigitte, touching his arm softly with her hand.

"I have to admit, I thought of entering but backed out the last minute," admitted Billy. "I wanted this day to go well, especially for Sheldon's sake. He's put so much into it."

When Bruno spied Brigitte and Billy conversing, he immediately marched over to them and jerked Billy by the arm. "Listen, you coward, I don't want you speakin' to my sister. You've caused me enough trouble."

"I'm afraid that's not up to you, Bruno. We're in the Prairie now, and we're free to speak to whomever we wish," countered Billy, pulling his arm away.

"Please, Bruno. I'm in no danger. If I need your help, I'll call you immediately," said Brigitte diplomatically, knowing that her brother was on edge before his last bout.

"Hah, when this is over, we'll talk again, Mr. Bones. You've done enough damage to our state already with your sweet talk!" barked the German shepherd as he strode back to where the other competitors were waiting.

"Brigitte, how can you tolerate this? Surely you must see...."

Before Billy could finish, Brigitte interrupted. "As I told you before, Billy, he thinks you're behind all the desertions. If I leave now, I can't promise what he'll do. But tomorrow's the three-state meeting. Maybe we can find time to speak then."

As Brigitte touched Billy's face gently with her hand and turned to leave, Sheldon Sheepdog called the championship round to order. "Good citizens of The Enchantment, I hope you're enjoying these matches as much as I am. We'll begin with Mr. Elk and Mr. Bison, and then Mr. Cur and Mr. Fox. After those two bouts we'll call on Mr. Running Deer and Mr. Big Horn and finish with Sheriff Lone Wolf and Mr. von Shepherd."

Sheldon stopped for a few moments and then gestured toward Angus Wolfhound and Conan Greyhound. "I especially want to thank our two referees for their fine work today in keeping these matches fair and clean. And now, Mr. Elk and Mr. Bison, if you'll come forward with your staffs, we'll start the championship round."

In the first match, Arthur Elk surprised Bison Bob with his quickness and agility. The slower bison was more experienced but could not quite keep up with Arthur's tenacity, and the big buffalo fell backwards, ending the struggle. He asked Angus Wolfhound if he could get up and continue, but Angus only laughed. "This is not a fight to the finish, Bob. This is just a match. And when you fall down or lose your staff, it's over."

Although Phineas was slightly larger than Neevil, the cur's innate savagery held him in good stead again, and he won quite easily over the fox, by tripping him up in less than two minutes. Either way, of course, the victory went to the North Woods.

The third bout between Victor Running Deer and Arnold Big Horn was a long, tedious affair with both animals becoming extremely fatigued. Arnold was stronger and more experienced, but Victor's natural athletic skills kept him in the contest. After a series of powerful blows from Arnold, his last swing put him slightly off balance, and Victor came down sharply with his staff, knocking the ram's staff out of his hand. When it was over, Victor approached Arnold. "You almost had me a number of times, Arnold. It could have gone either way. I just lucked out."

Since each state had one victory, there was a good deal of tension when Bruno von Shepherd and Walter Lone Wolf walked into the circle. By the time they took their shirts off and faced each other, the crowd was amazed at

how much they resembled each other. The shape of their heads and size of their bodies were very much the same, except that the German shepherd had more distinct markings on his face.

Even though Bruno seemed to exude more outward confidence, Walter had a quiet inner strength that held him in good stead. The bout started slowly with each canine striking down with their staff while the other easily warded off his competitor's blows. As the struggle became more ardent, the onlookers started tightening the circle around the players. After a particularly intense exchange, Conan and Angus finally stopped the bout and asked the crowd to back away so the two animals could continue safely.

Bruno had not expected Walter to be so skilled and tenacious. As was his custom, he had skipped a number of drill practices inside The Fortress because of his natural prowess over most of the animals. Walter, however, was at the top of his game, and Conan had worked with him especially hard, realizing his natural talent.

After the match went on for some time, Bruno finally let his guard down for a split second. The wolf came down on the dog's staff with a powerful blow, knocking it to the ground. Bruno, under the shock of losing, picked up his staff and gave the retreating wolf a sharp blow on the back of his head before Angus and Conan could interfere.

As the referees grabbed Bruno and removed his staff, the German shepherd began yelling, "What kind of match is this anyway? I could have easily finished him off if it weren't for your idiotic rules!"

Victor Running Deer and Billy Bones immediately raced over to help the fallen sheriff. They found him unconscious but still breathing. Fortunately, Dr. Muskrat was in the crowd, and after a quick examination asked Billy, Victor, Sterling, and Ernest to carry Walter back to his office. As they moved away toward Main Street, Billy could hear Sheldon apologize to the crowd and thank them for coming.

The shepherd dog wondered what would happen tomorrow during the three-state meeting scheduled to take place inside The Fortress. He felt especially bad for Sheldon on addition to Walter. Until that point the tournament had gone exceedingly well, allowing the competitors from the three states to compete in a completely safe and congenial manner.

# CHAPTER EIGHTEEN

# THE THREE-STATE MEETING

Although Billy Bones knew the Prairie City Council would leave from Main Street shortly before noon, he decided to go up to The Fortress by himself. After all, he was still a member of the Hill Country's Tribal Council, and it made sense for him to travel alone. Deputy Victor Running Deer would be the only constabulary behind the City Council, because Sheriff Lone Wolf was still at Dr. Muskrat's office recovering from the blow to his head.

When Billy got up to Beaver Dam Road, he saw Gerard Crow flying in from his father's farm. "He always seems to sense when I really need him," mused Billy to himself. "I wonder if he knows what a comfort he is to me." As usual, the crow circled the shepherd dog twice and then landed on his shoulder. As the two passed through South Court Street and then Court Street, a number of songbirds waved to them and wished them well.

Gerard stayed on the dog's shoulder or flew above him until they reached the gates of The Fortress, left open for the visiting councilors. Just before entering, the crow gently pecked Billy's neck and then flew back toward the Prairie.

"He doesn't like it here," thought Billy, "and I can't say I blame him."

Once through the gate, Billy was amazed again at the disparity between the beautiful mansion at the far end of The Fortress and the rest of the rough-hewn architecture that actually resembled a fort.

When Billy entered the large dining hall on the east side, he noticed that the tables were still arranged in a great C facing the fireplace. Sheldon Sheepdog and Brigitte von Shepherd were already at a desk in front of the fireplace preparing the day's agenda. Sheldon seemed untroubled, but Billy was sure he was deeply disappointed at yesterday's tournament and his leader's misconduct at the end.

Most of the council members had already arrived, except for Gaylord Cougar and Bruno von Shepherd. The Hill Country Tribal Councilors were sitting at the south table, and the Prairie's members were on the north side, leaving the west side for the North Woods. Behind each council were two representatives of the law, with the exception of the Prairie, where Victor Running Deer stood alone.

Shortly after Billy Bones took his place by Lucinda Vulture, she leaned over and whispered, "Bruno met Gaylord at the gate, and the two of them have been conversing inside the mansion. I don't like the looks of this."

When the two leaders finally arrived they were smiling, and Bruno looked as if he had never been in any kind of altercation the day before. As soon as he and the cougar were seated, Sheldon stood and opened the meeting.

"Council members, thank you for coming this afternoon and for being so punctual. As you remember, we left several things unsettled after our last meeting on November 1. Therefore, I would like to begin with the policy of open borders. Would you please take a few minutes to converse among yourselves and decide if you would like to continue that policy?"

During the discussion, Billy noticed that Sheldon joined the North Woods at their table. After several minutes the sheepdog returned to his desk and nodded to Brigitte to take the vote. Billy could see that Sheldon had a very determined look on his face and that he had spoken candidly with his council.

"We will start with the Tribal Council from the Hill Country," began Brigitte von Shepherd. "How do you stand?"

"Open borders have worked fine for the last six months, and we're okay with that…if the other states agree to it," announced Gaylord.

"And the City Council of the Prairie, what have you concluded?" continued Brigitte.

"We all agree that open borders are now a necessity, especially with the Grand Fair coming up next summer," declared Cornelius Van Mink.

"And now, the North Woods, what's your decision?" asked Brigitte, looking directly at her brother.

"We're somewhat divided on the matter," stated Bruno, glancing over at Sheldon. "But under the circumstances we agree to keep the borders open…until next November 2. Of course, that excludes The Fortress…when the gates are closed."

"Then the borders will stay open until our next meeting," declared Sheldon adamantly.

"With the exception of when our gates are closed!" added Bruno in a loud voice.

"Yes, with the exception of when our gates are closed," repeated Sheldon.

"It makes you wonder what goes on behind them gates!" cawed Jason Crow, not at all concerned about being controversial.

"Thank you for your remark, Mr. Crow. Now…moving on to the next question, we need to bring up the matter of union between the North Woods and the Hill Country. It was decided at our last meeting that a union would not be discussed until after this meeting." After a slight pause the sheepdog continued, "I suggest we abide by the same ruling at least through November 2, but I will give each council time to talk about this among themselves."

After this pronouncement, Sheldon returned to the North Woods table. Billy could see that he was again having a very agitated conversation with his council. However, Billy's own Tribal Council was having its own contentious debate.

"Bruno has assured me that we will both be in charge if a union is formed," announced Gaylord Cougar. "He also assured me that our council will be equal to theirs."

"And you believe that?" asked Lucinda Vulture,

turning to Gaylord. "Even after what Orville told you about Bruno?"

"I believe that we should not be restricted as to when we can discuss it—that's all." countered Gaylord. "We should be free to bring it up at any time."

When the vote was taken in the Tribal Council, only Lucinda Vulture, Billy Bones, and Maurice Rabbit voted to wait until November 2. Thus, when the role was called, both the North Woods and the Hill Country voted against waiting until the next meeting.

"The North Woods and the Hill Country are allowed to discuss union whenever they like," stated Sheldon without showing any emotion. "Now to the matter of Mr. Wise Owl's books. I see he's not with us today. I hope he hasn't given up on us. Please inform him that we'll take the matter up again at our next meeting. And to the three councils, I hope we don't let this business drag on," pleaded the sheepdog. "Now are there any more concerns that need to be considered?"

"We should probably discuss the Grand Fair," prompted Cornelius Van Mink. "Several changes were made last year, and then of course, we need to decide whether to add any drill competitions using the staff."

"Instead of just having the Prairie decide on the competitions, we were thinking we could invite a member from the Hill Country and also from the North Woods to join our planning committee. I therefore propose that each state should choose a representative," offered Mayor Beaver.

"I think that's a splendid idea, Mayor Beaver. If there

are no objections from the floor, I will personally see that a representative from each of our two states is selected," agreed Sheldon quickly. Billy could tell that the sheepdog did not want to discuss the addition of a competition with staffs until a little more time had passed. "Now, are there more concerns?"

"Yes," yelled Jason Crow, standing up on his seat. "I would like to address this question to you, Mr. Sheepdog, and to you, Mr. von Shepherd. After witnessing Mr. von Shepherd's disgraceful display yesterday at the tournament, I'm starting to believe that a contest of staffs should not be considered as part of the Grand Fair or for next May Day, for that matter—especially since a leader from one of the states cannot abide by the rules!"

After this outburst, there were several moments of absolute silence. Finally Sheldon addressed his pack leader. "Mr. von Shepherd, would you like to respond?"

When Bruno rose to speak he had a sarcastic smile on his face. "Mr. Crow, if you knew anything about real staff matches, you wouldn't have posed that question. Since we in the North Woods have real competitions, we know that a match is not completed until the winner is standing over the loser with his staff on the loser's chest. Since that was not the case with Sheriff Lone Wolf and me, you can see why I reacted the way I did and wanted to continue the match," explained Bruno.

"But you knew the rules, Mr. von Shepherd. I think you lost control and were just embarrassed at losin'. There ain't no other conclusion I can come to," countered Jason. "And

I think you need to apologize to our good sheriff for that unnecessary blow to his head and to every other contestant in that tournament who abided by the rules!"

"You need to mind your own affairs, Mr. Crow. I think my explanation was sufficient, and I don't owe you or anyone else an apology for my actions!"

With those final remarks, Bruno von Shepherd slammed his fist on the table and stormed out of the room. Sheldon tried to close the meeting gracefully by asking for any more concerns, but he was somewhat thrown by Bruno's outburst. Billy concluded afterwards that Sheldon was just as disgusted with his leader's excuses as Jason was, since he had ruined what was otherwise a very successful tournament.

Before Brigitte had a chance to leave, Billy caught up with her. "Please, stay for a moment. I know you're upset, but Bruno's leaving the room has given us a chance to talk."

"I know his little outburst pleased you, Billy. And I'm sure you think it's proved your point, but I'm afraid it just made things worse. Now he'll be angrier than ever. I'm afraid Sheldon and I are losing our ability to reason with him, but we've still got to try!"

"Perhaps you need to use it against him," suggested Billy, taking her hands in his. "Maybe if he thought that you and Sheldon were planning to leave, he might behave in a more rational matter and give up this insatiable ambition of his. And…selfishly, I want you to be free to be with me."

"That's what I want," agreed Brigitte softly, "but please give me time."

Before Brigitte departed, she kissed him on the cheek and gently touched his arm. When Billy finally left the empty room and made his way through The Fortress gates, he saw Gerard Crow flying toward him. When the crow landed on his shoulder, he reached up and petted the bird's silky feathers. "Thanks again, my good friend. You always seem to know when I need you around."

# CHAPTER NINETEEN

# A SCREAM IN THE NIGHT

On the evening of June 20, Winston Wise Owl and Hester Groundhog sat together at the ground-hog's outdoor table enjoying vegetables from her garden and fresh bread from her kitchen. Cornelius Van Mink and Mayor George P. Beaver had been with Winston earlier in the day, and the owl and Hester were discussing their many concerns.

"So Mr. Wise Owl, the councilors didn't talk about your missing books at their big three-state meeting. Did they say why?" inquired the old groundhog.

"Actually it was my fault. They said it was because I didn't attend. And I have to admit, I'd rather given up on the idea," admitted the owl. "I've come to the conclusion that nothing will happen while Bruno von Shepherd is aggravated about losing part of his pack. I think right now his anger is too great, and he's keeping my books out of spite to retaliate for the desertions."

"I understand they're still worried that the Hill Country and the North Woods might unite. I thought they had put that on hold," remarked Hester.

"It was, but now they're free to discuss it any time they want," answered Winston, finishing his cup of tea.

"And speaking of any time, isn't tomorrow the summer solstice, or is it the twenty-second this year?" asked the groundhog.

"No, it comes early this year. If my calculations are correct, the opening should occur as early as tomorrow morning," determined the owl.

"How early in the morning? Do I need to be on watch also?" asked Hester.

"I don't know what to tell you. It hasn't come at night for a long time, but I may sit out tonight if the weather's nice," decided Winston. "Usually nothing ventures in after dark."

"Maybe we should take turns," suggested Hester. "Then you could get some rest."

"I should be okay, but you might check on me," chuckled the owl, standing and heading toward his treehouse. "Well goodnight then. If I'm going to sit down here later on, I'll need to get some sleep."

Winston slept longer than he intended and didn't get down to his chair until after midnight. For some time he sat and listened to the sound of the crickets and enjoyed the night air. He still had his nightgown on and had brought a light blanket from the foot of his bed. He also had a lantern placed beside him, with its candle flickering softly in the night air. Finally after a couple hours, he dozed off in spite of his good intentions.

Sometime later Winston was awakened by a sudden scream of great pain. He looked up just in time to see a medium-sized animal dash by him and run far out onto the plain. By the time he picked up his lantern, Hester had joined him and was pulling the cord of her robe tightly around her waist. Behind them they could just make out a glorious opening between the trees, already starting to close. They knew immediately it was the mysterious passageway that opened for a few moments every summer solstice.

"What was that cry?" asked Hester, staring over at the owl.

"I don't know. I've never heard anything like it," returned Winston, in a loud whisper. "But it's out there somewhere, and we've got to find it!"

"For what seemed like half an hour Winston and Hester scoured the plain west of the two magnificent trees. Finally Winston found a piece of barbed wire, covered with blood and matted fur like it had been torn away from someone's body. When he raised his lantern he saw an animal several yards ahead of him, sitting on the ground. Its face had a great gash across its cheek, and it was covered with blood. Hester, who had been standing behind him, let out a sharp cry.

Suddenly the animal stood uneasily on its hind feet and screamed, "No, stay away from me!" and ran with some difficulty down the path toward the Prairie town.

The owl and the groundhog remained where they were in complete shock. Because of the dark they could not tell what kind of creature it was. They only knew it was in great pain.

"Do you know what that was?" asked Hester, taking hold of the owl's wing. "I couldn't tell, but it appeared to be badly hurt. I shouldn't have yelled though. I'm sorry!"

"It's not your fault, but let's take the barbed wire back to my place," decided the owl. "Then we must get dressed and tell someone. We can't let the poor creature come into a strange place and not understand why it can suddenly think and speak and walk on its back legs!"

"Yes, let's hurry," agreed Hester. "It will be dawn before long, and the light might help us."

# CHAPTER TWENTY

## BILLY'S VISION

"Tomorrow's the summer solstice, and I've got a meeting with the Tribal Council," Billy Bones remembered, as he pulled down his suspenders and removed his trousers. Finally he took off his blue shirt and laid it carefully on the dresser. "And I've gotta rise early and get down to the stream for a quick bath. I just hope Gaylord doesn't bring up union with the North Woods again. I was hopin' that battle was over for a while. Well anyway, off to bed."

Around three in the morning, Billy was suddenly awakened by a terrible scream in his head and a vision of an animal in immense pain. The creature was all covered with blood, and it appeared to be running away from the great trees at Land's End.

Billy had not had a psychic experience since last summer, and for a moment it confused him. "I don't understand what I just saw," he spoke out loud, "but whatever it was, I must get to Mr. Wise Owl as soon as I can."

Quickly the shepherd dog donned his shirt, pulled

up his pants, grabbed an apple, and rushed out the door. Instead of following the path to Beaver Dam Road, he cut across Gloria Meadowlark's open field and Jason Crow's cornfield to get to Land's End as swiftly as possible. When he arrived, Winston had just managed to get dressed and was coming down the circular staircase that led up to his doorway.

"Billy, what are you doing here?" wondered Winston, gazing down at the dog in amazement.

"I just heard this scream in my head, and I had a vision of an animal, bloodied and in distress, running from your trees," he explained. "I felt I had to come over here right away."

"But you must have seen him!" stated the owl. "He ran away from us toward the town. He was right in your path!"

"No, I'm sorry, but I came across the fields. I wanted to get here as fast as I could," said Billy. "How foolish of me…especially since I saw him running away from here in my mind's eye. But tell me, what happened?"

"This animal came through the solstice gateway," explained Winston, "I knew the opening would probably come early this year, but I was hoping it wouldn't happen until daylight. And I'm afraid I fell asleep."

"But then we both heard this terrible scream," said Hester Groundhog, who had joined them and was shaking her head in disbelief.

"But where did it go? It must have taken him or her some time to go through the change," suggested the shepherd dog.

"He was moving very fast, and he was able to get a long ways away. We looked for him for quite a while," said Winston. "By the time we found him, he could already think and speak."

"And we found this on the ground near him," continued Hester, showing Billy the piece of barbed wire. "Apparently he was in great pain when he entered, and he had to pull this wire off by himself."

"But did you get a good look at him? And are you sure it was a male?" inquired Billy again.

"Well, we think so," said Winston. "When he told us to stay away, it sounded like a male voice."

"How large an animal was it?" inquired Billy.

"About your size I'd say. It was hard to tell in the dark, and we only got a good look at his face with our lantern," admitted the owl. "But we've got to find him. He must be in terrible pain, and I'm sure he doesn't understand what's happened to him—I mean, after going through the change."

"I'd better follow him. He could be lying along the trail somewhere," decided Billy. "It will start to get light in about an hour, and it'll be much easier to spot him."

"I'll fly to Sheriff Lone Wolf's office," suggested Winston. "I understand he's well enough now to take up his duties again. Maybe we can wake up Victor Running Deer too."

"If I don't find him, I'll meet you later at the sheriff's office. I think eventually you'll have to take him to Dr. Muskrat's for his wounds," determined Billy before starting down the path toward the little town.

When Billy neared Jason Crow's farm, he looked for Gerard on the roof of the farmhouse but couldn't find him. "I'll hurry on to Percy's shop," he thought. "He's an early riser. Maybe he's seen something."

When Billy got to Percival Gander's shop, he found the gander sitting on the long ramp that led up to his entrance. "Percy, how long have you been awake? Did you see…."

"…He broke into my shop before I was awake. Yes, before I was awake. He took a long robe from my rack. I'm a light sleeper, so I caught him just as he was leaving," admitted Percival, rocking back and forth. "I would gladly have given him something if he'd just asked. Yes, if he'd just asked."

"But did you see him, Percy? What did he look like?" inquired the dog.

"By the time I entered that part of the shop, he already had the robe on. All I could see was his face, all bloodied and scarred. He looked almost like some sort of monster. Yes, a monster!"

"Then you didn't recognize anything else, like what kind of an animal he was, for instance?" questioned the dog even further.

"No, it was too dark and I didn't have time to light my candle," finished the gander.

"What kind of robe was it?" asked Billy, trying to get some idea.

"It was gray and very long, like a monk's robe. It even covered his legs and feet. And it had a hood that he pulled over his head." described Percy. "He was about your height, maybe a little smaller…yes, a little smaller!"

"Which way did he go?" asked Billy, looking toward the west.

"Yes, he was headin' for the dam. I tried to follow him for a ways. And I kept yellin' for him to come back, that I'd help him. But he just kept runnin'. Yes, he just kept runnin'."

"It's okay, Percy. I'll try to find him," promised Billy. "And Winston's gone to get help from the sheriff. I just feel bad. I think the poor animal's in a lot of pain. I was hopin' we could get him to the doctor's office."

Billy continued on the path toward the beaver dam and finally arrived at Main Street. At that point he turned south toward the sheriff's office at the end of the block. When he arrived he knocked on the door, but no one answered. He determined that Walter and Winston had probably gone to rouse Victor Running Deer out of bed. Since it was getting light, he finally decided that the most prudent thing to do was to sit on the sheriff's front step and wait for them. By this time the dog had completely forgotten about the Tribal Council Meeting that afternoon and soon fell fast asleep.

# CHAPTER TWENTY-ONE

# THE SEARCH FOR THE GHOST

Dawn had clearly broken by the time Winston Wise Owl, Sheriff Lone Wolf, and Victor Running Deer arrived back at the sheriff's office. The early light cast a long shadow from the shop across the street onto the sleeping Billy Bones, slumped back against the sheriff's front door.

"I guess Billy didn't find him," remarked Winston, as he gazed down on the shepherd dog.

"Now tell me once again. You say that Mr. Bones came to your place at 3:30 in the morning, shortly after this creature ran away?" questioned the sheriff, shaking his head in disbelief.

"He'd had one of his visions again, sheriff," explained Winston. "He said he heard the creature scream in his mind's eye and saw him running away from Land's End."

"That would be hard to believe, if I didn't know how he found Sandy Antelope after he'd been beaten," concurred the sheriff.

"And how he found me after the peccaries set my place on fire," continued the deer. "It's just a rare gift."

"Not to mention how he saved me three years ago during the summer solstice. He's a pretty amazing dog," added the owl. "Too bad he can't call upon that gift whenever he likes. Maybe he could tell us what happened to this wounded animal."

"Well, I'd better wake him up and find out what he knows," decided the sheriff. "Hey, Mr. Bones, time to get up!"

Winston could tell that Billy was embarrassed at being caught napping, but the dog just shrugged it off and stood up awkwardly. "Right…ready for duty, sheriff," said Billy, smiling sheepishly at the wolf.

"Yes, good morning, Mr. Bones. Did you have any luck?" inquired Sheriff Lone Wolf. "Winston said you tried to follow this animal we're lookin' for. He said the creature was wounded."

"Yes, he stopped at Percy Gander's place," said Billy.

"Is Percy all right?" asked Victor. "I understand the animal was half out of his head.

"Yes, Percy said he was upset, but he just took a long gray robe from his shop," related Billy. "He didn't try to hurt Percy at all."

"Did Percy get a good look at the animal?" asked Winston.

"No, I'm afraid not. He said the robe had a hood on it, and all he saw was his face, all scarred and bloody. He said he was close to my size, but he still had no idea what kind of animal it was," explained the shepherd dog.

"In other words, all we know is that we're lookin' for a

medium-sized animal in a hooded gray robe," decided the wolf. "And…oh yes, with a scared and bloody face!"

"So where do we go from here, sheriff?" asked Victor.

"I say we split up and find out if anyone else's seen the creature, either last night or this morning. Surely someone's seen something. I'll take the east side. Victor, you and Billy take the west," suggested the wolf. "And Winston, why don't you fly over to Eagle Butte and get Harold Eagle. We're gonna need his help on this one. Since it's daylight, maybe one of you will spot something from the air."

"But that leaves you by yourself, Walter. That's not such a good idea," warned the deer. "What if you find him, and he puts up a struggle?"

"I'll start in the southeast and maybe get Sterling to help. I'll be all right," insisted the sheriff.

"When do we meet?" asked Billy. "And if someone knows something, should we bring him back with us?"

"Use your judgment, Mr. Bones. I think, for the most part, you can just get the information," said Walter. "And let's meet back here in about three hours. That should give us time to cover a lot of ground."


By the time Winston arrived at Deputy Harold Eagle's cabin, he could tell that the eagle had already risen, since his door had been left ajar. He knocked, pushed it open, and found the eagle washing his face at the basin on his nightstand.

"Excuse me for busting in on you like this, Harold, but

we seem to have a bit of a problem and need your help," hooted the owl.

"Well, tell me about it, Mr. Wise Owl. It must be pretty serious if they've sent you," chirped the eagle as he put his plaid swath over his shoulder and across his chest.

After Winston explained his mission, the two great birds took to the air. Winston flew over the north part of the Prairie, and Harold took the south. When they landed on Main Street three hours later, neither had anything to report. The animals had fared better. They had talked to several eyewitnesses with much the same story.

Apparently several songbirds had been outside their houses before dawn, and they had seen the animal pass. They described him as a ghost-like creature in a long gray robe who came at them out of the dark and frightened them back into their houses. Elmer Prairie Dog said the animal broke into his store and took some food and a bucket. He said he yelled at him, but the creature scared him so badly he ran back upstairs. He also described the animal as a ghostly figure with a bloody face. After Winston heard the prairie dog's account, he feared the word would soon be all over town.

"Well, we better keep looking," sighed the sheriff. He probably needs a doctor. And Deputy Eagle, why don't you check up in the Hill Country. Maybe they've seen something."

By the end of the day, a number of other volunteers had joined the search, but the wounded newcomer seemed to have disappeared completely. Most of the citizens that participated traveled in groups, fearful of the ghost-like creature with the strange and terrifying face.

"Well, we tried our best," announced the sheriff finally. "If anyone sees anything, let me know. Victor and I will take it from here."

As Winston was heading for home, he noticed that Gerard Crow had caught up to Billy Bones and landed on his shoulder. It continued to amaze the owl at how well the crow and the shepherd dog got along. They seemed to have a real comradery, even though they could not speak with one another.

# CHAPTER TWENTY-TWO

# THE CAVE AT CASTLE ROCK

After Gerard Crow landed on Billy Bones' shoulder, the young bird seemed to be very agitated and started tugging on Billy's shirt with its sharp claws.

"What's the matter, my friend? Is something wrong?" queried the dog, turning his head toward the crow. Again Gerard started grabbing hold of his shirt and pulling him south toward the lower end of Main Street.

"You want me to go with you! Is that what you're tellin' me?" asked the shepherd dog. "Too bad everybody's left, but maybe we can handle this ourselves. I wondered where you had gone this morning. Well now I think I know. So lead on, my friend, and I'll follow as fast as I can."

By the time Billy reached Dry Gulch, the crow had circled over him a number of times.

"Whoa! Let me catch my breath!" barked Billy, gasping for air. By this time the crow had flown in the direction of Castle Rock and back again.

"So our creature's holdin' up behind Castle Rock somewhere. Is that what you're tryin' to tell me?" asked

Billy. After that question the crow seemed relieved and landed back on the dog's shoulder. "And they think we can't communicate. Well, what do they know?"

When Billy and Gerard reached Lonesome Road and were about to head south around Castle Rock, Billy noticed two birds flying toward them. When they got closer he realized it was Lucinda Vulture's two sons, Festus and Floyd.

"In the name of The Great Spirit, I forgot. Today was the meeting of the Tribal Council, and I just missed it!" cried Billy out loud. As the two vultures started to land, Billy could see that Floyd was having directional problems again and was heading straight toward him. Gerard escaped at the last minute, but Billy found himself flat on the ground in the midst of a pile of black feathers. Although Floyd had not scored a direct hit, he had managed a glancing blow that threw the dog off balance.

"Dang it Floyd, I thought you were gettin' better. Now look what you've done to Mr. Bones!" screeched Festus, helping Billy to his feet.

"Yes, the last time I visited you two, your landings were improving, Floyd," laughed Billy nervously.

"Sorry, Mr. Bones, it's just that Ma was anxious to get this message to yah, and we've been lookin' all over the Prairie," declared Floyd.

"Will there be another meeting tomorrow, or have I missed everything? We've been searchin' all day for an animal that just came into The Enchantment, and we think he's badly hurt," Billy explained

"Yeah, we heard," answered Floyd. "And so has Ma.

Deputy Eagle told us. But Ma says to come to the Hill Country in three days. They're havin' a big meetin' with Bruno von Shepherd and Sheldon Sheepdog to discuss a combined meetin' with the North Wood's Council. Ma says you need to be there."

"Then it looks like it might really happen," sighed Billy. "Well, tell your Ma…I mean your mother, I'm sorry about missin' today, but there's no way I could've made it. I'll be there in three days. Tell her she can count on it."

"She also wants you to know there's nothin' you coulda done to change things. So…see yah in three days!" returned Festus, as he and Floyd took flight and headed west again.

When Gerard saw the two vultures leave, he quickly returned and stayed on Billy's shoulder while they hiked around Castle Rock.

"Do you know where he's hidin'?" asked the dog. Immediately the crow flew up to a cavernous opening a ways up the hillside.

"I see," said the dog, as he started making his way up to the cave. Since he had climbed the path when Rodney Wild Deer abducted Melinda Doe three years ago, he knew exactly where the trail led. "It's amazing that he found this place," wondered the shepherd dog. "But I suppose when you're desperate, anything's possible."

When Billy got to the mouth of the cave, he carefully peeked inside. Surprisingly, Gerard remained on his shoulder. "Hello, in there! Can I come in? I want to help!"

After adjusting his eyes toward the back of the cave, he saw the injured animal sitting on a stone bench with his hood drawn discreetly around his face.

"No, stay away, I don't need your help!" the animal snapped back.

"But you're hurt. You need to get your cuts looked at. Let me take you to Dr. Muskrat and see what he can do," pleaded the shepherd dog.

"No, everyone's afraid of me! If I walk through town, they'll all gather around and try to stare at me. I couldn't stand that!" cried the animal.

"But it won't bother me, I promise," insisted Billy. "And you don't want your wounds to get infected. You could die!"

"Maybe that would be best. I saw myself in the mirror when I got my robe. I look horrible so what does it matter now?" moaned the animal, as Billy tried to get closer. "No, keep your distance. How do I know I can trust you?"

"You'll just have to take that chance. I came here by myself; didn't I?" insisted the dog. At that remark, Gerard gave him a quick peck on the neck. "Well actually, Gerard found you, and he can't tell anyone," stated Billy. "But I have an idea. Let me ask Dr. Muskrat if he'll see you around midnight. I'm sure we could sneak you up there without bein' seen. I'll go right now and ask him. And I'll bring you some more to eat. I understand you borrowed some food from the general store earlier, but that was quite a while ago."

"Swear to me you won't tell anyone. I couldn't stand it if you did!" snarled the creature, looking down at the ground.

"Yes, I swear," answered Billy. "But can you make it to Dr. Muskrat's office? It would be much better to see him there. He's got everything you need."

"Yes, I can make it. But I'll sleep until you get back. I'm very tired," admitted the animal. "And thank you. I'm totally in your hands...Yes, I'm totally in your hands. That's all I can say."

# CHAPTER TWENTY-THREE

# THE REVELATION

"You've asked me to do some weird things over the years, but this takes the prize, Mr. Bones. You mean you haven't even told Sheriff Lone Wolf?" inquired Dr. Muskrat, glaring at Billy over his glasses.

"This animal is very upset about the cuts on his face," declared Billy Bones. "Apparently all the citizens he met were afraid of him and ran away. He said he saw himself in the mirror when he took a robe from Percy Gander's Shop and was appalled at what he saw."

"But sneaking in here at midnight…that's highly irregular," said the muskrat.

"It was the only time we wouldn't be seen. Otherwise I couldn't get him to come. He's scarred up pretty badly, and he needs his wounds looked at, doctor."

"Well, it appears we'll have to see this animal. Though it goes against my better judgment," stated Dr. Muskrat.

"But you've got to promise, in the name of the Great Spirit, that you won't tell anyone," insisted Billy again.

"Yes, yes, very well, I promise!" answered the good doctor. "But you'd better be careful yourself. Something's not right about this."

After dark that night, Billy decided not to light his lantern until he got to the south side of Castle Rock. He brought a loaf of bread from his own cottage and a canteen pouch filled with water. Fortunately, there was just enough moonlight that he could easily find his way. Also, Gerard had not returned, making it easier for him to meet with the newcomer a second time. He wondered what must be going through the animal's mind, or if he remembered how he was wounded in the old world, or how he ended up in a totally different dimension—not to mention being able to think, speak, and walk on his hind legs.

There was something about the animal that troubled Billy. He seemed to know where things were—Percy's shop, Elmer Prairie Dog's store, and the cave behind Castle Rock. The store, of course, could be easily stumbled upon, and hiding behind a lone hill at the south end of The Enchantment would logically make sense, but Percy's shop?

"Maybe I'll get some answers tonight," Billy thought. "Or maybe this will always remain a mystery."

Billy lit his lantern before climbing up to the cave. When he arrived, he found the animal still sleeping. "Sir, I think we have to go soon," said Billy loudly, when he moved to the center of the room.

"What? Where?" moaned the animal, as he struggled to sit up. Because he was wrapped up in his robe and since the lantern gave off such weak light, Billy was still unable to see his new companion clearly.

After a few moments Billy handed the bread and pouch of water to the wounded newcomer and waited quietly. Because of the cuts around his mouth, the animal could only bite off small chunks of bread but devoured them hungrily. After that he drank thirstily from the pouch. When he had satisfied his hunger and thirst, he turned to the dog.

"Thank you. That was very kind of you. But I still hurt pretty badly, and I must see this Dr. Muskrat of yours as soon as I can," pleaded the animal.

When the wounded creature tried to stand, he momentarily lost his balance. Billy quickly moved in to assist him and grabbed his forearms.

"No!" cried the animal, trying to push Billy away, but it was too late. With the firm touch of the creature's arms, a vision of two men coming at them with a whip and a pole suddenly popped into the dog's mind. Immediately, in that dark little cave in the middle of the night, Billy knew who the newcomer really was. He knew because he had seen that same vision twice before when he was in The Enchantment the first time.

"Fabian! Fabian Lynx! I...I don't believe it! It's...It's you!" was all Billy could stammer, still holding onto the creature's forearms.

"Yes, Billy Bones, it...it is I," muttered Fabian Lynx, Billy's old enemy whom he had forced out of The Enchantment three years ago. "And now you see what's become of me!"

"But the cuts from the barbed wire—I don't understand?" continued the dog, still supporting the lynx.

"It's a long story, Billy. But now that you know who I am, I'm sure you'll want to leave, and I'll not blame you."

"We'll have none of that, Mr. Fabian Lynx. We're leaving together right now, if you're strong enough to walk. I should have guessed who you were once you took your robe from Percy's shop. That shows how dense I've become," said the dog perceptively. "Now come. The doctor's waiting for us."

"But how can you still want to help me?" cried Fabian Lynx, turning his head away.

"I would have learned when I got to the doctor's office anyway, so what's the difference when I found out?"

determined Billy. "We need to get you there as soon as possible…and why didn't you take a chance and tell me this afternoon?"

"I was afraid you'd leave me," said the lynx, still leaning against the dog. "But I needed your help, and I selfishly decided to keep it a secret. I was hoping that if you left me with Dr. Muskrat, I could get him to promise not to tell anyone, and it would be between him and me."

"But sooner or later, I…well, everyone would find out," responded the shepherd dog.

"I was hoping maybe I could just disappear. I guess I'm just too proud…or too vain. I didn't want anyone to see me this way," admitted Fabian, finally standing by himself.

"But where would you have gone?" inquired Billy.

"Maybe up into the Hill Country somewhere. I don't know," choked the lynx, losing his composure. "But now you know. As I said before, I'm in your hands. Ironic, isn't it!"

"Well, we'll talk about that later, once we've seen the doctor. But first things first," insisted the shepherd dog. "Now follow me, and watch your step. I'll give you as much light as I can going down this steep hill."

# CHAPTER TWENTY-FOUR

# THE DOCTOR'S OFFICE

Although climbing down the rocky path to the bottom of Castle Rock was difficult, the rest of the way was fairly easy. As they walked around the rocky hill and up to the New Meetinghouse, Billy's mind was racing through all the terrible interactions he had experienced with Fabian Lynx, or Brother Fabian, as he was known before. He had threatened to burn Winston Wise Owl's books…he had tried to confiscate all the other human artifacts...he had twisted the words of *The Great Book of Rules* to accomplish his own agenda…he had burned Mary McMink's furniture and caused five young creatures in The Enchantment to change back to their common animal forms, including Georgie Beaver and Gerard Crow…and finally, he had convinced the Prairie Council to sentence Winston Wise Owl to be banished into the old world and to cut the owl's wings so he would surely perish.

When the two unlikely sojourners got to Main Street, everything was dark and quiet except for a light in Dr. Muskrat's window. They had been walking in silence, but

Billy wondered what was going on in Fabian's mind. At one point the lynx stumbled, and Billy had to hold him up. As he glanced at Fabian he seemed different somehow. Of course they were both older, and time had certainly affected them both. But how had the lynx found his way back, and what did it mean?

When the two animals reached the doctor's office, Billy rapped softly on the door. By this time Fabian had his arm around Billy's shoulder, and the dog was supporting him.

"Dr. Muskrat we're here," said Billy quietly as the two of them helped Fabian through the door and onto a waiting table.

When Dr. Muskrat pulled the lynx's hood down, he leaned back in astonishment. "But…but I know you!"

"Yes, it's Fabian Lynx. I think you knew him as Brother Fabian Lynx," concurred Billy.

"But why didn't you tell me? Of course I'll treat him," remarked the muskrat, looking at the severe cuts caused by the barbed wire. "Brother Fabian, why didn't you come to me right away?"

"I…I was confused. And I didn't know how you'd accept me," said the lynx, turning away. "I was a pretty controversial figure when I left here three years ago, as you remember.

Besides, I didn't immediately realize how bad my cuts were."

"That has nothing to do with my responsibility as a doctor. Of course I would have helped you. Now Billy, the first thing we need to do is bathe this animal. I have hot water boilin' on the stove. If you help me we'll get his robe off and clean him thoroughly. Then we'll disinfect those cuts and stitch 'em up."

"But the one on my cheek, can it be fixed?" asked Fabian, "I mean, it's so long and deep."

"Well, you won't be as pretty as you were, and you'll have a scar. But it will heal in time, and you'll be fine," assured the doctor.

Billy Bones did most of the bathing of the lynx, who had blood all over his body. Afterwards the muskrat stood on a chair by the table and began cleaning, disinfecting, and stitching up the cuts. Billy found he was needed for most of the procedures, and had to hold Fabian down during the most painful moments. When Dr. Muskrat finally finished, Billy helped the lynx to a bed in the sick room, covered him with a warm blanket, and sat by him until he went to sleep.

"When did you realize it was Brother Fabian, Billy?" inquired the doctor.

"Not until a short time ago, I'm afraid no one could tell with that hood pulled over his head," responded the shepherd dog.

"But didn't you find it difficult to help him…I mean after what he did?" the muskrat began.

"Maybe for a moment, but then I realized what pain he was in—physically and mentally. "He's always been beautiful. I think the wounds got to him, and he became half crazed for a while."

"Well, you'll have to leave him with me for a time. I'll

need to tend those wounds for a number of days," explained the doctor.

"Is there any way you can keep his presence a secret, at least until he's better?" implored Billy. "I'm not sure how the citizens of the Prairie will act when they learn their ghost is in your sick room."

"I can try. But you'll have to let Sheriff Lone Wolf know something tomorrow. We can't have Victor and him lookin' for a missing creature that's already been found."

"Well, let's see what Fabian has to say in the morning and take it from there," suggested Billy.

"Since it's after midnight, why don't you just hole up on my couch, and we'll speak to him in the morning," suggested the muskrat. "Now I've got to get some sleep myself."


After Dr. Muskrat fixed Billy breakfast the next morning, they took a tray in to Fabian Lynx. When they explained the situation concerning the sheriff and his deputy, the lynx finally agreed to let them know his whereabouts, as long as they told no one else.

"And, Billy, will you also ask them not to visit me—at least not yet," begged the lynx.

"Yes, I guess I can do that. But they'll have to talk to you eventually. I think there might be a legal matter pending from your last visit."

"I wondered if that might be the case," answered Fabian.

"And now you promised to explain how you got back into The Enchantment. You know, outside of Georgie

Beaver and me and Lucinda Vulture's mother, it's never been done," informed Billy.

"Well, it all started back in the wildlife zoo. You know, when you forced me out of here, they caught me again and put me back into that terrible place. And…for a while, I'm sorry to say, I had the same two keepers who tortured me," recalled the lynx, turning his head away.

"Finally though, something wonderful happened. This young human woman took over their job." Fabian stopped for a moment. "I have to tell you, Billy, she was the sort of human you always talked about. She was always kind and gave me extra treats. I have to say, I was very leery of her at first, but then, I…well, I grew to love her. And later she even brought a male human around, and they would pet me and, you know, play games with me."

At that point in the story the lynx stopped and put his hand on his cheek where the largest bandage was. "Then… then something terrible happened. I got my old trainers back. But the woman and her friend came around to see me and caught those two bastards torturin' me again. You know, Billy, they used a whip and a long pole like you see in those visions of yours when you touch me. Then the woman yelled at them and they stopped… for a time."

At that moment, Billy Bones could see that it was becoming difficult for Fabian to continue. Without thinking, he reached over and took the lynx's hand and moved it away from the bandage on his cheek. "But then what happened, Fabian?"

"Well, finally last night, she came back with a wire

cutter and started cuttin' the barbed wire around my cage. I...I think she wanted to free me. But when she was in the middle of her task some other humans caught her and took her away. Then I saw my chance, and tried to get though the part of the fence she had just clipped. But that's when one of the loose pieces got caught on my face as I was jumpin' out. I had to run away with it hangin' on my cheek. When I finally stopped runnin' I found myself in front of the two trees at Land's End. And while I was tryin' to rub the piece of wire off my face, the barbs kept cuttin' deeper and deeper into my cheek...and into my paws...and into the front of my chest! Amazingly, the passageway to The Enchantment was just startin' to open. And because my cuts were gettin' worse instead of better, I...I started screaming in pain! Then suddenly I turned and dashed through the opening as hard as I could!"

By this time the lynx discovered that he was squeezing the dog's hand tighter and tighter. He let it go and continued, "And that's how I got back in, Mr. Billy Bones, completely by accident. And now...what will I do with this immense scar on my cheek that's sure to frighten everyone?"

"You'll wait until it's healed, Mr. Fabian Lynx," laughed Dr. Muskrat. "That's what you'll do. And then you'll learn from your mistakes and try to live a better life."

"I couldn't have said it better!" agreed Billy Bones.

# THE SUMMER VISIT

When Will Stuart brought his grandson, Billy Stuart III, home from the airport for his summer visit, he was still unsure how the boy would react to the new dog, Ringer. Before they got out of the Dodge pickup, Will broached the subject. "I've got a surprise in the house for you, Billy. I'm anxious for you to meet him."

"Bones came back! He came back!" cried Billy, sliding out of his seat and slamming the truck door.

"Well, not exactly, Billy, you see…" began the old man, following the boy out of the pickup.

As it happened, the first animal to meet the boy when he opened the kitchen door was the cat he had played with the first time Bones had disappeared. "Oh, Buttons, it's you," said the boy, expressing some disappointment. "Well, that's more than I expected."

Will entered the house just in time to see Ringer come running out of the great room, wagging his tail, and heading for the boy. Billy Stuart dropped the cat and started for the young dog. Suddenly he stopped in his tracks. "But you're not Bones! What is this, grandpa?"

"He's my new dog, Billy. I got him last November. He looks a lot like Bones. In fact, I call him Ringer because he's a dead ringer for Bones. Don't you think he looks like him?"

"No, you can't do that, grandpa. There's only one Bones," insisted the boy. "What if he comes back?"

"I don't think that's gonna happen, Billy. Not a second time," said the old man in a reassuring voice. "Now go ahead and pet him. He's a really nice dog and almost as smart."

Billy Stuart III was not mean to the young dog, but he did not give him much affection either. In his mind, he was staying true to his friend, Bones. Even when his friend Danny Red Feather came over to play, he gave the cat more attention. Danny, however, adored young Ringer, and fawned over him whenever he had the chance.

"He's a great dog, Billy. I wish he was mine," said Danny. "Your Grandpa's right. Bones isn't comin' back a second time."

# PART II

# THE FINAL CONFLICT

# CHAPTER TWENTY-SIX

# THE SHERIFF'S RESPONSE

True to Winston's predictions, stories of the ghost with the terrible face spread like wildfire—first inside the Prairie and then in the other two states. As reports of the various sightings circulated, talk began to surface about hunting the creature down. By the time Billy Bones spoke to Sheriff Lone Wolf on the morning of June 22, the good sheriff was already worried about an uprising.

"Both Dr. Muskrat and I thought we should let you know that the wounded animal is recovering in the doctor's sick room," informed Billy, after hearing about the sheriff's concerns. "Dr. Muskrat's stitched up his wounds, but he's still heavily bandaged, and he's worried about what he'll look like once the bandages come off."

"But we need to get the word out that he's not a ghost, just a badly wounded animal," insisted Sheriff Lone Wolf. "Who found him anyway?"

"Actually it was Gerard Crow. He had me follow him up to the cave behind Castle Rock," said Billy.

"But why didn't you tell me right away?" questioned the sheriff.

"Well, there were extenuating circumstances, sheriff," said Billy. "I didn't know much about him until late last night. And as it turned out, he was someone we all knew, and he's terribly worried about how our citizens are going to react to him—not only because of his past, but because of his appearance. Therefore he wants his whereabouts kept a secret, at least for now."

"But what if he's discovered? As I said before, there's already talk about forming a posse and hunting him down. Wouldn't it be better to let our citizens know who he is and how he got hurt?" rebutted Walter.

"You don't understand, sheriff. He doesn't want anyone to see his face the way it is now," explained Billy.

"Come to think of it, there's only one animal I can think of who fits your description, Mr. Bones, someone who would come back who everyone knows," determined the sheriff, "and that's Brother Fabian Lynx!"

"I'm afraid you're right, sheriff. It is Fabian Lynx," admitted Billy.

"And you're helping him after what he tried to do to Winston Wise Owl, not to mention those poor change-lings?" howled the wolf. "And to you!"

"What was I supposed to do? He was seriously hurt and half out of his mind," responded the shepherd dog. "Besides, his entry back into The Enchantment was an accident, like some of the rest of us who stumbled into this place. But unlike us, he was badly wounded, trying to get out of a cage at a wildlife zoo."

"I tell you what, Mr. Bones, you go back and tell Mr.

Lynx that I insist on coming to see him as soon as Victor gets here. We all need to sit down and have a serious talk," said Sheriff Lone Wolf. "So…he doesn't want anyone to see his face! Can you believe that?"

"Fine, I'll tell him. But imagine if you were Fabian. He always got by on his charm and his good looks, and now they're gone…at least for the time being," explained Billy.

"I still can't believe you're helpin' him, Mr. Bones—after what he tried to do to you," returned the wolf. "But all right. I won't repeat what I know except to Victor when he comes. But it sounds like a pure case of vanity to me!"

When Billy returned to Dr. Muskrat's office, he explained Sheriff Lone Wolf's reaction.

"But didn't you tell the sheriff that I didn't want to see him or Victor Running Deer?" asked Fabian.

"He was having none of that, Fabian," said Billy. "I'm sorry, but I was afraid that would be the case. But it's better this way. He said that stories about you as a ghost were spreading all over The Enchantment, and he's afraid there might be an uprising."

"But to have them see me this way!" bemoaned the lynx. "It's what I was tryin' to avoid."

"I hate to tell you this, Fabian, but all you look like now is a bunch of bandages," grinned Billy in spite of himself.

"Billy's right, Brother Fabian," agreed Dr. Muskrat. "We're the only ones who've seen your scars. And remember, you'll look much better in a couple of weeks after your stitches have been removed and you've started to heal.

"It's just Fabian now, but thank you," said the lynx quietly.

A few minutes later the expected knock was heard at the front door, and Billy let Sheriff Lone Wolf and Victor Running Deer into the office. Fabian Lynx sat in a chair next to his bed, wrapped himself up in his blanket, and pulled it part way over his head. He had asked for his robe, but Dr. Muskrat had already washed it and laid it out to dry in the back room.

"Well good morning to you again, Mr. Bones; is he ready to see us?" began the sheriff.

"Yes, he and Dr. Muskrat are waiting for you in the next room. Just follow me," said Billy.

When Walter and Victor entered the sick room, Dr. Muskrat met them and gestured to the bed. "Please just have a seat here. Fabian wanted to meet you sitting up, even though he's still recovering from his injuries."

"Mr. Lynx, I'm sorry to hear about your wounds. Mr. Bones told me you got them tryin' to escape captivity," began Sheriff Lone Wolf. "But I'm glad he got you to see Dr. Muskrat. I can't imagine why you didn't come here yourself."

"I'm afraid I wasn't thinking clearly, sheriff. I guess I…I just wanted to hide somewhere. I seem to have frightened everyone I met," answered Fabian. "And I don't blame them. I got a look at myself in Percy Gander's shop."

"Well, the question is, where do we go from here?"

asked the wolf. "As I told Mr. Bones, there's already talk about gettin' a posse together and huntin' you down. I think if you let it be known what really happened, we could avoid that. In fact, maybe if you went before the City Council."

"No! That's out of the question...at least for now. Give me some time, sheriff," begged the lynx.

"It's against my better judgment, Mr. Lynx," continued Walter. "The sooner everyone knows the truth, the better."

"I'm just asking you to give me a couple weeks. At least till I start to heal. That's all I ask," implored Fabian again.

"But if you're discovered, you might be in real danger," suggested Victor, who had been silent up to that point.

"No, Victor. You don't understand. I'm now a member of The Enchantment. I can't be thought of as some ghost or monster," pleaded Fabian. "It will be hard enough for our citizens to accept me again without appearin' to them like this!" said the lynx, pulling the bandage away from his worst scar and showing them the extent of his injury.

"Careful, Mr. Lynx!" shouted the muskrat. "Don't touch anything."

"All I can do is play it by ear," decided the sheriff, turning away in spite of his better judgment. "But if any trouble occurs, I'll have to let them know what happened, for your own safety."

"That's all I ask," responded Fabian. "Although I think our good citizens will soon forget about their ghost after a few days."

"I don't know. Word spreads quickly here," warned Walter. "And who'll take care of you after you leave Dr.

Muskrat's office? You'll still have to survive for a while."

"Maybe we could arrest him, sheriff, and keep him in the jail until he's well enough," suggested Victor, smiling. "At least that would keep him safe."

"You keep talking about keeping me safe. You mean my life might be in danger?" inquired Fabian.

"Well, there are those in the Prairie who are not fond of you, but I think Victor's talking about Bruno von Shepherd," stated Billy. "You see, Bruno and his pack of wild dogs entered The Enchantment during the same time that we left. When Bruno found out how you manipulated *The Great Book of Rules* to get rid of the human antiquities and then tried to get rid of Winston Wise Owl, he decided he didn't want to live under the laws of the Prairie. At least, that was the excuse he gave for starting a new state up in the north woods. I'm afraid when he finds out you've returned, he just might try to come after you."

"As I said," repeated Victor, "he might be better off in a jail cell until he's better."

"The only problem is there isn't a warrant for his arrest—at least not yet. 'Course after the City Council meets, they may well come up with something," indicated Walter.

"So for now, can we keep my whereabouts a secret?" inquired the lynx again.

"We'll try. But it's against my better judgment," consented the wolf. "We'll all keep our ears to the ground and be ready to respond if trouble occurs. Now, I think we need to slip out of here one at a time, so as not to raise any suspicion. Billy, why don't you go first, and then we'll follow a little later. I still want to talk to Dr. Muskrat about some safety issues."

"I'll look in on you later and bring some food," said Billy, looking over at Fabian.

"Thank you, Mr. Billy Bones," said Fabian; then he added unexpectedly. "I…well, I'll never forget this."

# CHAPTER TWENTY-SEVEN

## THE VULTURE'S CONCERN

It seemed to Billy Bones that whenever Lucinda Vulture waited for him at his cottage, she would perch on his roof and pull the hood of her robe down over her head. From a distance she resembled a dark specter ready to pounce. This morning proved no exception. When Billy neared the cottage, she uncovered her head and flew down to meet him.

"I was ready to give up on you, Mr. Bones, but I was worried and decided to stay longer," stated the vulture.

"I'm sorry, but a lot's happened in the last couple of days," answered the dog.

"Yes, we heard about the wounded animal that came through the opening from Deputy Eagle," informed Lucinda. "But I felt your spirit soar erratically yesterday morning, and when Harold told us about how you went to Land's End to help Winston, I realized immediately what had happened."

Once again Billy was amazed at the vulture's ability to pick up his prophetic dreams, and how closely their spirits were connected. "Yes, the vision was very vivid, but unfortunately I couldn't see clearly and only knew the animal had been wounded and was bleedin' profusely.

"So you went looking for the animal and discovered he'd taken a robe from Percival Gander's shop," continued the vulture. "But then my sons told me they found you with Gerard near Castle Rock. "You must have been chasing him.""

"It seems you know more than most," smiled Billy. "Only Victor and Walter Lone Wolf and Dr. Muskrat know more."

"So you were able to find him?" inquired the vulture.

"Yes, but we're keeping it a secret. No one else knows," confided the dog.

"And you'd like me to keep it a secret too, I take it," determined the vulture. "But there was something else, Mr. Bones, even more troubling. I felt your spirit stir even more erratically last evening close to midnight. Something far greater happened to you at that time, and I felt I had to see you about it. Are you all right? Is it something you can talk about?"

"You're right. Somethin' very traumatic did happen last night. It happened when I finally convinced the wounded animal to see Dr. Muskrat," admitted Billy. "But the animal doesn't want anyone else to know."

"Then perhaps you shouldn't...."

"If it were anyone else, I wouldn't say anything, but since you're already aware that somethin' disconcerting did happen, I think you need to hear the truth," decided the shepherd dog. "'Course, Dr. Muskrat knows, as well as Sheriff Lone Wolf and Victor Running Deer, so they wouldn't keep lookin' for this animal."

"It has something to do with the identity of this ghostly creature; doesn't it? You know, word's already spreading about him all over the Hill Country and the North Woods."

"Well…it started when the animal was standing up to go to the doctor. He suddenly started to stumble, and I caught him. When I took hold of his arms, the vision of two men comin' at us with a whip and a pole rushed into my mind's eye, and I knew immediately who it was."

"Brother Fabian Lynx! Of all animals!" exclaimed the vulture. "But how did you react?"

"There was nothin' I could do 'cept take him to Dr. Muskrat's. You must understand that he is still in a lot of pain," said Billy, looking away. "As you can imagine, he doesn't want anybody lookin' at him—even though all you can see now is a bunch of bandages 'round his face and head."

"But what does the sheriff think?" asked Lucinda.

"Walter tried to warn him about the gossip that's goin' round. You know, the stuff about wanting to hunt this ghost-like creature down," answered the dog. "But somehow Fabian convinced him to keep his whereabouts a secret. At least until he's better."

"And I'm afraid Orville Bat is one of those gossipers," warned Lucinda. "He's already talking about a disturbing force that's invading The Enchantment and how it needs to be eradicated. He says he's felt its presence since early yesterday."

"Well, let's hope he doesn't act on it!" cried Billy, "'specially now that the tension's so great between the three states."

"I think it will be at least two days before anyone listens to him," continued the vulture. "That's why this upcoming meeting is so important. Bruno von Shepherd, Sheldon Sheepdog and Angus Wolfhound will all be there, and Orville will have the audience he wants."

"So you think he plans to recruit a posse from the ranks of the Hill Country and North Woods drill groups?" inquired Billy.

"Those and more," said Lucinda. "I think he believes it's his time to shine. And of course, he has a well-developed insight. I'm sure he picked up on this catastrophic happening just as I did. He's quite gifted that way."

"And we can't tell him the truth. Not for a while anyway," lamented the shepherd dog. "Maybe we can at least stall him."

"I think they're planning to have both councils meet after our meeting—a sort of trial run for a united state. Perhaps we can put it off until then," suggested Lucinda. "But there's one other problem that I need to discuss with you. It has to do with Orville and what he and I know that could change the whole balance of our little world."

"Somethin' that important?" questioned Billy.

"Something that I hoped would never be revealed," conceded Lucinda. "But now that Orville's been caught up in Bruno von Shepherd's ambitions, I think someone else needs to know. And I believe that someone is you!"

"You certainly have my attention. Is it somethin' we should talk about now?" asked Billy.

"We could, but I think it might be better to wait until the meeting. Maybe I can figure out a way of showing you as well," concluded the vulture. "And maybe we'll have to get Maurice Rabbit involved. Let me see what I can do."

"Very well, I'll see you in two days then," responded the shepherd dog.

"Yes, in two days," agreed Lucinda Vulture.

# CHAPTER TWENTY-EIGHT

# THE DREAM OF VICTOR'S MOTHER

Later in the afternoon after Lucinda Vulture's visit, Billy brought food over to Dr. Muskrat's office. He discovered that Victor Running Deer had preceded him and was conversing with Fabian Lynx about the animals that had entered The Enchantment as Fabian and Billy were leaving. He also discovered that the lynx was more at ease and extremely interested in hearing about Bruno von Shepherd.

"So Billy, I understand that you spent some time in the North Woods, but you had a disagreement with this Bruno von Shepherd of whom I should be concerned about. And…as I understand it, a number of his followers have just recently had similar problems. He sounds worse than I was," deduced the lynx.

"Well, he's a different animal than you were, let's say," answered the dog, not wanting to get into a confrontation.

"But from what Victor tells me, the Prairie might be in some danger," continued Fabian. "And it sounds like because of that, I wouldn't be too safe either."

"As Victor may have explained, we're unsure about

Bruno's next move," responded Billy. "We do know that he'd like to take over the Hill Country, and he may have ambitions toward the Prairie as well."

Billy found it uncomfortable talking to Fabian Lynx about another animal's ambitions, but he reasoned that the lynx needed to know what was happening for his own safety. Before he left, he reiterated Sheriff Lone Wolf's warnings about the possibility of an uprising against him. He did not mention Orville Bat's premonitions, since it involved his conversation with Lucinda Vulture and her knowledge of the lynx's return.

"I might not see you for a couple days, Fabian, since I'll be attending a meeting with the Tribal Council and some members of the North Woods. And as you probably guessed, Lucinda Vulture and I are trying our best to keep the Hill Country from makin' any political changes," informed Billy. "But please remember to stay safe and be extremely watchful."

Since the following morning was Sunday, Billy attended the Old Meetinghouse and heard Thaddeus P. Turtle explain to his congregation that there was no such things as ghosts, and that when the wounded animal was eventually found, he should be treated with kindness and understanding. Afterwards, a number of members tried to corner Billy concerning his knowledge of the creature, but he excused himself and escaped as quickly as possible.

Since Sunday evening meant the routine visit of Nosey Coon and Needles Porcupine, he knew he would be inundated with questions. Of course, he had to inform them about the escape of the wounded animal from Land's End, and his taking a robe from Percy Gander's shop. Even though he felt guilty, he skirted around the rest of the story and pretended he was ignorant about the creature's whereabouts. He did repeat Counselor Turtle's admonition to his congregation about not believing in ghosts, however, and the importance of treating the animal with kindness once he reappeared.

Later that night, as fate would have it, Nosey and Needles awakened Billy after hearing him cry out in his sleep. Afterwards, while the three of them were sitting around the table, the dog repeated what was more like a real happening than a dream.

"For some strange reason, I started dreaming of Victor Running Deer when he was only a fawn. I know that sounds weird, but I knew it was him," related Billy. "He was with his mother and they were feeding together in this beautiful meadow. Suddenly two men came out of a wooded area close by. They were carryin' rifles, you know, like the ones you read about in Winston Wise Owl's books. As they got closer to Victor and his mother, I began yellin' at the top of my lungs for them to stop, but of course they couldn't hear me."

"That's probably what Nosey and I heard," interrupted Needles, putting his chin down on the table and gazing up at the dog.

"Yes, I imagine you're right," agreed Billy. "But that's

when Victor's mother raised her head as if she heard some-thin'. Then she nudged Victor, and the two of them started runnin' back into the woods, but it was too late. The two hunters shot and killed her, but Victor escaped. And that's when you awakened me…and…well somehow, I knew that that's how it really happened all those years ago."

"Maybe you dreamed it that way, 'cause Victor had told you about it," suggested Nosey.

"Perhaps, but I don't think so. It wasn't like my other dreams. It was like seeing the real thing," concluded Billy. "Now I'm just wonderin' why I had it."

"Do you think it means somethin'?" asked Nosey.

"For the life of me, I can't think of what that might be, but I'll ask Lucinda Vulture tomorrow. Maybe she'll know," decided Billy. "Now come on; let's try to get some more sleep. I've got a busy day ahead of me."

# CHAPTER TWENTY-NINE

## ORVILLE'S REQUEST

Before leaving for the Hill Country the next morning, Billy Bones decided to drop by the boardinghouse on Main Street. He had not seen Whiskers for some time and wanted to know how he was doing. Except for Georgie Beaver, the old cat was the only animal Billy had known outside The Enchantment. When the shepherd dog was just a pup, the old cat had strayed away from Will Stuart's barn and accidently wandered through the opening between the two trees at Land's End on June 21. Billy found Whiskers on the long bench that sat on the boardinghouse porch. He was leaning heavily on his cane.

"Why…why if it isn't little Bones," greeted the cat, looking up wearily. "I…I was hopin' I'd get to see you. It's…it's harder and harder for me to get down here. Mrs. Badger helps me downstairs."

"I'm sorry it's been a while. A lot's happened, old friend. In fact, I'm on my way to the Hill Country now to keep them from joinin' with the North Woods…for all the good it'll do," complained Billy.

"And I keep hearin' rumors about this ghost," chuckled the old cat. "Now that's one for…for the books. I bet that'll be quite a story…when it comes out! But I…I've seen you several times with the good sheriff. I have a feelin' you… you both know somethin' you ain't tellin' us."

"Well, you're a wise old codger. I'll let you know the whole truth as soon as I'm allowed," grinned Billy. "Now you have to excuse me. I have to be on my way. So take care of yourself and be careful comin' down those stairs."

"I will as long as I can, you…you young whippersnapper!"

By the time Billy slipped on his blue robe and took his seat inside the Hill Country's sacred lodge, Lucinda and Maurice were already in their places. The other Tribal Councilors were still over by the great doors greeting Bruno von Shepherd, Sheldon Sheepdog, and Angus Wolfhound. Billy noticed right away that chairs for the three visitors had been placed across from the Tribal Councilors, making a complete circle.

"Mr. Bones," greeted Lucinda, "if you wouldn't mind waiting around after the meeting, I have something to show you; but keep your robe on."

"Of course," whispered Billy. "I see our friends from the North Woods are already here, so I guess there won't be any discussion beforehand."

"I'm afraid that was done three days ago when you were out chasin' your ghost," added Maurice, leaning over and jabbing the dog with his elbow.

"Then what can we do?" inquired Billy.

"Try to put off any idea of uniting until we meet with the North Woods Council. Once we're all together, I think things may look different to some of our councilors," suggested Lucinda. "The one I'm concerned about now is Orville Bat."

After everyone was seated and Gaylord Cougar had made the proper introductions, he called on Bruno. "Mr. von Shepherd, I know you're anxious to speak to our council, and we're most anxious to hear your ideas. The floor is yours."

"Thank you, Chief Cougar," began the German shepherd. I would like to formally invite your Tribal Council to meet with our council next Friday to see if our two states can govern as one. I know you haven't decided to unite with us, but I think you'll find we're of the same mind. Neither of us like certain parts of *The Great Book of Rules*, and we both prefer your code and *The Vulture's Appendix,* as interpreted by your own Orville Bat. Since we seem to be in basic agreement, I see no reason we can't be one state.

"But how exactly would that work?" questioned Lucinda Vulture. "Our two states have different problems. We have hills and you have woods, and we're separated by geography. It seems to me it would be better if we both took care of our own needs and just remained friends. What would be the advantage of joining with you?"

"Well, for one thing we would both be stronger if we were united," reasoned Bruno.

"Stronger? But for what reason? We've always managed to get along with the Prairie, and they've never shown any aggression towards us," declared the vulture.

"Then why the closed borders? There must've been something you were afraid of," rebutted the German shepherd.

"Yes, I remember," joined Lucretia Lizard. "In the old days, they wanted us to follow their *Great Book o' Rules.* That's why we separated in the first place."

"But they never tried to forcibly intervene, Lucretia," continued Lucinda. "And having two states has always worked well. And now we have open borders."

"But things could always change for the worse," said Gaylord, trying to support Bruno. "How about when Brother Fabian Lynx was using their *Great Book of Rules* for his own purpose? We were more than a little worried?"

"Even then it was better to have two states," commented Maurice. "That way we weren't directly affected."

"But that's just it," stated Bruno. "We have the same beliefs."

"I think Maurice and Lucinda are right. Havin' three states is a better idea," remarked Billy for the first time. "And since we already have our separate councils, we wouldn't have to worry about disagreements that arose with your state either."

"Well, so we finally hear from the famous Mr. Billy Bones," said Bruno sarcastically, "and you don't even live in either of our two states! Isn't that interesting!"

"Well, why don't you all join us on Friday and see how comfortable you are?" intervened Sheldon Sheepdog, trying to diffuse the uncomfortable situation.

"I think there's no reason we can't vote on the idea of meetin' with you right now. I think we can do that by a simple show of hands. All those in favor," began Gaylord. "All right, I see Ms. Lizard, Mr. Bat, and Mrs. Big Horn, and counting me makes four. And now those against? I'm afraid I see only three, Ms. Vulture, Mr. Bones, and Mr. Rabbit. So congratulations, Mr. von Shepherd, it looks like we'll be seeing you next Friday. Now Mr. Bat, I believe you had something you wanted to discuss."

Before the bat started to express his views, he stood on the seat of his chair. "I know you've all heard about the terrifying animal that just came into The Enchantment during the summer solstice. Apparently he frightened a number of citizens inside the Prairie and then completely disappeared. I understand that Mr. Bones here had a vision that was so strong that he went to Mr. Wise Owl's aid. Well, I felt the disturbing presence as well, but being at The Fortress at the time was unable to respond. Since then I've determined that for the good of all our states, we should raise a band of deputies and force this creature out of hiding!"

"And just who would you use?" asked Gaylord.

"We could start with the animals in the various drill groups in our three states and then add anyone else who felt compelled to join us."

"But wait a minute, Mr. Bat. I thought this animal was badly wounded. Maybe he's just trying to recover some-where," suggested Lucinda.

"Yes, from what Mr. Wise Owl and Percival Gander told me, this animal was in great pain," continued Billy Bones.

"If that were the case, he would have sought help by now," determined Orville. "And Ms. Vulture, I'm sure you felt his presence too. I think this creature must be hunted down and dealt with."

"Mr. Bat, why don't we wait until at least Friday? At that time, we'll bring it up before the two councils, and I think you'll get a much better response. Until then, let's let Sheriff Lone Wolf and Victor Running Deer handle it," suggested Sheldon Sheepdog.

"But the sooner we strike, the better!" screeched the bat.

"Perhaps, but you'll need time to get your deputies together," suggested Angus Wolfhound. "By Friday you can get the word out, and maybe we'll know more…."

"Then until next Friday, when we'll have a full house, so to speak," announced Gaylord Cougar before adjourning the meeting.

# CHAPTER THIRTY

# THE SMALL CHEST

After the other council members took off their robes and left the lodge, Billy waited for Lucinda Vulture by the great stone fireplace on the south wall. Lucinda and Maurice Rabbit had gone outside with Arthur Elk, and when she finally returned, she addressed the shepherd dog. "Last night, I felt another disturbance in your spirit, Billy. Could that possibly be right?"

"I wondered if you might pick up on my dream," said Billy. "I didn't understand it myself, but it was very real." For the next few moments, Billy recounted his dream of the two hunters shooting Victor Running Deer's mother. "I've never dreamt about guns before. It was very strange, yet I'm sure that's how it really happened. In fact, I can still hear the sound of gunfire in my ears." recounted the shepherd dog.

"Yes, it is strange, especially in light of what I have to tell you," admitted Lucinda. "But before we go back into the robing room, there's something I think you should be cognizant of—something no one else knows except Orville Bat and me. But because of Orville's erratic behavior and his closeness to Bruno von Shepherd, I think you must now share in this secret."

Billy was still in awe that over the years his spiritual connection with Lucinda Vulture had grown stronger and stronger. As she spoke, he could almost see her standing before a cool, clear lake. Because of this admiration, he was almost fearful of the secret she was about to divulge. "Yes, if you feel I should know," said the dog, summoning up his courage.

"When the ancients first collected the pioneer possessions along the Old Wagon Trail, many of these artifacts were eventually stored in our Sacred Chamber. Among the many pieces was a small wooden chest that contained an article unlike anything else found along the trail. My mother and another animal who lived in the Hill Country decided to lock the chest up and never tell anyone what was inside. To this day, no one else knows about it except me and that animal's grandson."

Lucinda stopped for a moment and took a deep breath before continuing. "There are two keys. That grandson has one, and I have the other."

"But who…" began the dog.

"That's what I'm coming to," said Lucinda, taking another deep breath. "That other animal, as you might already have guessed, is Orville Bat."

"And what's in this small chest?" asked Billy.

"A very dangerous weapon, I'm afraid," warned Lucinda.

"But I thought all weapons were forbidden by *The*

*Great Book of Rules* and even *The Vulture's Appendix*!"

"Yes, that's true. But they didn't want to destroy any human artifacts for fear of how it would affect the well-being of The Enchantment," explained Lucinda. "You saw what happened when Fabian's lieutenants burned five pieces of furniture belonging to the humans."

"But what kind of a weapon is it?" questioned Billy.

"I'm afraid it's a gun, Mr. Bones. That's why I was so surprised at your dream," said Lucinda. "I've been worrying about it for some time."

"You mean it's a rifle like the hunters used?" asked Billy.

"No, it's what they called a six-gun, and it has a holster and six bullets," informed the old bird.

"Yes, I've read about them in one of Winston's Wild West books. And I also remember that the old man in the outside world had one. He would sometimes shoot cans off fence posts just for practice," recollected the shepherd dog. "But what must we do now?"

"I think we have to remove that weapon and hide it someplace where Orville can never find it," continued the vulture. "With his new closeness to Mr. von Shepherd, I fear it might fall into the wrong hands."

"The Great Spirit forbid," whispered Billy.

"So, Mr. Bones, that's why you still have your robe on. As you remember, the spirit is very strong inside the Sacred Chamber, and it's better that we're properly attired," instructed Lucinda as she entered into the robing room.

When the vulture reached the door that led back into the mountain called Spirit Dwells, she lit a candle and picked out the right key from her key ring. "We must be very quiet inside, so just follow me. The chest is hidden under a table in the far left corner," the old bird whispered as she unlocked the door and stepped inside. The chamber still looked much the same to the shepherd dog except for shelves that had been built along the north wall. The dog knew that many of Winston Wise Owl's books had been placed there to hide them from Brother Fabian's lieutenants. All the other artifacts were still stored around the room in an orderly manner.

When Lucinda got to the table, she had Billy reach underneath it and pull out the small chest. Again she took another key off her key ring, bent down, and unlocked the chest. After she opened it, she suddenly stood up in great dismay. "Mr. Bones, it's empty! He beat us to it! How could I have been so careless!" hissed the old vulture, forgetting her own insistence on being silent. "Here, let me lock it up, and please, Mr. Bones, put it back the way you found it. No one must know this chest is empty except for perhaps Maurice. Hopefully, Orville hasn't already given the gun to Bruno von Shepherd!"

When Lucinda and Billy left the lodge, they were met by Maurice Rabbit, who had been standing guard. By the vulture's demeanor, the jackrabbit knew something had gone very wrong. "Maurice, can we meet at your place?" the old bird requested. "Mr. Bones and I have just witnessed a disaster, and you must help us rectify it!"

For almost an hour the three councilors met at the jack-rabbit's dugout. Lucinda spent the initial time informing Maurice about the revolver, and then Billy decided to tell him about the wounded animal and Fabian Lynx's return. The dog hated to let another animal in on the lynx's plight, but he felt the rabbit needed to know everything if he was going to help save the two states from Bruno's ambitions. And like Lucinda, Billy thought he could trust Maurice completely, even with his own life.

It was finally decided that the best time to approach Orville was either right before or just after the meeting with the North Woods Council. Since the bat was now staying inside The Fortress, there seemed no better time without calling attention to their evident concern.

# CHAPTER THIRTY-ONE

## A MATTER OF PRIDE

Even though the weather on Wednesday morning was already hot, attendance for drill practice inside the Prairie was at full capacity. Conan Greyhound began with the usual warm-up exercises, and then went into the one-on-one matches with staffs. During the first break, Billy Bones noticed that Orville Bat had come down from the North Woods and was crouching in the shadow of a nearby tree. Eventually he slithered over and asked Conan if he could make an announcement.

"Thank you. Thank you for allowing me to speak," began Orville, glancing nervously at Conan and then at the rest of the group. "As you're all aware by now, an animal entered The Enchantment five days ago during the summer solstice. I'm…I'm sure you all know that your own Billy Bones felt the presence of this animal and rushed over to Land's End to help, but unfortunately the animal had already escaped. Now…neither Mr. Wise Owl nor Ms. Groundhog was able to identify this animal, 'cause it came at night, and its face was bloody and unrecognizable. However, I too felt the presence of this creature as far away as the North Woods and…and knew immediately he could be a threat to our community! Now…I'm told he was spotted several times and described as a ghost-like figure with a terrible face. It was also reported that he frightened those eye witnesses back into their homes."

At this point the bat felt a little more comfortable and hopped up on the steps of City Hall. "Since then I've talked to the drill groups from the Hill Country and the North Woods, and they agreed to form a band of deputies. However, Bruno von Shepherd and Gaylord Cougar asked us to wait until our joint meeting on Friday so they can officially declare this creature a criminal and authorize our attempt to hunt him down. Now…we plan to start inside our two states and then search the Prairie as well. Since the open border policy is still in effect, this should be acceptable. And…we invite your group to join our search as well. So…do you have any questions?"

"As Lucinda Vulture mentioned to you at our Tribal Meeting in the Hill Country, you should probably wait until this wounded creature decides to make an appearance on his own," ventured Billy Bones.

"But…as I told you, Mr. Bones, the presence I felt last Friday was a powerful disturbance. And I'm not wrong about this! I'm as gifted as you are, Mr. Billy Bones!" squealed the bat.

"But perhaps you picked up on the creature's pain," rebutted the dog.

"No! I think I would have known the difference! And since he's already terrorized some of your own citizens,

I believe we need to find him as soon as possible!" cried Orville.

"Do you plan on carrying weapons?" asked Sheriff Lone Wolf, trying to calm the bat down, "and when would you start your search?"

"I imagine we'll have clubs. But that's not been determined yet," responded the bat. "If he hasn't shown himself by Friday, we'll probably begin our search the following morning."

"Since Mr. Bones will be at your combined meeting on Friday, we'll send word with him if anything's changed," declared the sheriff. "I think the use of clubs for one wounded creature is hardly necessary. But thanks for informing us."

After the bat flew away, Sheriff Lone Wolf addressed the group. "If these deputies come down from the North Woods on Saturday morning, I hope you'll be willing to help Victor and me if any trouble arises. I know Mr. Bat would like to have you join his band of deputies, as he calls them, but I hope you won't get carried away by his rhetoric or get caught up in a mob mentality."

"Do they have the right to come into the Prairie and look for this animal?" asked Ernest Buck.

"It's been a standing policy, I'm afraid. If a creature's been judged to be a criminal in one state, they're allowed to search for him in another state as well. As most of you remember, when our own Billy Bones escaped our council three years ago, we searched inside the Hill Country," explained Sheriff Lone Wolf.

"Should we bring clubs?" asked Sterling Buck.

"I would say it wouldn't be a bad idea to have them on you somewhere," answered Walter Lone Wolf. "But don't carry them openly unless things go badly."

After the practice was over, Sheriff Lone Wolf asked Billy Bones and Victor Running Deer to remain. "I think the three of us need to talk to Mr. Lynx this afternoon. This whole thing's gettin' out of hand. I suggest we meet at Dr. Muskrat's office at different times. Victor, why don't you arrive at 1:00? I'll come at 1:30, and Billy, why don't you sandwich in between us...say at about1:15? Hopefully we won't cause any suspicion that way."

By the time Billy arrived at the doctor's office, Fabian Lynx was telling Victor about the humans that were kind to him at the wildlife zoo. The lynx was wearing his robe, and the bandages were still on his face, but the hood of his robe lay around his shoulders. "I know you and I had bad experiences with humans before we entered The Enchantment, Victor, but I have to say this human woman and her friend were very kind to me, and I didn't even belong to them. Billy was right about that. I'm just sorry I hadn't experienced that before I entered the first time."

"As I told Billy, I imagine the human animals are like creatures everywhere; there are some good ones and some not so good," smiled Victor.

Sheriff Lone Wolf arrived soon after Billy Bones, and the three of them told Fabian what had happened earlier in the day.

"I'm concerned, Mr. Lynx, that these deputies of Orville Bat will be coming to the Prairie sometime on Saturday. That is, if they get permission from their councilors, which they very well might. We'll probably be all right unless they discover you're here at Dr. Muskrat's. It would be safer if you introduced yourself before that time—perhaps to the City Council."

"I'd still like to wait 'til Friday after next. My bandages will be gone and my stitches out, and I'll know what I have to live with," countered the lynx. "Besides, I see no reason for them to look here."

"Perhaps we should just inform the council then?" suggested the sheriff.

"No, too many would know, and the word would surely get out," returned Fabian. "And they might want to arrest me—especially for burning the human artifacts and what happened to those five young changelings. But my hate was so strong…."

"Yes, you should have known better," admonished the wolf, "especially since it was clearly stated in *The Great Book of Rules*. And didn't Mr. Bones try to warn you?"

"I wasn't listening to anyone; my head was so full of loathing. Besides, I didn't think anything would happen if we destroyed that furniture. Something like that would never occur in the outside world. It's beyond reason—beyond understanding or rational thought."

"But you forget where we are, Fabian," insisted Billy Bones. "The rationales of the outside world don't apply here."

"Speaking of Winston Wise Owl, that's my real crime. It was bad enough that I was going to send him into the other world, but having his wings clipped! That was unforgiveable, and I need to be held accountable for that," concluded Fabian, hanging his head.

"Again, that'll be for the council to determine. In the meantime we need to decide what to do about your safety. They'll probably bring clubs. And I'm sure Orville Bat will have them all worked up," warned Sheriff Lone Wolf. "Are you positive you won't go before the council until your stitches are out?"

"No, I still feel I'll give a much better account of myself if I wait until I'm healed," insisted the lynx.

"But we have to consider Dr. Muskrat's safety too," cautioned the deer.

"No one will hurt me, Victor," responded the muskrat. "And Fabian is in no condition to go anywhere. We'll just have to ride out the storm."

"Then until after Saturday, we must stay away from this place, in case someone's watching," ordered Sheriff Lone Wolf. "And Fabian, when patients visit the doctor, please stay in the back room. If the sick room door is closed, they may get suspicious."

# CHAPTER THIRTY-TWO

# THE TWO COUNCILS

The Tribal Council and the North Woods Council met again in the large dining hall inside The Fortress. Billy Bones and Lucinda Vulture were anxious to catch Orville Bat before the meeting, but he did not arrive in time. Brigitte von Shepherd did make an early appearance and approached Billy immediately.

"Mr. Bones, I'd forgotten that you were a councilor in the Hill Country. What an unexpected pleasure! I'm not sure how Sheldon plans to seat us, but maybe we can sit together," suggested Brigitte.

Billy happily stood and offered her the chair next to him. As the other councilors dribbled in, they noticed Brigitte and Billy sitting together. They continued the trend and sat wherever they pleased.

When Sheldon finally arrived, he was delighted to see the various councilors sitting randomly about the room. Earlier he had arranged the three tables in a large C again and placed himself in front of the fireplace on the fourth side

When Gaylord Cougar and Bruno von Shepherd

entered, they took seats next to each other facing Sheldon. All told, there were fourteen councilors besides Sheldon. For this special meeting, Angus Wolfhound had taken Sheldon's place so the sheepdog could remain neutral. Orville Bat showed up last and took the only vacant seat, near the fireplace.

After Sheldon Sheepdog's welcome, he introduced the subject of union between the two states. Again, Bruno von Shepherd was the first to express his opinions. "Since we've adopted your code and *The Vulture's Appendix* from *The Great Book of Rules,* and since we're a stronger body together, I feel it's time we finally joined forces."

After a number of other councilors from both states offered their thoughts, Lucinda rose to state her objections. She reiterated her concerns about the geographical differences and the problems they presented. At the end, she touched on the matter that was most prevalent on her mind.

"My main disagreement with Mr. von Shepherd has to do with the two states becoming stronger once we're united. It almost sounds like a threat to our friends inside the Prairie. The idea of any type of aggression is repugnant to me, and I think we need to stay away from anything that would point us in that direction," the vulture asserted. "Of course we could still remain aligned and enjoy the close spiritual relationship we've already developed and meet from time to time to discuss matters that concern both of our states, like we're doing today."

"I would hope, Ms. Vulture, that we would never initiate aggression ourselves. However, we could ask Mr. von

Shepherd or Mr. Cougar if they care to respond to your concern," suggested the sheepdog.

"It's hard to speak to your concern, Ms. Vulture, with Mr. Billy Bones sitting right next to you," growled Bruno.

"What could he possibly have to do with my concern?" questioned Lucinda.

"Hasn't it ever occurred to you why so many of our pack members left the North Woods, Ms. Vulture?" snarled Bruno, glancing over at Brigitte. "And look, he's even got my sister eating out of his hand. Can't you see that he's subtly weaning them away from us so he can become their new leader?"

After this unexpected outburst, there was a moment of complete silence. Finally Lucinda spoke. "Mr. von Shepherd, not everyone desires that kind of power, and certainly not Mr. Bones."

"Ha! I see he's fooled you too! He even got you to try to elect him chief of the Hill Country! And besides, he shouldn't even be here. He's not a citizen of either of our states," barked Bruno.

"As I explained to you before, Mr. von Shepherd, it was not his idea to be chief, it was mine," answered the vulture. "And I still believe it was a good one."

Following Lucinda's remarks, a question arose from an unexpected source. "Mr. Sheepdog, who would be the leader of our combined states?" wondered Hilda Big Horn. "Would it be Bruno von Shepherd or our elected leader, Gaylord Cougar?"

"Mr. Cougar, would you like to answer that question?"

asked Sheldon, trying to shift the direction of the debate.

"As I understand it, each of us would control our own state. Otherwise we'd make decisions like we're doing now—with a mediator," answered the cougar.

"Yes, but what if there was a conflict…say with the Prairie. Who would make the final decision?" asked Colonel Eddie Crane.

"That would depend on what state the conflict was with," stated Bruno. "If it was in Mr. Cougar's area, it would be him. If it happened against the North Woods, then it would be me."

"I think we need to move on to the next subject," declared Sheldon, trying to prevent more talk of aggression. "Mr. Bat has an immediate concern that he wishes to bring to the floor. He's been talking to the three drill groups about the animal that entered The Enchantment during the summer solstice. He feels that this animal could be a danger to all of us and should be found as soon as possible. He needs our permission, however, to deputize these animals before taking them into the different states. Ah…Mr. Bat, do you have anything to add to that?"

For the next few minutes, Orville Bat described the entry of what he now referred to as an "evil force" into The Enchantment. He then went on to relate how it had already frightened a number of the Prairie citizens and should therefore be considered a criminal. He explained how he, as well as Billy Bones, had felt its presence. He finally finished by saying, "We feel we need a lot of deputies in case we run into resistance of some sort, but we need the council's permission to do this."

"Then what I need is a show of hands from each state," said Sheldon finally.

"Excuse me, Mr. Sheepdog," interrupted Billy, "but I need to say a word before you vote."

"Yes, Mr. Bones, what's your concern?" asked Sheldon.

"As I've said a number of times, this animal was badly wounded. I think he should be allowed to show himself whenever he's ready," implored the shepherd.

As he was speaking, Billy suddenly realized that the majority of the councilors had been moved by Orville's plea and were already somewhat fearful of this unknown entity. And since he could not tell them the whole truth, he was fighting a losing cause. After a few moments, Sheldon called for a vote.

When the sheepdog finally calculated the results for the North Woods, Bruno von Shepherd, Angus Wolfhound, Colonel Eddie Crane, Willie Wild Cat, Milton Brown Bear, and Old Ma Peccary immediately responded in favor of an intervention. Only Brigitte von Shepherd voted against the deputies. Among the Hill Country councilors Gaylord Cougar, Lucretia Lizard, Hilda Big Horn, and Orville Bat supported the request, while Billy, Lucinda, and Maurice Rabbit rejected it.

"It looks like you've got your permission, Mr. Bat. When would you start your search?" inquired Sheldon.

"We plan to meet tomorrow morning," answered Orville with some elation.

"Excuse me again," called Lucinda Vulture before

Sheldon could continue. "I believe that Gaylord Cougar and Bruno von Shepherd should not be allowed to be part of this group. If they show up in the Prairie with these deputies, it would surely look like an aggressive action on our part, and we certainly don't want that."

After a second vote, and to the consternation of Bruno von Shepherd, both groups agreed that the two leaders should not be among the deputies. It was also decided that the councilors needed more time when it came to uniting, especially after Lucinda's objections and Bruno's outburst. Therefore the matter was tabled until the two groups could meet separately.

After the meeting Lucinda and Billy failed to corner the bat, who quickly escaped. "I think he's aware that we know about the six-gun. I just hope he's hidden it in a safe place. He also knows that *The Vulture's Appendix* forbids him to use it," determined Lucinda. "But you have other problems on your hands, Mr. Bones, with those deputies showing up tomorrow. Orville says he plans to search our two states first, but we both know he'll go directly to the Prairie!"

# CHAPTER THIRTY-THREE

# STANDOFF AT CASTLE ROCK

Early Saturday morning, Billy Bones met Sheriff Lone Wolf and Victor Running Deer at the sheriff's office on lower Main Street.

"All we can do for now is keep an eye out for Orville's deputies. If we see them headin' for Dr. Muskrat's office, we'll have to join 'em," ordered the wolf. "But since we decided not to expose Fabian, we'll have to remain neutral unless, of course, things go badly and he needs our protection."

During the early hours Billy noticed that most of the Prairie's drill participants were scattered up and down Main Street or in front of City Hall. Finally around midmorning, the gang of deputies arrived from the north. After a quick calculation, Billy counted eighteen strong: six from the Hill Country including Angus Wolfhound, and twelve from the North Woods, including the four peccary brothers and Orville Bat. Billy was glad that Bruno von Shepherd and Gaylord Cougar kept their part of the bargain and stayed away. He was also pleased that Sheldon Sheepdog and Fritz Terrier were not with the other dogs and that

Maurice Rabbit stayed home. To Billy's chagrin, however, they came straight down Main Street and stopped in front of Dr. Muskrat's office.

By the time the sheriff, Victor, and Billy joined the band, so had Conan Greyhound, the two Buck brothers, Arnold Big Horn, Sandy Antelope, Philip P. Fox, and Lenny Coyote. When Orville approached the muskrat's door, Sheriff Lone Wolf called out to him. "Mr. Bat, I see you haven't had any luck. And you've brought quite a crowd with you, and they're armed!"

"That's because we just reached our destination," answered the bat somewhat sarcastically.

"So why are you stopping at the good doctor's office then?" continued the wolf.

"Because that's where you told me to go!" squeaked that bat, puffing out his cheeks.

"I said no such thing!" rebuked the sheriff.

"Oh, but you did," contradicted Orville.

"When was that, may I ask?" questioned the wolf, walking up to the door and towering over the bat.

"Wednesday after I left your drill practice, I thought maybe I should come back and wait to see how you reacted to my announcement. My hunch was right. Early that afternoon, your deputy, then Mr. Bones, and then you, my dear sheriff, entered Dr. Muskrat's office. Of course I soon put two and two together. I reasoned that if you knew where the creature was, you'd lead me straight to him…and so you did!" squealed the bat again in a show of delight. "Now would you care to knock on Dr. Muskrat's door, or should we break it down?"

As the deputies took out their clubs and started to surge forward, the door suddenly opened, and Dr. Muskrat confronted them. "I'd prefer you didn't break my door down, Orville Bat. If you want to come in, please leave my doors and windows alone."

As the doctor stepped aside, a number of Orville's deputies rushed inside. After pushing furniture around, tipping over beds, and making a general mess, Phineas T. Fox rushed back outside. "Orville, he's not there, but the back window's open. I'm afraid he escaped."

Before Sheriff Lone Wolf could stop Orville, the bat took flight and started circling the area. Before long he returned and perched on the office roof.

"He's behind the buildings on Main Street and headin' south. After him! Quick, don't let him escape!" screamed the bat in a high-pitched voice. "He's got a head start, but don't let him scare you! He's pretty horrible to look at!"

"Wait! Have you lost your reason?" cried Walter Lone Wolf. "This animal's wounded. In the name of The Great Spirit, put down your weapons and go home!"

"He's getting away, you fools! Stop him before he gets out of sight! Don't listen to the sheriff or you'll lose him!" screeched Orville again.

After the bat's final urging, the mob mentality prevailed, and the deputies from the Hill Country and the North Woods jubilantly joined the chase with the bat circling frantically above them and shouting out directions. Close behind them, Sheriff Lone Wolf, Victor Running

Deer, and Billy Bones followed, and interspersed among Orville's deputies raced the members of the Prairie's own drill group.

When the pursuers got beyond Dry Gulch, they could see that the robed creature's hood had slipped down over his shoulder, and his heavily bandaged head was bobbing up and down as he hobbled along. As the lynx started to circle south around Castle Rock, great cries of "There he goes!" and "Don't let him escape!" rang out as they picked up their collective pace.

By the time the hunters reached the south side of the rocky hill, they began wandering around in ragged confusion. The ghost-like creature seemed to have vanished. Suddenly above them Orville began screaming. "There he is! He's climbing up to that cave! After him! Don't let him escape!"

"In response to the bat's cry, Bison Bob threw a rock at the robed animal, knocking him down. As howls of victory began to ring out, the creature picked himself up and started limping toward the mouth of the cave.

During the chaos Billy showed the sheriff and Victor where the path that led to the cave was located, and they quickly blocked it. At the same time Sheriff Lone Wolf cried, "Over here, friends! Lend us a hand! We can't let them harm him. He's done nothing wrong!"

When the other members of the Prairie drill group heard their sheriff, they quickly positioned themselves on either side of the three defenders, pulled out their clubs, and formed a solid blockade in front of the entrance.

At first Orville's deputies searched for another way up the rocky hillside, but they soon discovered that large impassable boulders covered the rest of the hill. Finally, in desperation, the deputies turned and rushed the line of Prairie defenders, their clubs raised.

"Stop! Have you gone mad?" howled Sheriff Lone Wolf. "Can't you see that he's wounded? Have you lost your senses? What kind of creatures are you anyway?"

The sheriff's outburst immediately slowed down the deputies' charge. When the bat saw what was happening, he began squealing, "Don't listen to him! You outnumber them. Break your way through!"

"No! Stop, I say! We don't want to fight you, but we will if we have to! You're not savages! Now behave your-selves and go home!" howled the wolf again.

The first animal to respond was Arthur Elk. "The sher-iff's right! What are we doing? Have we lost all decency? Besides, they're our friends. I'll not fight them!" the elk yelled, looking at Billy and Victor, and throwing his club to the ground. "If that animal up there's wounded, I'll have nothing more to do with this!"

Slowly the other animals from the Hill Country started putting their clubs away and leaving the area. Finally when no one was left except the deputies from the North Woods, Angus Wolfhound spoke. "I'm sorry too, sheriff, I'm afraid Orville here talked us into this with his 'evil creature' scare. Arthur's right. We need to go home. I'll have no more of this."

"Nor I," chimed in Milton Brown Bear, "But I would like to know who that creature is."

"When he's better, I'm sure he'll tell you himself," answered Billy Bones, finally entering the explanation. "But as you can see, he's in no shape to see anybody for a while."

After the animals from the Hill Country had also departed, including the disgruntled bat, Sheriff Lone Wolf turned to the Prairie defenders. "Thank you for standin' with us. You have no idea what your loyalty means to us. And I think we've seen the last of Orville's deputies…for a while anyway. As Billy said, that poor animal up there will explain everything as soon as he's able. In the meantime, thanks again for trustin' us."

After much hubbub and as soon as everyone had gone except Billy, Victor, and Sheriff Lone Wolf, the shepherd dog glanced up at the cave, "Guess we'd better see how Fabian's doin'. That rock hit him pretty hard."

"Good idea, and thanks to you both. This turned out better than I thought," said the sheriff, turning and heading up to the cave.

"I wonder what they'll say when they find out who he really is?" questioned Victor, following the sheriff.

"He'll have a lot of explaining to do," decided Billy, hurrying after the sheriff and his deputy. "And so will we!"

# CHAPTER THIRTY-FOUR

## THE CONFESSION

Because Rodney Wild Deer had used the cave at Castle Rock as a hideaway three years before, it had certain amenities. Besides the stone bench, a table and several chairs sat in the middle of the room, a dresser stood against the west wall, and cupboards had been built into the east wall.

"Why don't I go back to my office and get some food? And, Victor, why don't you and Billy stay with Mr. Lynx," suggested Sheriff Lone Wolf. "Hopefully by this evening he'll be strong enough to walk back to Dr. Muskrat's office. I don't think anyone will try to bother you, but be on your guard. We don't know how Bruno von Shepherd will respond when he finds out his deputies failed to take the unknown stranger by force."

Although the stone that Bison Bob threw had not broken any of Fabian's bones, it had bruised his left leg pretty badly. "And they still don't know who I am, do they?" remarked the lynx, as soon as the wolf had departed. "I'm afraid they reacted worse than I imagined."

"That's because Orville Bat painted such a grim picture

of you as a terrible creature," explained Billy. "Apparently his psyche felt you enter into The Enchantment, and he kept insisting you were an evil force. I believe he just picked up on your pain. Whatever the case, the animals from the Prairie came to your rescue. For that you can be thankful."

"Maybe…until they find out who I really am. What then? And my lieutenants, where are they?" asked Fabian.

"I'm afraid most of them live in the North Woods under Bruno von Shepherd," replied Victor. "They're among the deputies who chased you, but…perhaps when they know who you are…."

"Yes, that's a thought, Victor," said Billy excitedly. "Maybe when Fabian's feeling better he can wean them away from Bruno and put a damper on his eagerness to take over the Prairie…as well as the Hill Country."

"If I'm still recognizable after my stitches are out," sighed the lynx. "Only the Great Spirit knows what I'll look like—or if they'll accept me."

"Your charm wasn't just in your good looks, Mr. Lynx," laughed Billy. "As I remember, you had quite a persuasive way about you, even if you used it to further your own agenda."

"Don't have any delusions. I'm still that same animal, Billy. Even though I've changed how I feel about humans, I still wonder if my own ambitions will drive me in the wrong direction—even though I now know better."

"Then maybe it's time for your redemption, Mr. Fabian Lynx. Maybe The Great Spirit is giving you a second chance," suggested the shepherd dog.

Victor nodded in agreement with Billy, "We've all grown and learned from our experiences, Mr. Lynx, and you can, too."

"Well, if The Great Spirit is giving me a second chance, he's certainly going about it in a very harsh way," responded the lynx.

The four animals didn't get back to Dr. Muskrat's office until late that evening. The doctor had already straightened out his home office and was expecting them. "Will one of you stay here for a while?" requested the doctor. "I'd feel much safer if you did, at least until the bandages are off and the stitches removed."

"I'll stay tonight," decided Sheriff Lone Wolf.

"I'll come in the morning and stay the rest of the day," promised Billy. "But you and Victor will have to take over after that. I've got a Tribal Council meeting on Monday, and I think it's gonna be a rough one. They'll be deciding whether to join the North Woods. And this time, if Orville Bat's there, I don't think we can stop them."

Two days later, Lucinda Vulture was waiting for Billy when he stopped by Maurice's dugout on his way to the council meeting. "Mr. Bones, I was hoping we'd get a chance to talk. We've got some important issues to discuss, especially concerning Orville Bat."

"I'm sure you heard that Orville's deputies found Fabian Lynx and chased him all the way to Castle Rock. Fortunately, they didn't try to get past the blockade we set up. And of course, they still don't know who he is."

"We also heard that Sheriff Lone Wolf shamed them into going home, even after Orville told them to stay and fight," added Maurice.

"Speaking of Orville Bat, we must find a way to delay him after the meeting. Whether he likes it or not, we've got to find out what he's done with that six-gun," implored Lucinda.

"Can we get Arthur Elk to help us?" inquired Maurice. "I think he will if you ask him, Lucinda."

"I'll try, but hopefully we can corner Orville before he leaves," determined the vulture.

"Perhaps I can get him to talk about Saturday's fiasco after the meeting," suggested Billy. "He might be just angry enough to confront me."

"Then there's the problem of the big vote on unifying the two states. We might not be able to stop them this time, but we've got to try," insisted the vulture.


Luckily, just before the council meeting Billy was able to corner Orville Bat. "I know you're angry with me, Mr. Bat, but I still feel I must ask about your vision. Please, if you'd be so kind as to see me after the meeting. When the creature you chased Saturday goes before the City Council, it'll be important for them to know what you felt…as well as what I experienced."

"I really don't want to talk to you, Mr. Bones. But I would like to know about that 'creature,' as you call him," spat the bat.

"Thank you. I'll see you right after the meeting then," responded the shepherd dog, taking his seat between Lucinda and Maurice.

Before the vote on uniting with the North Woods, both sides repeated their arguments again. When all was said and done, Billy knew that the cougar was still in Bruno von Shepherd's corner. The dog could also tell that Hilda Big Horn was satisfied that Gaylord Cougar would be on an equal footing with Bruno. When the vote to unite with the North Woods was finally taken, Gaylord and his followers won by a margin of one, as Billy feared. Now all that remained was the decision by the North Woods Council, which would likely go the same way.

While the other councilors were removing their robes, Orville stayed in the great hall with Billy, as he had promised. "So, Mr. Bones, you finally agree that I had a vision as well as yourself?"

"I have no doubt of it, Mr. Bat," answered Billy. "But don't you think it's only fair that we wait until this creature can speak for himself? Perhaps if you came to our next meeting at City Hall, you could hear for yourself."

"And when would that be?"

"I would say by the weekend or the first of next week," responded Billy.

When the other council members were leaving the robing room, Billy and Orville went inside. While they were taking off their robes, Lucinda reentered the small room, and Maurice stood guard outside.

"Mr. Bat, might I have a word with you?" Lucinda

began, leaving Billy out of the confrontation and locking the door. "I have something I need to discuss with you."

"What is this?" Orville replied, starting to get nervous.

"Last week I got worried and unlocked the chest that contains the weapon that has remained a secret between us."

"Hush, Lucinda, Mr. Bones here should not be part of this conversation!" squealed the bat.

"No, I think he needs to hear this, Orville. This is a very serious matter, and a third party must be present—someone I can trust," insisted the vulture. "That weapon was to remain hidden forever, and only you and I had a key."

"Lucinda, you must not go on!" squealed the bat again.

"No! Orville Bat, you have broken a very sacred trust. The weapon is gone, and you are the only one who could have taken it. Now you must tell me what you did with it!"

"I...I put it in a safe place so no one can find it. Not even you, Lucinda Vulture!" cried the bat.

"But that wasn't your prerogative, Orville. You must return it at once. What if Bruno or Gaylord or Sheriff Lone Wolf were to get ahold of it? Someone's sure to get killed!" warned Lucinda. "That was the whole reason our two ancestors wanted it to remain a secret."

When the bat looked away and put his head down, Billy knew instantly that he had already placed it in the hands of another animal.

"Who has it, Orville?" asked Billy grabbing the bat by his wrist. "I know you've given it to someone!"

"I...I thought Bruno should have it. He said he promised

to protect us in case the Prairie marched on us!" screamed the bat, trying to free his wrist.

"You gave it to Bruno!" yelled Billy. "But he wants to control everything, and you just made it possible! Surely you know that!"

Orville Bat suddenly stopped struggling and faced Billy. "That's not what he told me, Mr. Bones. He said that you were the dangerous one. He said you were takin' away all his pack from him so you could be the leader!"

"Mr. Orville Bat…and you believed him?" asked Lucinda incredulously. "I thought you had more insight that that. Surely you can see by now that Bruno is the one to be feared."

"But I've already given it to him," whined Orville. "There's nothin' I can do now."

"Yes there is, Mr. Bat. You must find it and return it to its rightful place, or I will tell everyone about the weapon and how you betrayed your trust—to us and to our ancestors!" cried Lucinda.

"But I'm afraid of him. What if I get caught?" whined Orville, scrunching his feet under him and collapsing to the floor.

"That's something you should have thought of before you decided to betray us," hissed the vulture. "Now go and get it back before that weapon changes everything inside The Enchantment forever!"

After the bat left, Lucinda and Billy stepped slowly into the great room. When Maurice observed them he asked, "What did you find out? Did he take the weapon?"

"Worse than that, Maurice," responded Lucinda. "He's given it to Bruno. And now we're united with the North Woods and under his leadership."

"Perhaps if I talked to Sheldon…or Brigitte," suggested Billy, trying to come up with a solution.

"No, let's see if Orville can find the weapon. In the meantime, no one else must know about it. If that doesn't work, than I…I don't know. I guess everything's on the table," whispered Lucinda.

# CHAPTER THIRTY-FIVE

## THE FIRST STEP TO RECOVERY

Dr. Muskrat decided to take out Fabian's stitches on Friday morning. He asked Billy Bones if he would assist him in the process. "If you'll help me take the bandages off his head, Mr. Bones, I'd appreciate it. They're a little hard for me to reach," determined the doctor. "We'll take the stitches off his face first and then off the smaller cuts on his chest and hands."

For the next half hour, the two animals worked without much conversation. When they finally finished, Billy was surprised at what an excellent job the muskrat had done. Although the scars were visible, they did not change the shape of Fabian's face. There was still some redness, especially around the large gash on his cheek, but the lynx was not disfigured.

"Here's a mirror, Mr. Lynx," offered the muskrat. "Quite a difference from the first time I saw you! Thankfully we got to the cuts before they had a chance to heal improperly. You can thank Mr. Bones for that."

"I guess that scar on my cheek will remain with me always," observed Fabian.

"Yes, but the smaller ones should pretty much disappear in time," assured the doctor.

"It gives you a mark of distinction, Fabian. If you choose to think of it that way," laughed Billy. "Now it's time for you to meet your public."

"How about Monday? Maybe some of the redness will have gone by then," reasoned Fabian.

"Let's talk to the sheriff and try to arrange a meeting with the City Council," suggested the shepherd dog. "But first we need to talk to an old acquaintance of yours and see if we can make things right. I think we've waited long enough."

"You mean Winston Wise Owl, of course," responded Fabian. "You're right, the sooner the better. But I must say I'm not looking forward to it."

"I'll leave right now," said Billy. "I'll look in on the sheriff first, and then I'll see if Mr. Wise Owl will return with me."

"Will you tell him who I am?" inquired Fabian.

"Yes, I think that would be the wisest thing," answered Billy. "In any case, I'll be back this afternoon…with or without Mr. Wise Owl."

----------------------------------------------------------------

Winston Wise Owl had just finished his lunch and was resting in a chair beneath his treehouse when Billy Bones arrived. The owl had been expecting the shepherd dog for two weeks and was disappointed that all his news of the wounded animal had come from other sources. He knew

Billy probably had good reasons for not telling him exactly what happened, but his ego was bruised anyway.

"Mr. Wise Owl, may I have a word with you?" asked Billy.

"Mr. Bones, I've been expecting you for some time," said Winston, sounding a little disgruntled.

"I'm sorry for not coming sooner, Mr. Wise Owl," apologized the dog, "but there was so much I couldn't explain until today."

"Oh?" said the owl. "And does this have something to do with the wounded animal that came screaming through here two weeks ago?"

"Yes, it does," admitted Billy.

"Then what was it about this animal that you couldn't divulge until now?" continued the owl, not letting the dog off too easily.

"Well, that's what I've come to explain, sir," admitted Billy. "You see, there's a reason only a few of us knew who the animal was. It's because he asked us to keep his identity a secret until he had a chance to heal. In fact, Dr. Muskrat and I just removed his stitches this morning. And now he asked to see you before going to the City Council."

"This gets more intriguing as you speak," commented the owl. "And why does he want to see me first, may I ask?"

"Because you know this animal, and he's done you a great wrong!" barked Billy finally.

"Brother Fabian Lynx!" exclaimed the owl. "But why? I should be the last animal he'd want to see!"

"Well let me explain. You see, after I forced him into the old world, he was recaptured and sent back to the wildlife zoo. However, his experience was much different this time. A human woman and her friend treated him well and even helped him escape. In fact, his wounds were the result of getting caught in some barbed wire, which cut him pretty badly, as you're well aware."

"I still don't understand. Why does he want to see me?" insisted Winston.

"In short, he no longer hates humans as he once did. He seems much changed, Mr. Wise Owl, and he would like to apologize to you if you'll give him a chance. In fact, he was hopin' to see you this afternoon."

"I see," was all the owl could utter for a few moments. "Well, this is an interesting turn of events."

"Then you'll see him, sir?"

"Under the circumstances, I suppose I must."

Winston allowed Billy time to get back to the doctor's office. Even though the owl still had doubts about the lynx's sincerity, he screwed up his courage and left half an hour later. When he arrived, Fabian was in a conversation with Sheriff Lone Wolf and Billy Bones. When the lynx turned around, the owl was somewhat shocked. Instead of the wounded animal he had seen rushing through Land's End, he saw a handsome lynx with a rakish scar on his left cheek. Instead of the white robe he used to wear as the spiritual counselor of the New Meetinghouse, he wore the gray robe he had taken from Percival Gander's Shop.

"Mr. Wise Owl, thank you for coming," began Fabian. "Billy told me that he already explained what happened to me…so I won't go into that. I'm just glad I could talk to you before going to the City Council. As I told Sheriff Lone Wolf, I realize I'll be held accountable for what I did…and I'm ready to answer for that. However, I wanted to apologize to you first. What I did to you is unforgiv-able—especially trimming your wings so you couldn't fly. Thank goodness Mr. Bones was brave enough to interfere."

For a moment Winston said nothing. He was quite aware of the lynx's charm and charisma, which he still seemed to possess in abundance. He also knew that Billy, Doctor Muskrat, Sheriff Lone Wolf, and apparently Victor Running Deer were all taken in by his magnetism, especially since they bowed to his vanity and allowed him two extra weeks to heal. Finally he addressed the lynx. "I appreciate your apology, Brother Fabian, and I thank you for seeing me before meeting with the City Council. I hope, for all our sakes, you've really had a change of heart. As for me, I'm certainly willing to give you a chance to redeem yourself."

"That's very kind of you, Mr. Wise Owl, and it's just Fabian now since I'm no longer the spiritual leader of the New Meetinghouse and certainly don't deserve to be after the things I did. And…I've had a lot of time to think, and I feel quite ashamed of my blind hatred that caused so much pain," admitted the lynx. "I only hope I can be forgiven. And I'm also hoping I can be of some help in the Prairie's dispute with the North Woods and with this Bruno von Shepherd."

Winston stared at the lynx for a long while, his mind racing. "He does seem different," the owl thought. "I guess only time will tell. But as far as Bruno von Shepherd is concerned…."

"In the meantime, Mr. Lynx," began the sheriff, inter-rupting the owl's reflection, "I guess you'd better stay with me at the jail, at least until we find a home for you. There's no one in either cell, and they're nice and clean. You can lock yourself in at night if you wish. I don't think we should lean on Dr. Muskrat's kindness any longer."

"Yes, that's getting to be a problem," agreed the doctor. "Have you thought of a place to live? I'm sure that cave behind Castle Rock isn't really suitable."

"Is anyone staying in the big room behind the New Meetinghouse? I know Sister Sarah Mourning Dove has her own treehouse," suggested Fabian.

"I don't know if that'd be such a good idea," said the sheriff. "There might be a lot of complaining by the congregation, since you were their counselor."

"Well, it was a thought," said Fabian. "I bet my street clothes are still there."

"Well, we could ask Sarah, I guess, since it wouldn't be permanent," said the wolf. "But first, I'll inform Chairman Cornelius Van Mink of your desire to meet with them on Monday so he can make arrangements. Mr. Wise Owl and Mr. Bones, I think you better attend also. A lot of questions need to be answered. And Mr. Bones, you need to tell the members what happened at the last Tribal Council meeting. I'm sure they'll be upset, but they need to know."

# CHAPTER THIRTY-SIX

# INTRODUCING THE GHOST

Word soon got around that the Ghost of Castle Rock was staying at the jail and would appear before the City Council on Monday afternoon. Winston Wise Owl arrived early so he could watch the lynx's journey to City Hall. He soon discovered that most of the Prairie's citizens had come to the same decision and were scattered up and down Main Street.

When Fabian Lynx and Sheriff Lone Wolf finally left the sheriff's office, the lynx proved to be like the Pied Piper of Hamelin whom Winston had read about in one of his fairy tale books. As it was in the story, when the lynx journeyed forth, the crowd systematically fell in behind him. The lynx had pulled the hood of his gray robe over his head. However, his handsome face was still visible, and he walked along proudly, as murmurs of his identity quickly spread.

When the owl entered the hall after the lynx and the wolf, he discovered that the councilors had decided to meet in the east wing of the Entrance Hall. They had posted Victor Running Deer at the front door, since the session was not open to the public. Once inside, he noticed that Mayor Beaver and the councilors and Billy Bones were already situated around the long oak table. As usual, the councilors sat on the north side except for Cornelius Van Mink, who decided to position himself next to the mayor on the east side. Winston took a seat between Billy and the sheriff on the south side, and the single chair on the west side was saved for Mr. Fabian Lynx.

"Thank you, Sheriff Lone Wolf, for instigating this, ah…this very unusual session. And thank you, Mr. Lynx, for agreeing to meet with us," began Cornelius. "We are most anxious to hear about the circumstances surrounding your reentry into The Enchantment. We've heard about your wounds, and we're glad that Dr. Muskrat was able to attend to them. And… we're sorry about the animals who chased you and tried to harm you. Of course, I'm sure the rumors of a ghost roaming the streets certainly contributed to your, ah…misfortune…. "

The chairman paused for a moment and then glanced at his fellow councilors. "As you can see, many changes have taken place since you left. For one thing, our present council is vastly different. But before we get into their issues, we'd like to hear your story and why we're just learning your true identity."

Before Fabian spoke, he lowered his hood so everyone could see him clearly, but he chose not to stand. Winston noticed again how his scar seemed to add a new dimension to his charismatic demeanor. For the next ten minutes or so the lynx related his ordeal, beginning with his experience with his human zookeepers. He then described how he couldn't remove the barbed wire with his paws and how it made his cuts even worse. Then he detailed all the things that happened to him inside The Enchantment and how Billy finally convinced him to see Dr. Muskrat. When he finished, Jason Crow immediately began asking questions, but not to the lynx.

"Mr. Billy Bones, how is it that you continued to help Mr. Lynx once you knew who he really was? I mean, after what he tried to do to you—not to mention what he did to my son!" cawed Jason loudly.

"Because he was in great pain," answered Billy simply. "I had no choice. You would have done the same thing."

"I ain't so sure about that, Mr. Bones," insisted the crow. "I think I'd have gone to the sheriff right away. And you, Sheriff Lone Wolf, you found out the next day. Why didn't you arrest him?"

"I guess for the same reason, Mr. Crow," admitted the sheriff. "When I first encountered Mr. Lynx, he was still recovering from surgery and needed to stay under the doctor's care."

"Is that true, Dr. Muskrat?" asked Robin Red Breast. "Did he need to remain under your care?"

"Yes, for several days. And I couldn't remove his stitches for at least two weeks because the cuts were quite severe," answered Dr. Muskrat.

"But you did nothing for two weeks, Walter Lone Wolf! Surely you could've kept him in jail for more than two days," argued the crow.

"I really had no reason to put him in jail, Mr. Crow. You see, there was no warrant for his arrest, and no formal charges had ever been made."

"But you knew what he'd done before he left The Enchantment," chimed in Sylvester Turtle. "Wasn't that reason enough to at least let us know who and where he was?"

"Yes, sheriff, why did you wait two weeks before notifying us?" inquired Cornelius.

"I can answer that," interrupted Fabian. "I asked them to wait until I healed. I did not want to appear before this council with bandages around my head and sutures over my cuts. They were waiting because I asked."

"For your vanity, you mean. And they let you get by with it!" yelled the crow. "And Mr. Bones, you, of all animals should have insisted, especially since he had you arrested so you couldn't help Mr. Wise Owl. I'm ashamed of you…and you too, sheriff, and you also, Dr. Muskrat!"

Winston was startled at the crow's outburst but knew Jason had hit upon the reason for the delay. It was the lynx's charm. Even when bloodied and covered with bandages, he always seemed to get what he wanted.

Before the chairman returned to the question of charges against the lynx, he discredited Jason's concerns as well as his own. "I have to remind you, Jason Crow, that the decision to burn the human artifacts was the council's own decision. Those on the council at that time, including you and me, bear just as much responsibility as Brother Fabian. However, his injustices against Mr. Bones and Mr. Wise

Owl could still be adjudicated. Mr. Bones, Mr. Wise Owl, would you like to press charges against Mr. Lynx?"

Winston was taken by surprise. He had been certain that a number of other charges would be made before his own. Finally Billy answered for himself. "No, Mr. Van Mink, not at this time." By the time Cornelius turned to Winston, all he could do was shake his head, "No."

"Then, for the time being, Mr. Lynx, you're free to go. And if you wouldn't mind, please wait in the main hall while we finish our meeting."

After Fabian left, Cornelius asked Billy to give his report on the Hill Country's last meeting. Although the members knew that union with the North Woods was a strong possibility, they had hoped it would never happen. And of course, Winston knew that getting his books back from the Hill Country would now be just as difficult as reclaiming them from the North Woods.

As soon as the mink closed the meeting, Jason Crow left the grounds, but the other councilors lingered out in front, looking for Fabian. When the lynx finally appeared on the steps of the beautiful old hall, a sudden hush came over the crowd as they waited for him to speak.

As the lynx was reintroducing himself, Winston could not help but notice how the afternoon sun caused the lynx's eyes to flash and his white teeth to sparkle. All in all, the large cat soon cast a spell over the entire assembly.

"Citizens of the Prairie, I feel privileged to speak to you again, and I'm sorry that I frightened some of you when I first returned. I too heard rumors of the Ghost of

Castle Rock. That's why I waited until my wounds healed before I came to see you. And before I go any further, I want to express a special thanks to Mr. Billy Bones, who befriended me and took me to Dr. Muskrat's office. And also, many thanks to the good doctor for stitching up my wounds."

At this point the lynx stopped and pointed to the wound on his cheek. "As you see, I will always wear this scar, but it will remind me of the kindness of the animals who saved my life. Among them I include Sheriff Lone Wolf and Victor Running Deer, and some of your local citizens who came to my defense at Castle Rock."

Again the lynx paused. "But most of all, I wanted to tell you, the good citizens of the Prairie, how sorry I am for the hurt I caused some of you three years ago. During my time back in the other world, I had different experiences that forced me to take a hard look at how I behaved. And I've come to see the error of my ways. From now on I will try to do everything in my power to help the City Council and you bring a sense of peace back into The Enchantment. I hope you will allow me to do this, and that you will forgive me for my past misjudgments."

When Fabian Lynx finished, no one made a sound. Slowly one of the bystanders began to clap, and that was picked up by another one, and then another until the whole group joined in the applause. Just before Winston left, he heard the wolf speaking confidentially to the lynx.

"Sister Sarah says you may stay in the room behind the New Meetinghouse until you find another place. She also said that your street clothes are still there," added the sheriff. "At least this will give you a start."

Instead of flying home, Winston decided to walk. The afternoon had not turned out exactly as he had expected. Although the lynx had charmed the citizens assembled to see him, he could not help but remember his early confrontations with the lynx at Percival Gander's Shop when Fabian threatened to burn his books because they had been left by the human animals. He appreciated the lynx's promise to change his ways but worried that his natural inclination was to take charge, just as Bruno von Shepherd was trying to do. "Oh my! What have we gotten ourselves into?" he whispered to himself. "Can Fabian really redeem himself?"

# CHAPTER THIRTY-SEVEN

# THE INVITATION

Instead of going to the Old Meetinghouse on Sunday morning, Billy Bones and Victor Running Deer joined Fabian Lynx at the New Meetinghouse. Billy noticed immediately that the lynx had changed from his gray robe to a white shirt and homespun pants. They were the same street clothes he had worn three years ago. The shepherd dog and the deer had put on their white shirts for the occasion as well.

Even though Fabian had lived in the back room for six days without incident, Billy and Victor were still concerned about his reception by the congregation. Billy knew that Sister Sarah Mourning Dove had been extremely generous in letting Fabian stay in the room but wondered how she would handle the situation during the Sunday service.

After Sarah's welcome, she immediately explained the situation to the congregation. "I realize that Mr. Lynx's request to stay in our back room has caused some concern. However, Mr. Lynx is trying to make a new life for himself and regrets his past mistakes. He has also offered to clean the meetinghouse and tend to the grounds. I hope you'll give him a chance to redeem himself."

Nothing was said about the lynx after the dove's initial remarks, and she did not give him a chance to speak, which Billy thought was wise. After her lecture, many of the members took time to greet Fabian, and were gracious to Victor and Billy as well. Among the most welcoming were many prairie dogs. Billy knew they had been Fabian's most faithful followers, but he was not sure how they would respond after his three-year absence. Another problem was that one of their own, Patsy Prairie Dog, had become a changeling during The Great Burning, as it was now called.

Before Billy left for his cottage, Fabian asked the shepherd dog to do him a favor. "Mr. Bones, I understand you'll be going to the first session of the Hill Country and the North Woods."

"Yes, it's this Friday," informed Billy.

"Would you do me a favor and talk to my old lieutenants, especially Phineas Fox and Lenny Coyote's three brothers? Ask them to come and see me. Maybe in some way, I can wean them away from the North Woods and the clutches of Bruno von Shepherd. I know you're concerned about Bruno's designs against the Prairie—and this might help. It probably won't work, but it's worth a try."

"I think it's a great idea!" exclaimed Billy. "They were very loyal to you, and it would certainly deplete Bruno's forces. The only problem is getting them to talk to me. They've been angry with me ever since I returned because I was responsible for your expulsion. In fact, I might even pay the Peccary Brothers a visit, even though I'm loath to be around them."

"Well, they'll probably all hear about my return before Friday. That might help," suggested Fabian.

Billy Bones arrived at The Fortress gate around noon on Friday. As he had hoped, it had been left open to accommodate the councilors from the Hill Country. From his earlier experience, the shepherd dog knew that the extended pack would be at lunch. He slipped in as quietly as he could in case someone had been left on guard. When he saw no one about, he quickly entered the cabin belonging to the Coyote Brothers and Phineas T. Fox on the west side of the yard. His plan was to wait patiently and hope that someone would return before the start of the meeting between the two states. He realized he was on dangerous ground, since the four animals never warmed up to him like the other pack members had. His intention was to get Fabian Lynx's message to them before they threw him out or raised a ruckus.

As it happened, Lester and Leon Coyote arrived at the same time. Billy was sitting on Lester's bed, and both coyotes backed off when they saw him.

"Mr. Billy Bones, in the name of The Great Spirit!" was all Lester could utter.

"You've got some nerve…" continued Leon.

"Please, just listen to me," begged Billy. "Mr. Fabian Lynx asked me to give you a message. I'm sure you heard he's returned. In fact, he was the ghost-like creature you were chasin' three weeks ago. He couldn't make himself known 'cause he was severely wounded."

"Yes, we heard," answered Lester. "But we couldn't believe what they were sayin'."

"Well now you know," assured the shepherd dog.

"But why you?" asked Leon. "The last we heard you were mortal enemies."

"Because I happened to be the one who found him, and like you, I only knew he was a seriously wounded animal who needed a doctor's attention," explained Billy. "Since then one thing led to another, and I encouraged him to go before the City Council—and he did."

"But you said you had a message for us," continued Lester.

"Yes, he was hopin' to see all his lieutenants again. He wants you to visit him," said Billy, finally feeling it was safe to get up from the bed. "He's especially anxious to meet you three brothers and Phineas.

"But where's he stayin'?" inquired Leon.

"Sister Sarah's letting him stay in the room in back of the New Meetinghouse where he lived before," informed the dog.

"Should we tell Bruno?" questioned Leon, glancing over at his brother.

"No, definitely not," said Lester. "He wouldn't want us to, I'm sure. But I'd like to see Brother Fabian. When should we go?"

"Just let me know what's good for you, and I'll let him know," suggested Billy.

"Tell him next Tuesday afternoon after lunch. Nobody'll be watchin' us then."

"And how about Bison Bob or Milton Brown Bear?" questioned Billy.

"No, they're too close to Bruno, and they'd let him know, especially Bob," determined Lester. "No, it'll be just the four of us."

"And the Peccary brothers?" asked Billy.

"No, definitely not them—there's not a trustworthy bone in their bodies!" yelped Leon.

"Then I'll tell him Tuesday afternoon," stated Billy, crossing to the door. "Now I've got to slip out of here before anyone sees me. I don't want to get you into trouble."

While Billy nonchalantly strolled over to the dining hall, he contemplated his strange meeting with Lester and Leon. "They really missed Fabian. I'm truly amazed at how anxious they were to see him again," he thought. "But I know one thing. I'm not going to visit those blasted pigs...."

# CHAPTER THIRTY-EIGHT

## FINALLY UNITED

By the time Billy Bones reached the dining hall, most of the councilors were already in their places. When he looked around for Brigitte von Shepherd, she waved to him from the south table. In fact, it seemed to Billy that the seating was similar to what it had been during their first meeting. The only new face was that of Neevil Cur, who had positioned himself next to Bruno von Shepherd.

"Brigitte, what's Neevil doin' here?" whispered Billy, sitting beside the German shepherd.

"My brother chose him to be on the council while Sheldon acts as mediator," explained Brigitte.

"But Neevil? I don't understand!" responded Billy. "He's a loose cannon."

"Neevil goes everywhere with him now. I think it's a matter of trust," explained Brigitte.

"But I thought Angus Wolfhound was takin' Sheldon's place," continued the shepherd dog.

"All I know is that he feels more comfortable with Neevil," said Brigitte, shaking her head, "especially after that botched affair with Orville's deputies."

As Billy watched Sheldon open the meeting, he could not help but wonder about Neevil Cur. There was no doubt that the angry little dog was completely loyal to Bruno. After all, Bruno used the cur to spy on Brigitte and him when they went on their picnic, and he was responsible for injuring Sandy Antelope before the Grand Fair. Neevil's worst crime, however, was totally out of meanness—breaking Alvin Muskrat's arm.

At the end of Sheldon's opening remarks, he alluded to the present state of affairs. "This morning Gaylord Cougar and Bruno von Shepherd signed an agreement of unity that must be ratified by this entire body," announced Sheldon. "According to the agreement, each state will still handle its own affairs. However, both states will be under the rules of the Hill Country code and *The Vulture's Appendix* and will act as one when it comes to its dealings with the Prairie."

Immediately several hands shot up. Sheldon called on Colonel Eddie Crane first.

"Does that mean that the three-state agreements are no longer valid?" inquired the crane.

"I don't think we've broken any of those yet, Colonel Crane," answered Sheldon. "But at the next meeting in November, we would act as one state."

"In other words, our borders would remain open," mused the colonel.

"May I answer that, Sheldon?" asked Bruno.

"Yes of course, Mr. von Shepherd," said Sheldon.

"I see no reason to close our borders except if there's a conflict. Then of course, we would have to do so," stated the German Shepherd.

"What kind of conflict could possibly close our borders," asked Willie Wild Cat, "especially since we've already given our word?"

"Well, for instance, let's take this latest fiasco. We sent deputies down to the Prairie to find an unknown animal who had just entered our world. Orville Bat warned us that this animal was a bad spirit, and as it turned out, he was right. In fact it was the same animal that Mr. Bones had forced back into the other world in order to save Winston Wise Owl's life. And…it was the same animal who was responsible for burning the human artifacts that caused five of our youngest citizens to revert back to their animal forms and become changelings. Now, thanks to Mr. Billy Bones, we find ourselves facing a new danger."

"And why is it Mr. Bones' fault?" asked Willie Wild Cat.

"Because when we sent deputies down to find this animal, it was Mr. Bones and his friends Sheriff Lone Wolf and Victor Running Deer who protected Fabian Lynx," barked Bruno. "Now they're allowing him to roam freely and do whatever he likes."

"You know that's not quite right," interrupted Billy. "When Fabian first came back into The Enchantment, no one knew his true identity. And when we did find out, we had to tend to his wounds. When your deputies came looking for him, he was still in no shape to defend himself.

That's why we had to protect him, as you probably know too well."

"But what do we do now, Mr. Bones?" asked Gaylord Cougar. "Apparently he's free to do whatever he pleases, thanks to your City Council."

"He tells us he no longer has a hatred for all human things, and he's sorry for his previous misjudgments," concluded Billy.

"But how can we believe him?" inquired Gaylord again. "He's still the same animal. It's pretty hard to change one's nature."

"That's true," agreed Billy, glancing over at Bruno, "but I think it's only fair that we give him a second chance. He's gone through a lot these past three years."

"But my dear councilors, if Mr. Bones is wrong, we might have to go after this animal ourselves, before he infects our two states," warned Bruno.

"I don't like the sound of that, Mr. von Shepherd," declared Lucinda Vulture, standing up and pushing her chair back. "That sounds very combative to me, and I don't think we should ever go in that direction!"

"Fortunately that's not your choice, Ms. Vulture," grinned Bruno sarcastically, "now that we're a united body. Maybe you and your precious Mr. Bones need to go elsewhere. In fact, while we're on the subject we should decide whether Mr. Bones should still be part of this council, since he's not a member of either state."

"My dear brother," exclaimed Brigitte, also rising to her feet, "that's the Hill Country's affair. We cannot interfere in their choice of councilor, according to the agreement you just signed with Mr. Cougar."

"Well, it seems you want to protect your precious Mr. Bones too," snarled Bruno. "But I guess I should defer to you this time, my dear sister, and allow Mr. Cougar to handle it."

Sheldon Sheepdog quickly entered the dispute at this point and called for a show of hands to ratify the new agreement. It ultimately passed by a vote of eight to six. Since Neevil had voted in favor of the agreement, Billy wondered if things would have gone differently if Sheldon still had a vote.

After the meeting, Lucinda found a moment to speak to Billy alone. "Hopefully, Gaylord won't call for a special meeting to consider your dismissal before the autumn equinox," remarked the vulture. "We need you here when Bruno finally strikes. And we both know he'll try. But I'll be in touch. There's too much at stake, especially while he still has that weapon."

After the delegation from the Hill Country left, Billy stayed behind to talk to Brigitte, waiting for him just outside the door.

"Come. Let me walk with you to the Beaver Creek Bridge. It'll give us a chance to talk," suggested Brigitte von Shepherd.

"Won't Bruno object to your leaving The Fortress with me?" asked Billy, taking her hand.

"I don't think so. He's in the mansion now, talking to Gaylord Cougar. "But we probably shouldn't hold hands 'til we get through the gate," smiled Brigitte, removing her hand and slipping it around his arm. "There. That looks more polite."

Before the two dogs left the yard, Milton Brown Bear approached Billy. "Mr. Bones, may I speak with you for a moment?"

"What is it, Milton? We were just leaving," stated Billy.

"That's all right, Billy. I'll wait for you by the gate," said Brigitte, moving on ahead.

"I just wanted to ask you about Brother Fabian, Billy. I know he was badly cut up. Is he all right?" asked the bear.

"Thanks to Dr. Muskrat, he's healing nicely. He'll wear a scar on his left cheek, but it doesn't look bad on him. In fact it gives him some rugged character," responded Billy.

"It's just that I was hopin' to see him. Is that's at all possible?" inquired Milton.

"Do you think Bruno would approve? I mean, after what he said today?" questioned the shepherd dog.

"As far as I'm concerned, he doesn't need to know," declared the bear, looking around.

"Why don't you visit him on Tuesday afternoon? And I might as well tell you that you'll run into some of your friends," said Billy, breaking into a smile.

"I guess you're referrin' to the coyotes," responded the bear. "Well, I'll let them know that I'm joinin' them. And don't worry. I won't let the word out. By the way, where is Brother Fabian staying?"

"He's at the New Meetinghouse where he lived before. But of course, he's not their counselor anymore," grinned Billy, as he turned and headed for the gate. "He calls himself just Fabian now."

"What was that all about?" inquired Brigitte as the two dogs were leaving The Fortress.

"He asked how seriously Fabian was wounded," said Billy, leaving out the other details.

"I can see why he's interested. He was one of Fabian's lieutenants, wasn't he?"

"Yes he was, but Sheriff Lone Wolf appointed him to the job," informed Billy. "It's probably better if you don't tell your brother that Milton talked to me. After today, I get the impression that wouldn't go over well."

"My lips are sealed," laughed Brigitte. "Besides, I'm more worried about you. Do you think the Hill Country will actually revoke your position with them? I'm sure Bruno is talking to Gaylord about it right now. If we're going to avoid a confrontation with the Prairie, we really need your voice."

"What will you do if I'm gone and the two states decide to march on the Prairie?" inquired Billy, stopping and drawing her close to him.

"I'll threaten to leave. And if that doesn't work, I'll be the next animal to desert, if you'll have me. I'm sure Sheldon will come right after me," said Brigitte, putting her arms around him in a warm embrace. Unfortunately, at that moment she glanced back in the direction of The Fortress and spotted Neevil Cur. "Why that...."

"What is it, Brigitte?" asked Billy.

"Neevil Cur. He's been following us," frowned the German shepherd.

"Maybe I'd better walk you back to the gate," wondered the shepherd dog.

"No, he's no threat to me, Mr. Bones. I'm too close to my brother."

"Why do you think Bruno puts so much faith in Neevil?" inquired Billy. "I mean, having him around all that time. Has he become that insecure?"

"All I know is that after he lost Conan and Arnold and Sterling, he's never been the same," concluded Brigitte, taking Billy's hand again and leading him toward the Beaver Creek Bridge. "Anyway, if Neevil's spying on us, we might as well give him something to report."

Before Brigitte von Shepherd left Billy, she kissed him on the cheek and then waved as she headed back toward The Fortress. Just as the shepherd dog turned and started down Main Street, he noticed Gerard Crow circling above him. "Well, come on down, my friend. I haven't seen you for a while. I know you don't like Fabian too well, but I've got a message for him, and it might be a good time for you to meet him."

# CHAPTER THIRTY-NINE

## A MEETING OF LIEUTENANTS

At the end of Main Street, Billy Bones decided to go around the New Meetinghouse and knock on the back door that led to Fabian Lynx's room. The last time he had visited the lynx at the meetinghouse, he had gone through the front door. The lynx had found him at the podium in the main hall, looking at *The Great Book of Rules*. He remembered how he had planned to convince the lynx of the importance of Winston Wise Owl's books but was outwitted by the lynx at every turn.

Gerard Crow stayed on Billy's shoulder until Fabian opened the door.

"I have some news for you, Fabian," stated Billy. "But first I want you to meet Jason Crow's son, Gerard. He's one of the changelings, as you already know. He's my traveling companion from time to time, and he's very bright. He's the one who followed you to Castle Rock. If he hadn't shown me the way, I never would've found you that first night."

"Well I guess I'm in your debt, Gerard," said Fabian, trying to pet the bird's silky back. Gerard would have none of it however, and flew off to the closest tree.

"He's an excellent judge of character, I must say," grinned the lynx, as he stepped outside into the sunlight with the shepherd dog. "So what's the news?"

"It looks like you're gonna get company on Tuesday afternoon. Lenny's three brothers and Phineas Fox and even Milton Brown Bear are all comin' to see you," informed Billy. However, during our two-state meeting, Bruno von Shepherd took time to mention all the offenses you committed just before you and I left this place three years ago. It sounded like he was puttin' you on the 'most wanted' list."

"But they're still comin' to see me?" purred the lynx. "Well that's a positive sign, I must say. Maybe I can do some good after all. And how about you, Mr. Bones? Bruno probably wasn't too pleased that you helped me."

"No, I can't say that he was. In fact he suggested that I should no longer be a councilor for the Hill Country, since I never lived there," admitted Billy. "And, on top of that, I think he believes I want to be leader of the pack."

"Why don't you join us on Tuesday? Maybe we can convince some of my old lieutenants that we're on the same side now," suggested Fabian. "And I'm anxious to see what they really think of Bruno."

"I can tell you that they were extremely loyal to him at first. Recently he's been actin' strangely, though. Brigitte tells me that after last year's desertions he's never been the same," explained the shepherd dog.

"Well then, join us on Tuesday, my dear old enemy, and we'll see how the land lies," said Fabian.

As soon as Billy turned to go, Gerard flew down and landed on his shoulder.

"It's gonna take a long time to win Gerard over, I'm afraid," grinned the lynx. "He's a lot smarter than you."

By the time Billy arrived on Tuesday afternoon, the three coyote brothers, Phineas T. Fox, Milton Brown Bear, and Fabian Lynx were all under the trees in the big yard behind the New Meetinghouse. Fabian had laid the meetinghouse picnic table with bread and jams of various sorts and was already charming them with the story of how he reentered The Enchantment.

"Ah Billy, I was just telling them how I scared everybody with my bloody face and how you found me and took me to see Doctor Muskrat," said the lynx jovially. After he finished explaining why he waited two weeks before going before the City Council, he told them about the woman at the zoo who had helped him. After that, the lynx went into some detail about how his experience with this human gave him new insight.

"This is hard for me to admit," said the lynx finally, "but Mr. Bones was right. Not all humans are evil. And now that Mr. Bones and I agree about this, I'm hoping we can work together. But I'm concerned about your leader up in the North Woods. From what I've heard, this Bruno von Shepherd has designs on the Prairie as well as on the Hill Country. Is there any truth to that?"

"We're not privy to his intentions," answered Milton Brown Bear, "but from his remarks, I'd say he's not too fond of Mr. Bones here and the other members of his pack who deserted to the Prairie. And it sounds as if he'd like to settle the score."

"But will you go along with him if he does? I know he got you to chase after me when he thought I was some sort of evil ghost," contended the lynx.

"I'm afraid we're pretty obligated. We signed those loyalty oaths to be faithful to him," confessed Lester Coyote.

"But didn't Conan and Sterling and Arnold sign the same oaths?" asked Billy.

"Yes, I guess they did," agreed the coyote.

"It seems to me then that they were following their consciences," stated the shepherd dog. "When it comes down to war or peace, you might have to do the same thing."

After more serious conversation, Fabian's lieutenants started reminiscing about their adventures together three years ago. Before it was time to leave they had been completely captivated again by the lynx's flashing eyes, sparkling teeth, and charismatic personality.

"Is there any way you could visit us in the North Woods?" asked Phineas T. Fox.

"I don't think that would be such a good idea," responded a deep voice.

When the group turned around they saw Bison Bob coming from behind a large tree just west of the meetinghouse. He was shadowed closely by none other than Neevil Cur. "So Neevil was right. Mr. Bones did coax you down here to see Mr. Fabian Lynx." As the buffalo and the cur entered the circle of lieutenants, he spoke to them harshly. "At least you could have informed Mr. von Shepherd about your plans. Now it looks like you had questionable motives for sneakin' down here."

"So…Mr. Bison, it's good to see you again too," intervened Fabian, holding out his hand. "And why do you suppose they hesitated to tell your Mr. von Shepherd?"

"Because they knew he didn't like the way you misled the City Council three years ago, or how you misused *The Great Book of Rules,*" answered Bob, refusing to take the lynx's hand. "Not to mention, how you mistreated Mr. Wise Owl and Mr. Bones here. But I see you've worked things out with Mr. Bones."

"I explained my reasons, and Mr. Bones knows I've had a change of heart and want to do better," retorted the lynx, "but I still want to know why your comrades are afraid of this Bruno von Shepherd. There must be something else goin' on."

"For one thing, he's concerned about losin' more of his pack to the Prairie," determined the buffalo.

"But why restrict their freedom to do what they like? Why should they have to ask?" inquired Billy, entering the argument for the first time.

"And another thing…he doesn't trust you, Mr. Bones," continued the bison. "And when I look around and see my friends down here, I can't say that I blame him."

"But why shouldn't they want to visit Mr. Lynx? You were all very close at one time," insisted the shepherd dog. "And Mr. Neevil Cur, I take it you're the informer—still spyin' for Mr. von Shepherd, eh? What demon drives you to do that, I wonder?"

"Because he knows where his loyalty lies, Mr. Billy Bones!" bellowed Bob, "as should the rest of you! Now I think you should all follow me back to The Fortress. This visit is over!"

When Bison Bob started marching to the north, closely followed by Neevil Cur, Fabian Lynx turned to the stunned group of former lieutenants.

"You'd better go with him. I don't want you to get into trouble on my account. But just remember, you can always visit me here," smiled Fabian, turning on his charm. "I am now and will always be at your service. Considerin' your loyalty to me in the past, what else can I be?"

# CHAPTER FORTY

## TERMINATION

The dreaded invitation to a special meeting of the Tribal Council came a week later. Billy Bones knew that Bruno von Shepherd had received a full report concerning Fabian's lieutenants and the part he played in it. He also knew that the meeting was for his benefit. He reasoned that Gaylord Cougar finally had the votes to oust Billy from his role as councilor. He also knew that after Omar Mountain Goat's passing, his spot on the Tribal Council had always been tenuous, to say the least.

On the day of the fateful meeting, Billy noticed that storm clouds were building up in the southeast, and a stiff breeze was already howling through Echo Canyon. "Well, this certainly adds to the drama of the situation," observed the shepherd dog as he made his way to the lodge.

Once inside, Billy quietly slipped into his seat. The only salutations on his arrival were a nod from Lucinda Vulture and a wry smile from Maurice Rabbit. None of the other councilors glanced his way or paid any heed to his arrival. This apparent snub plus the darkening atmosphere caused by the oncoming storm only added to the dog's anguish. He wondered why he had decided to attend in the first place.

When the session was called to order, Billy thought that Gaylord Cougar would begin by enumerating the reasons for his dismissal. Instead he introduced Bruno von Shepherd, who sat facing the Tribal Council with the ever-present, Neevil Cur.

"Members of the Tribal Council, thank you again for allowing me to speak at your special session," began Bruno. "As you all know from our combined meeting, Fabian Lynx has returned to The Enchantment. And…as you also know, your own Orville Bat warned us that an evil spirit had invaded us. Unfortunately, when our deputies went down to the Prairie to hunt this creature down, they were thwarted by Sheriff Lone Wolf and some of his conspirators, including Mr. Bones here. Since then the Prairie's City Council has allowed this creature, who we now know was none other than Fabian Lynx, to get off scot-free. I have already discussed this with our councilors, and they've agreed with me that this lynx is guilty of a number of crimes and needs to be punished."

At this point Bruno stood and picked up a pamphlet he had been holding. "I will not reiterate the crimes against Mr. Wise Owl and Mr. Bones, because you know them all too well. But I will read to you several passages from their *Great Book of Rules*, some of which our state accepted when we joined forces. By the way, these passages support our belief that the destruction of any human antiquity is strictly forbidden and is therefore considered a crime."

As Bruno read, he slowly strolled in front of the Tribal Council members, stopping from time to time to emphasize a certain point. "First of all, let me read from *The Mink's Appendix*: Artifacts found along the old wagon trail are of the highest quality and must be safeguarded at all cost." At this point a clap of thunder shook the log building. Bruno hesitated for a second and then continued. "And now, from our own *Vulture's Appendix:* If any of the human artifacts are destroyed, a great disaster will likely occur." Instantly as if on cue, a second clap of thunder, louder than the first, shook the lodge. Bruno von Shepherd only smiled and looked upward, as if The Great Spirit was punctuating his statements.

Before continuing, Bruno stopped in front of Billy Bones and leaned over so he could gaze directly into the shepherd dog's eyes. "Now if we add those readings to your own visions, Mr. Billy Bones, we can come to only one conclusion: The burning of those five artifacts, which caused five of our youngest and brightest to become changelings, was a crime of the highest order. And may I remind you, that Ms. Vulture's own son was a victim of this senseless burning."

After this last remark, a gush of wind blew the windows on either side of the entrance wide open. Quickly Arthur Elk pushed them shut and locked them as securely as he could.

After this third interference from the outside storm, Bruno returned to his seat and concluded his argument. "As I said before, our council has already discussed this, and we've concluded that Mr. Fabian Lynx needs to be held accountable for these crimes—even though the Prairie Council failed to accomplish this. And…our council has agreed that it is our responsibility to apprehend this Fabian Lynx, by force if necessary, and bring him back to the North Woods for trial. But, according to our agreement, we need your consent so we can act as one body."

"This is what I've been warning you about, my dear friends!" declared Lucinda Vulture, standing in front of her chair. "What we're talking about is an excuse to march on the Prairie, and please, Mr. von Shepherd, don't use my son as an excuse to foster your ambitions!"

"But Ms. Vulture, Mr. von Shepherd's arguments are sound, and I think we must all be free to make our own judgment on this matter. If we agree that these are crimes, it's up to us to handle the situation," concluded Gaylord Cougar.

At this point the sound of rain pounding against the roof made it harder for Gaylord to be heard, but he pushed on in a louder voice. "But before we do, we need to take care of another matter, something we've put off for a long time. That is the legitimacy of Mr. Bones' position on this council. Mr. Bones has never been a member of this state and was only brought on because of his apparent psychic abilities. However, in light of our union with the North Woods, this can no longer be acceptable, since he's not a member of either state."

"I say that we resolve the situation," hissed Lucretia Lizard above the pelting of the rain. "I move that Mr. Billy

Bones be removed from his position as a member of this Tribal Council immediately."

"And I second the motion!" bleated Hilda Big Horn.

"So…is this a plan hatched by you and Mr. von Shepherd, Mr. Gaylord Cougar? After all it will be much easier for Mr. von Shepherd to get his way with Mr. Bones out of the picture," decried Lucinda, still standing by her seat. "How convenient for you both! But let me tell you, Mr. Cougar, you will rue the day you allowed this to happen!"

"I think there's a motion on the table, Mr. Cougar. And I call for the vote," demanded the lizard, trying to cut off the vulture's complaint.

"And you, Orville Bat, are you going to sit there and go along with this? You know better than anyone that this should never happen," insisted the vulture, turning to the little animal. "This is your opportunity to finally do the right thing!"

Billy could see that the bat had been pushed into a corner and that he probably did not have the courage to assert himself. Instead, as was his way of escaping, he closed his eyes, pulled his feet under his little body, and tucked his head tightly against his chest.

"Do I get a vote," yelled Billy finally, smiling over at the cougar, "or have I already lost my right to do that?"

"Yes, he should still have that right," stated Maurice, knowing it was a lost cause.

"Yes, you may vote, Mr. Bones. You haven't been ousted yet," agreed the cougar, starting to wonder if he was doing the right thing, after nature's dramatic interference.

When the vote was taken by a show of hands, Orville at first would not respond. Finally in desperation he shot up his hand in support of the yea votes. When Gaylord ultimately broke the tie, Billy's place on the Tribal Council was finally terminated, and the rain stopped as suddenly as it had started.

Nothing was said when Billy took a seat by the door and waited for Lucinda and Maurice. In fast order the council decided to join the North Woods in their decision to go after the lynx if it proved necessary. It was also decided that the Hill Country's drill group would join the North Woods in their next practice session, so they could get used to working together.

On his way out, Bruno approached Billy and snarled, "Glad to see your friends are finally seeing your true colors. You know, it should be you we're goin' after, but all in good time, my friend…all in good time!"

After the others had gone, Lucinda and Maurice joined Billy by the window.

"You'd better warn the City Council right away, Mr. Bones," decided Lucinda. "Bruno will probably formally ask them to turn Mr. Lynx over to the North Woods sometime tomorrow. If that doesn't work, I'm sure they'll march down to get him. And if they succeed, Bruno won't stop until he gains control of the Prairie as well."

"But how about the weapon?" asked Billy. We can't really hide that from the council any longer."

"No, it's only fair to caution them," agreed Lucinda.

"And I have a feeling that Bruno will use it if he has to. The council might decide to give Fabian up if they know someone might get killed. That might depend a lot on you and Sheriff Lone Wolf and the members of your drill group."

"Yes, we can't put the council or the Prairie in further danger. But we'll have to talk to the practice group and tell them about the six-gun. It's not fair to subject them to a weapon like that," determined Billy. "But how about you? Will you stay on the Tribal Council?"

Lucinda then spoke up. "I wanted to leave some time ago, but Maurice and I still might be able to do some good. I don't know if Bruno will try to get the combined councils together again, but I would like to talk to Sheldon Sheepdog. Maybe there's still a chance he can help, or you could contact Brigitte. Her brother probably no longer listens to her, but it's worth a try."

Billy replied, "I would imagine that Bruno will send Sheldon down to speak to the City Council. He might send Brigitte as well. Of course, what he really wants to do is take charge of things in the Prairie too—especially now that he has that revolver."

"You think he'll wear the holster if he goes down to the Prairie? And does he know how to use the revolver?" wondered Maurice, joining the conversation for the first time.

"Well…he only has six bullets," replied Billy. "Come to think of it, he'll have to practice, and that means he'll use one or two bullets at least."

"You're right. Even Bruno wouldn't be fool enough to take that gun along without firing it first," agreed Lucinda. "I think he'll use at least two bullets just to orient himself."

# CHAPTER FORTY-ONE

# WITH THE SHERIFF

It was late afternoon by the time Billy Bones reached the office of Sheriff Walter Lone Wolf. The shepherd dog knocked and entered before the wolf could reach the doorway.

"I'm sorry to push in on you like this, sheriff, but I think we may have a crisis on our hands, and I thought I should come to you first," puffed Billy, sitting in the chair in front of Walter's desk.

"Why don't you just slow down, Mr. Bones, and collect your thoughts," grinned the wolf, sitting behind his desk. "It seems we've had our fair share of crises lately. But you had a meeting with the Hill Country this morning, didn't you?"

"Yes, that's true, and they kicked me out as we expected. But that's not the dilemma," continued the dog.

"Well, take a deep breath, Mr. Bones, and tell me what happened," ordered the sheriff. "I take it this has something to do with Bruno von Shepherd."

"I'm afraid Bruno's convinced both states that Fabian's a criminal, and they're going to demand that we release him into their custody," responded Billy.

"But that's a matter for our City Council to decide, isn't it? And they've already made a judgment. My guess is they'll refuse to let him go, since Fabian's a citizen of the Prairie."

"Under normal circumstances I'd agree with you. However, if the council doesn't hand him over, they plan to march down here and take him by force," explained Billy.

"They plan to do what?" inquired Walter, sitting up in his chair.

"Bruno wants to deputize the drill groups from their two states and use them to carry out his agenda. I imagine they'll be armed with staffs and clubs," deduced Billy.

"If that's the case, it looks like we have to alert our drill group and see if they'll help us again. We held them off at Castle Rock. Maybe we can get some of their deputies to back off like before," reasoned Walter.

"But there's one overriding problem that no one in the Prairie knows about," warned Billy, standing and pacing about the office. "It's something I wasn't aware of until just recently because it was a well-guarded secret."

"It sounds ominous, Mr. Bones," said Walter.

"Yes, it does, Walter. But we've all got to know about it now before we stand up to Bruno and his deputies," stated Billy, shaking his head.

"In the name of The Great Spirit, Billy Bones, tell me what it is!" demanded Walter, raising his voice and swinging his chair around to face the dog.

"When the pioneers abandoned some of their belongings along the Old Wagon Trail, one of them left a six-gun and a holster and six bullets. Until now, only Orville Bat and Lucinda Vulture were aware of this. Unfortunately, Orville's taken it upon himself to turn the gun over to Bruno von Shepherd. I guess he wanted to impress him. I'm not sure. But now the question is: will he bring it with him when he comes to arrest Fabian?"

"I've heard about guns of all sorts, but, of course I've never seen one except in pictures," admitted the wolf. "But does Bruno know how to use it? It's different from those long rifles, you know. Apparently they were easy to aim… but this thing?"

"I imagine he'll try it out first. I think you have to be fairly close to your target," concluded Billy. "But then again, he only has six bullets. Lucinda and I reasoned that he'll probably use one or two of them just to practice. The problem is he'll still have enough bullets to shoot someone if he chooses, and he could kill someone. That's why we've got to warn the City Council and the members of the practice group. Staffs won't be much protection."

"So our first job is to find out what the council wants to do. They could release Mr. Lynx or they could ask our drill members to protect him. And of course, our members might refuse to back us up, considering the danger. No matter what, though, Victor and I will have to carry out the council's request."

"And Fabian: will he have any say in this?" asked Billy.

"Good question. I don't know," admitted the sheriff.

"The problem is that this is really an excuse for Bruno to march on the Prairie," reasoned Billy. "I can almost guarantee that he wants to be in charge here as well as in the Hill

Country and the North Woods, and this'll be his best chance."

"I'll get Cornelius Van Mink to call a special session tomorrow afternoon, and we'll talk to our drill group in the morning at practice. They need to know exactly what we're up against," determined Walter. "And Mr. Bones, you need to decide whether you want to stand with Victor and me if it comes to a showdown. Legally you're not obliged. And you could find yourself a target for a third bullet. Of course, there's always the chance that Bruno will play fair and leave that six-gun at home. Even then we'll probably have to fight him and whomever he deputizes."

"There may be another way," speculated the shepherd dog. "Maybe we could mess with his ego and get him to fight one of us using staffs, of course. If nothing else, that might work."

"Yes, that might just work," agreed the wolf. "Well, you'd better get home and try to get some sleep. It looks like we're in for a heavy day tomorrow."

"Maybe we ought to invite Winston Wise Owl and Thaddeus P. Turtle and Sister Sarah Mourning Dove to the council meeting. We might need some wise heads there," suggested Billy, heading for the door.

"Good idea. And I need to get word to Sheldon Sheepdog. I think we need to find out when all this is gonna take place," determined the sheriff.

"I have a feeling that if Bruno decides to march on the Prairie, Sheldon will leave him," determined the shepherd dog. "Come to think of it, Bruno may lose his sister as well."

# THE FATEFUL DECISION

Winston Wise Owl arrived at City Hall at the same time as Billy Bones.

"I'm glad you're here, Mr. Wise Owl," greeted the shepherd dog. "We've got some serious problems to discuss, and we may need your input. I think we'll be in the main hall today."

Winston had never seen Billy quite so agitated. "Are you okay, Mr. Bones? You seem very tense."

"You'll soon hear why, sir," scowled Billy uncharacteristically.

"And who's coming to the meeting?" asked Winston

"Well, besides you and the City Council, there'll be Counselor Turtle and Sister Sarah and the members of the drill group," informed Billy. "And I'm hoping Sheldon Sheepdog will come down from the North Woods."

When Winston and Billy came into the main hall they could see that Cornelius Van Mink had decided to seat the councilors on stage and the other guests in the first two rows.

"I hope Mr. Sheepdog will join us before long. Until

then I'd like Mr. Bones to bring us up to date on exactly what's transpired," began the mink.

As Billy explained the situation before them, Winston could see that he was full of trepidation. When he got to the part about the secret weapon, however, Winston started to understand why the dog was so anxious. The owl knew that there were secret artifacts in the Sacred Chamber, but the revelation of a six-gun shocked him immensely. Winston had always hoped that Bruno would stop short of actually marching on the Prairie. But adding a gun to the equation made it infinitely more likely.

After Billy concluded his report, Chairman Van Mink asked Sheriff Lone Wolf to discuss the council's alternatives. "If Mr. Sheepdog concurs with Mr. Bones," began the sheriff, "then the council has to decide whether to turn Mr. Lynx over to the North Woods for trial or refuse their request. And if you refuse their request, do you authorize Victor and me and our drill group to protect Mr. Lynx? This morning I explained to the group sitting in front of you the dangers of defending the council's decision, if it should come to that. They all agreed to stand with us no matter what the consequences may be."

"Well, this is one heck of a mess Mr. Fabian Lynx's got us into, ain't it?" interrupted Jason Crow. "And this damn business about a gun! Why, Mr. von Shepherd could kill anyone of us if he came down here half-cocked!"

"Yes, I guess he could," agreed the wolf. "I think that's why it's important for the council and other citizens of the Prairie to stay out of harm's way if there's an invasion."

"Unless we turn Fabian over," continued the crow.

"But would that be the end of it?" questioned Winston, standing and joining the conversation. "I think if we showed this kind of weakness, it would be just a simple step for Mr. von Shepherd to take control of our council as well. I don't think we should ever get to the point where we can be blackmailed out of fear of a weapon or even overpowering odds. I think we have no choice but to stand up to them."

"But is it worth someone getting killed?" asked Cornelius, glancing down at the bird everyone admired.

"It depends on whether we want to give up our freedoms. Once you bow to tyranny, it's hard to ever stand up again," warned Winston.

After Winston sat down, the only sound was the ticking of the great clock in the tower above them. Finally Cornelius asked for a recess until Sheldon Sheepdog was due to arrive.

When the sheepdog finally came, the owl could see that he was as anxious as Billy had been earlier. After the mink's introduction, Sheldon stood erect in the center of the aisle facing the council. "I know of no other way to say this than to tell you that our combined councilors have deemed Mr. Lynx to be a criminal. Therefore, they've requested that you turn him over to the North Woods for trial."

"And if we refuse?" cawed the crow. "What then?"

"Then they've directed me to tell you that they will march down here and apprehend him with or without your permission," said the sheepdog, looking straight ahead.

"And do you go along with this?" asked Dr. Muskrat, hoping to find out where the sheepdog stood.

"I've advised against it," stated Sheldon, "as have a number of other councilors. But I'm afraid we are in the minority."

"So…you would like us to give you an answer one way or the other, I take it," stated Cornelius Van Mink. "And are you and your council aware that Bruno von Shepherd has a gun that was left by the humans? If you are, do you have any idea whether he plans to bring it with him when he and his deputies march down into our territory?"

"No, I'm not aware of any such thing," gasped Sheldon, showing complete ignorance of the matter.

"Mr. Bones, will you elucidate?" asked the mink.

"Apparently this six-gun was left by humans before the Great Rift, and only Lucinda Vulture and Orville Bat knew about it," began Billy, standing in the aisle next to Sheldon. "But it seems that Mr. Bat took it and turned it over to Mr. von Shepherd. This six-gun, or revolver, as some call it, has six bullets. I'm sure you're aware that weapons like that are forbidden by both *The Great Book of Rules* and *The Vulture's Appendix*."

"So that's the noise I heard!" exclaimed the sheepdog, shaking his head in disbelief. "In fact I heard it two separate times—sort of a loud bang. I'd never heard anything quite like it. All I know is that it came from in back of The Fortress."

"I'm afraid that means Bruno probably plans to bring it with him," concluded Billy.

"Yes, it would seem so," admitted Sheldon, turning to Billy. "And your answer to your other question is no; I'm sure no one else knows about this six-gun except maybe Neevil Cur. They are constant companions these days."

"All right, Mr. Sheepdog. Please go into the entrance hall and wait until we can give you an answer," sighed Cornelius finally.

Even though Winston could not vote, he was suddenly concerned about putting the young animals in the drill group in harm's way but decided to say nothing.

"Sheriff Lone Wolf, I ask you one more time. Are you sure you're willing to stand up to this threat, knowing that one or even several of you could get killed?" asked Cornelius, looking down at the sheriff and his soon-to-be deputies.

"We'll take all the precautions we can if he has the weapon on him," answered the wolf. "And we'll defend Mr. Lynx against Mr. von Shepherd's deputies if that is your wish."

"Well, my dear councilors, it looks like we're at a crossroads here, but I must ask for your vote," said the mink finally.

"I say…I say, Fabian Lynx ain't worth it," stammered Jason Crow. "But like Mr. Wise Owl says, we can't allow Bruno von Shepherd to march down here and intimidate us. And it could very well mean the loss of our independence to those two other states. I say, we ain't got a choice."

"Then who votes that we won't allow them to seize Mr. Lynx, a Prairie citizen in his own right, and take him back to the North Woods?" inquired Chairman Van Mink.

One by one all the council members raised their hands. Winston knew that they all felt conflicted because of the weapon and the hostility that was sure to follow. But everyone in the room seemed to understand the gravity of it all.

When the sheepdog was called back into the room and given the news, Mayor George P. Beaver spoke to him for the first time. "Mr. Sheepdog, when do you suppose this will happen?"

"My guess is very soon, possibly tomorrow, so as to not give Sheriff Lone Wolf much time to prepare," responded Sheldon.

"Then we'll put someone on the border to sound the alarm," decided the sheriff. "We'll ring the bell here at City Hall as a warning, if that's all right with you, Counselor McMink." As soon as Cornelius nodded in agreement, Walter continued. "Then…I would like all my new deputies to meet with me after this meeting. I imagine we'll have to set up our defense in front of the New Meetinghouse, since that's where Mr. Lynx is stayin'. But the first thing I have to do is warn him. I don't think he'll try to hide, since there's really no place he'd be any safer."

"And what do you plan to do, Mr. Sheepdog, if I may be so bold to ask," inquired Billy, rising from his seat.

"I'll probably come back here and stand with you," answered Sheldon. "And…if you'll be kind enough, please tell Molly that I'll see her tonight."

# CHAPTER FORTY-THREE

# BRIGITTE'S ARRIVAL

"Something must have gone wrong," concluded Billy Bones. The shepherd dog had waited with Molly Sheepdog and Conan and Clara Greyhound at Clara's cottage until late in the evening. He had already informed them of everything that had occurred earlier in the day. "Sheldon was very clear about wanting to come down to the Prairie this evening, but I know he was very concerned about the six-gun that had fallen into Bruno's hands."

"If I know Sheldon, he probably tried to find out where that gun was hidden," decided Molly. "Maybe he got caught, or maybe Bruno was afraid he might defect. I'm sure he knows Sheldon was against any type of aggressive action toward the Prairie."

"Speaking of aggressive action, how are you planning to protect yourselves against this gun? I mean, it's bad enough that you might have to fight Bruno's deputies," asked Clara. "Maybe the whole community should come out and defend Mr. Lynx."

"I thought of that," answered Billy, "but if he has that six-gun on him, it's just too dangerous."

"But do you really think he'll bring the gun with him?" questioned Molly.

"Knowing Bruno, I think he probably will—for a back-up anyway. He no longer has that much advantage with his deputies. He used to really outnumber us, but that's not quite as true as it used to be," concluded the shepherd dog.

At this point in the conversation there was an impatient knock on the door. When Conan opened it, Brigitte von Shepherd rushed in, carrying a small satchel that seemed to have been packed in a great hurry. "Good. You're all here. I was hoping I'd find you all together."

"Brigitte, what's wrong?" asked Billy, hurrying to her side and removing the satchel from her tired hand.

"You must have come down here in the dark. Are you all right?" asked Molly, taking Brigitte's satchel from Billy and setting it by the fireplace. Her entrance was especially poignant, since it reminded Molly and Clara of their midnight escape almost a year ago.

"Yes, I had to be extremely careful, since my brother was concerned that I might try to leave," said Brigitte.

"What's wrong? Has it anything to do with Sheldon?" asked Molly. "We were expecting him tonight, but he hasn't come yet."

"I'm afraid my brother's put him in the guest chamber and has it well guarded. He caught Sheldon going through his things, and there was quite a row," puffed Brigitte, sitting at the table.

"But was he able to tell you anything?" asked Molly with great concern.

"I only saw him briefly, but he said for me to escape when I could and come down to see you, and you'd explain," answered Brigitte, still out of breath. "All I know is that your council refused to turn Fabian over and that Bruno and Gaylord and their deputies plan to march down here in the morning and arrest him."

"Did he tell you about the gun?" asked Clara.

"Gun? No, I'm afraid not," gasped Brigitte, turning to Billy Bones.

"You better tell her, Billy," decided Conan. "I think maybe that's why Sheldon's been locked up."

Billy Bones explained about the six-gun that Orville had turned over to Bruno. Afterwards, Brigitte was greatly disturbed. "And do you think Bruno might bring this six-gun with him tomorrow?"

"That's what we're concerned about," admitted Billy. "We know he's got at least four bullets left. Of course we're hopin' he won't bring it, but Sheldon heard him firing it in back of The Fortress a couple days ago."

"I'm really sorry, Billy. I just never thought it would come to this. I know you tried to warn me, but I hated to think that my own brother would go to such lengths," cried Brigitte. "So what do you plan to do?"

"The members of our exercise group and Sheriff Lone Wolf plan to congregate in front of the New Meetinghouse where Fabian stays and try to protect him as best as we can," answered Conan.

"But how about this six-gun?" inquired Brigitte. "Aren't you concerned someone will get killed?"

"The council decided that we have to take a stand. They're afraid that Bruno wants to take over the City Council once he gets his way with Fabian," cautioned Billy.

"Then I'm going with you tomorrow morning," decided Brigitte.

"No, it's much too dangerous. We have no idea how it will turn out. And I don't know what I'd do if something happened to you. You know how much I love you," pleaded Billy, taking both her hands.

"I know you do, and I love you, too. But I don't think my brother would hurt me, and I might be able to do some good if he'll only listen to me. And besides I may be able to save lives," insisted Brigitte.

"I still wish you'd reconsider," said Billy, bowing his head. "The fact that you came to the Prairie may inflame your brother even more. To lose you and Sheldon in the space of one night may be more than he can take."

"But maybe I can influence some of his deputies, get them to lay down their weapons," argued Brigitte. "You've got to let me come with you. And besides, if you don't, you know I'll go by myself. Wouldn't you feel safer if I was with the two of you?"

"Well, in that case, but...."

"Then it's settled, and no more talk about it. And Molly, do you have room for me tonight? I'm afraid I'm here to stay, and tomorrow...well, tomorrow will bring what it brings!"

# CHAPTER FORTY-FOUR

# THE ENCOUNTER

The warning bell in the City Hall tower rang at nine o'clock the next morning. By the time Billy Bones got down to Clara's cottage, Conan Greyhound had his club and staff in hand and was already outside. Before they started south along the East Wagon Trail, Brigitte joined them.

"I still don't like the idea of putting you in harm's way," cautioned Billy.

"I know," Brigitte replied, kissing him on the cheek, "but this is my fight, too. And I've got to try…."

Reluctantly Billy took Brigitte's hand as they hurried on after Conan. By the time they arrived at Victor Running Deer's lean-to, they knew by his half-open door that he had already left. When they got to East Main Street, they were joined by Sterling Buck and his brother Ernest.

"At least it's a cool mornin'," yelled Ernest. "I was afraid it might be an oven like it was yesterday."

Sheriff Lone Wolf and Victor were already in deep conversation when they arrived, and Sandy Antelope and Arnold Big Horn were just coming into the yard from the west.

"Ms. von Shepherd!" exclaimed Walter Lone Wolf, seeing Brigitte. "Please, this is no place for you. Billy, what were you thinking?"

"She's hopin' to talk to her brother," said Billy. "She's convinced he won't harm her, and besides, if we didn't bring her, she was comin' on her own."

"Well, if the fighting starts, you're to go inside," ordered the wolf. "Is that clear? I have enough to worry about without lookin' after you. And please stay behind us until it's time to speak."

"Yes, I promise, sheriff," answered Brigitte. "But please let me try to stop this. I used to have some influence over Bruno."

"So how many do you think your brother will bring?" asked Victor.

"I'd say about twenty, if the Peccary Brothers come," answered Brigitte. "But they're not very trustworthy, and they don't like to get hurt. How many do you have?"

"Well, let's see. We're still missin' Lenny Coyote and Philip Fox—so that makes ten," said Walter. "Now that's not countin' Alvin Muskrat and Georgie Beaver. They're the ones that spotted Bruno and his deputies about fifteen minutes ago just north of Beaver Creek Bridge. I tried to send them home because of their size, but they wouldn't leave, so I sent them inside to guard Mr. Lynx."

"So without them, we're only ten," bleated Arnold, "Got any bright ideas, sheriff?"

"For one thing, I'm hopin' a number of Bruno's deputies won't fight us, as at Castle Rock," replied Walter.

"And Mr. Lynx wants to speak to his old lieutenants. He's hopin' some of them will come over to our side."

"But they're comin' to arrest him. Will they let him defend himself?" wondered Sandy Antelope.

"I'm hopin' they will. And...I'm hopin' that most of them don't wanna be here," added the wolf. "Two things

SANDY ANTELOPE, PHILIP P. FOX, ARNOLD BIG HORN, LENNY COYOTE, VICTOR RUNNING DEER

we've got goin' for us: we've got no weak links, and we stand together with one resolve."

As soon as Lenny Coyote and Philip Fox arrived, Sheriff Lone Wolf asked the Prairie's drill members to close ranks around him. "Before we do this, my friends, I just want you to know how appreciative Victor and I are

SHERIFF LONE WOLF, CONAN GREYHOUND, BILLY BONES, ERNEST BUCK,  STERLING BUCK

for your help and for placing yourselves in harm's way. As Mr. Wise Owl put it yesterday, our freedom is very precious to us, and it's our responsibility to protect that freedom."

When the sheriff paused, each animal automatically put his arms around his neighbors' shoulders. "No one knows what this day will bring," continued the sheriff. "All I know is how much we value your friendship and your loyalty. No matter what happens, that will always remain in our hearts. But remember, stay alert. If Bruno draws the gun, don't do anything that will cause him to shoot. Hopefully we can talk him out of it."

As the sheriff was lauding his drill members, Billy spotted Bruno and his deputies advancing down Main Street. "They're comin', sheriff. We better form up."

At that point, the friends closed ranks around the front door of the meetinghouse. When Bruno and Gaylord and their deputies got closer, Billy could see that the Peccary Brothers were not with them, and the group was only sixteen strong. After they came to a halt some twenty feet or so in front of them, Billy noticed that Arnold's two brothers, the two smaller deer, Arthur Elk, and Angus Wolfhound, stood to Gaylord's right and Neevil Cur, Heinz Rottweiler, Bison Bob, Milton Brown Bear, Phineas Fox, and Lenny's three brothers lined up on Bruno's left. As was the case with the Prairie's deputies, all the animals carried staffs and had their clubs tucked into their trousers.

"You might as well turn around and go back home!" stated the wolf firmly. "Our City Council has not charged

Mr. Lynx with any crimes, and you have no jurisdiction here."

"Sorry, sheriff, but the North Woods was part of the Prairie when Fabian Lynx was here before, and we've issued a warrant for his arrest for his many crimes. So move aside and let us take him," barked Bruno, even louder than the wolf.

At that moment Fabian Lynx, Georgie Beaver, and Alvin Muskrat came out of the meetinghouse doors and stood on the steps with Brigitte von Shepherd. Victor Running Deer, Sheriff Lone Wolf, and Billy Bones had placed themselves in front of the steps and their deputies formed a blockade on either side of them.

"I see, Mr. Bones, that you've persuaded my sister to leave me. And Sheldon, you had him too until we locked him up last night," growled Bruno. "Now tell your friends to get out of our way, so we can accomplish what we came here to do!"

"I didn't win Brigitte over," retorted Billy. "You drove her away. Can't you see that she wants no part of this encounter? And, I'd be willing to guess, that neither do most of your deputies."

While Billy was talking, Brigitte took advantage of his lead and stepped down between him and Walter. "He's right, Bruno, this has gone far enough. You know that Sheldon and I stayed with you as long as we could. And we'd still be there if you and Mr. Cougar hadn't instigated this little altercation of yours. Now I beg you, if you have any feelings for me, go home before anyone gets hurt."

"I'll add my voice to that," remarked Fabian Lynx, moving down between Sheriff Lone Wolf and Victor Running Deer. "As I told the City Council, I no longer have a hatred for human artifacts because of my experience these past three years in the outside world, and I've realized the terrible mistakes I made when I was here before. So they've given me a chance to prove myself, and I was hopin' you would too. Besides, a number of your deputies are my friends, and I was hopin' that out of love for me, they wouldn't join this posse of yours."

"Yes, that's true," yelled Milton Brown Bear, as he and Phineas Fox and the three coyote brothers moved to join the Prairie deputies. "We want no part of this!"

"Hold your position!" barked Bruno as he pulled out the six-gun he had strapped beneath his vest and fired a shot in the air above the bear's head. Fearful after the gunfire, Fabian's old lieutenants moved back into formation. "Remember, I have this revolver, and I will not hesitate to shoot any animal that breaks ranks."

"Bruno! In the name of the Great Spirit, what are you doing?" cried Brigitte, taking a step forward.

"Hold it there, my dear sister. That goes for you too. I'll have no insubordination," shouted Bruno again.

"Bruno, please," pleaded Angus Wolfhound, "I have no stomach for this either."

"And you too, Mr. Wolfhound, this is no time for cold feet. We've come this far, and we're gonna finish what we started even if I have to use this six-gun!" shouted the German shepherd. "Now prepare to advance!"

"Wait, Mr. von Shepherd! Listen to your deputies. They don't wanna get hurt any more than my deputies," howled Sheriff Lone Wolf, taking several steps forward. "If you insist on fighting, why don't we make it a one-on-one between you and me?"

"No, I'll not fight you, Sheriff Lone Wolf…but I will fight Mr. Bones there. He wants to be leader of the pack. Let me show him what that really means," snarled Bruno.

"No, if you want to fight somebody, you'll have to fight me," persisted Walter.

"But my argument's not with you, sheriff. You're not the one destroyin' my pack. It's that back-stabbin' Mr. Billy Bones. Either I fight him or we attack now."

From his previous bouts with Bruno, Billy knew he could very well lose. Bruno had an innate savageness he could not match. Sadly he knew that many animals would be hurt or even killed if he refused to fight.

"All right Bruno, I'm yours. But put down your six-gun. I don't want anyone accidently hurt," demanded Billy.

"I'll let my friend Neevil hold it. He'll know what to do if anyone tries to pull any shenanigans," agreed Bruno. "But we'll play it my way—we fight to complete submission."

"No Billy, he's goading you," interrupted Brigitte, trying to hold Billy back. "He won't play fair."

"She's right, Mr. Bones, I play to win," snarled Bruno. "And I plan to beat you up pretty badly—so everyone here can see who's the better animal!"

"Are you afraid of me then?" inquired Walter Lone Wolf, trying to change Bruno's mind.

"No, sheriff, it's Mr. Bones for me. In fact I'll just have target practice with this Mr. Fabian Lynx of yours, if he doesn't agree," warned Bruno, pointing the revolver at the lynx.

"Before you do anything rash, Mr. von Shepherd, let's have at it," stated Billy, moving out in front of Fabian and into the designated space between the two sides. "But let's use just staffs. These clubs are too bulky."

"Fine with me," agreed Bruno. "My staff is all I need for such a small job. But remember, if I win, Fabian Lynx comes with us!"

CHAPTER FORTY-FIVE

## THE DUEL

As Billy Bones and Bruno von Shepherd began circling each other clockwise around the grassy knoll, Billy could not help but notice how cool and crisp the air was. It was the kind of morning where the eye could see everything more clearly. The trees were greener, and the edges of their leaves seemed to almost sparkle in the sunlight, and the sky was a deeper blue with white clouds floating freely in its simple glory.

The shepherd dog almost laughed to himself that he had suddenly become so cognizant of his surroundings. During this fateful morning when he should be focusing on his combative skills, he was seeing everything about him in a new light. A sudden melancholy gripped him as he realized how much the gift of clarity really meant to him. During this crucial moment in his life there was no roll of thunder, no sheets of rain, no driving winds to spur him on to victory, only the realization of how precious and beautiful life was.

"So Mr. Bones, it's come down to the two of us, like I always thought it would be in the end," declared Bruno, jarring Billy back to the task at hand. "You thought you were being so clever, gradually weaning my pack away from me. But what did you ever do for them, may I ask? Were you there in the other world to protect them or keep them fed? Were you there to see that they lived to see this world? No…you were not. It was I who brought them here, not you and your phony goodness. You had no right to take them from me. I'm their true leader!"

"You're wrong, Bruno. I never wanted to take them from you. I wish you could believe me. That's not how my mind works," insisted Billy. "So why don't we just stop this foolishness and go home before one of us gets hurt? And…if we can live in peace and freedom, I'll even bring Brigitte back to The Fortress and live with you there, if that's what it takes."

"But will that bring Conan back? Or Sheldon? Or Molly or Clara? No, I don't think so," snarled the German shepherd. "We need to settle this right here and now, just you and me…here and now…for once and for always."

After his last words Bruno went on the attack. He handled his staff with the utmost ease and was totally in his element. As the two dogs continued to move clockwise, the two lines of deputies gradually started to close around them in a great circle. Billy finally realized he had to use every skill he had learned in the past year just to survive.

"I've got to remember that I'm not only fighting for Fabian but for the soul of The Enchantment. Do we want to live in freedom, or do we want to live under Bruno's thumb and fulfill his personal agenda?" thought Billy.

A sudden onslaught of blows by Bruno von Shepherd brought Billy back to the moment at hand. He could see that Bruno was playing with him, sensing a weakness that could quickly end the match and the Prairie's freedoms.

Just as Billy was losing hope, he began to sense a new strength welling up inside. With a renewed onslaught of his own, he changed the complexion of the match and started driving Bruno back toward his own deputies. It seemed a new force had taken hold of him and was pushing him along, giving him a potency he never knew he possessed.

Ultimately as the duel dragged on, both dogs started feeling an overwhelming fatigue. By this time Bruno had again forced Billy back toward the steps of the meeting-house. Unintentionally, after this latest attack Billy was the first to let his guard down and received a mighty blow to his right shoulder that spun him around. This latest move gave Bruno a clear shot to the back of Billy's head. At that same moment, a voice within Billy's mind's eye screamed, "Duck and dive around him, Billy. You've got him!" Unhesitatingly, Billy Bones obeyed the voice and ducked under and around Bruno's mighty swing, catching the back of the German shepherd's knees with a desperate blow of his own. The sudden strike caused Bruno to fall on his knees and lose control of his staff.

As Billy was about to finish the fight with another powerful blow, he was suddenly pushed to the ground by Fabian Lynx just as a gunshot rang out behind him. When he looked around he saw Bruno von Shepherd clutching his chest and falling to the ground. He realized instantly that the bullet was meant for him. As he started to rise, he saw Neevil Cur running toward him, waving the six-gun wildly in the air.

"No, no, no!" was all that the devastated cur could yell as he fired another bullet, striking Fabian in the chest as well. During the tumult, Angus Wolfhound tried to stop the killing and managed to tackle Neevil from behind. This unexpected movement caused the final bullet to discharge and strike the cur under the chin and upward through the head. In one terrifying moment, Neevil Cur had managed to slay his pack leader, mortally wound Fabian Lynx, and kill himself.

The first animal to react was Milton Brown Bear, who rushed to Fabian's fallen body, helped him sit up, and cradled him in his arms. He was closely followed by the three coyote brothers and Phineas T. Fox. After telling them how much he loved them and how sorry he was to leave them, the lynx turned his head toward Billy Bones.

"Be kind to them, Billy," whispered the lynx, glancing back at his lieutenants. "They…they mean so much to me. And I'm…I'm sorry for all this. So… so do you think I've finally…redeemed myself…so I can become one with The Great Spirit?"

"Yes, Fabian, you've redeemed yourself, and thank you…thank you for saving my life as well," uttered Billy softly.

"Goodbye then," said the lynx, glancing around at his lieutenants one last time before passing on. "I'll…I'll miss you all…terribly…."

When Billy finally left Fabian's side, he saw that Brigitte, Heinz Rottweiler, and Angus Wolfhound were kneeling by Bruno's body. "I'm so sorry, Brigitte. The last thing I wanted was for him to die."

"I know, Billy. And it's not your fault. But I've got to go back to The Fortress with Heinz and Angus for now. They're the only members of the original pack who stuck by my brother after we all deserted him. It looks like even Fritz Terrier refused to be one of his deputies. And poor Neevil, he loved my brother so. He just went out of his mind."

When Billy finally took time to look around, he noticed that many residents of the Prairie had started to move into the combat zone. He realized that most of them had been watching the whole time but had stayed hidden as they were told to do. Beside them he thought he saw the young human again who had smiled at him each time he entered The Enchantment. He was standing by the corner of the meetinghouse and nodding appreciatively to Billy. When he looked a second time, however, the human was gone, and he realized he had only seen him in his mind's eye.

"So Jimmy Stone helped me once again when I needed him," whispered Billy. "But I'd better keep that to myself. They all think I'm a little wacky as it is."

# CHAPTER FORTY-SIX

# TWO MONTHS LATER

Winston Wise Owl had not visited with his friends Mayor George P. Beaver and Chairman Cornelius Van Mink for some time. He was anxious to show them the books that had been returned to him from the North Woods. Although some volumes still remained in the Hill Country, his library had taken on a whole new look. He was also interested in what the City Council had decided after the tumultuous day when the North Woods and the Hill Country deputies tried to march on the Prairie.

"Are you thinking of giving Billy Bones a special award?" asked the owl.

"We tried," answered Cornelius, "but he would have none of it. He did suggest, however, that we honor Sheriff Lone Wolf and the drill group for their collective bravery. I think he felt that since his duel with Bruno von Shepherd ended in three deaths, it was not right to honor anyone, but we must all remember how aggressive action almost destroyed the peace of our little world."

"Those are wise words," said the owl, "but I'd expect

nothing else from him."

"Has he reunited with Brigitte von Shepherd?" inquired Cornelius. "I know that after her brother's death she went back to the North Woods."

"Counselor Turtle informed me that there's to be a ceremony joining Billy and Brigitte in marriage, and also Victor Running Deer and Patience Doe sometime next month. He said it might have to be held outside, since the Old Meetinghouse couldn't hold everyone who would want to attend," chuckled the owl. "Of course, I had to go to Thaddeus for the information. Mr. Bones never said a word about it."

"Well, if Brigitte leaves the North Woods, who'll lead their council?" asked the mayor. "I know Sheldon Sheepdog's gone back down to the Prairie, and he and Molly are having a cottage built across from the greyhounds."

"I can answer that," stated Cornelius, "They've elected Angus Wolfhound for the job, and they've officially separated from the Hill Country. In fact, they both requested a three state meeting again on November 2, which of course we agreed to."

"And Winston, what did Mr. Bones tell you about Fabian Lynx's lieutenants?" asked Mayor Beaver. "I know they were pretty devastated after losing Fabian. I think they thought he might lead them again."

"They went back to The Fortress and are doing fairly well," said the owl. "Apparently they like their jobs and the camaraderie they have together."

"Do you think that if Fabian were still alive, he would

have resorted to his old ways?" wondered Cornelius. "I mean, he did like to be in control, and he had a very magnetic personality. Can an animal change that much?"

"That's something we'll never know," commented Winston. "In fact, I warned Mr. Bones about that when he was deciding to befriend him. Even with his scar, he had a lot of charm and charisma. But I guess we shouldn't dwell too much on what might have been. After all, he did save Mr. Bones' life. And we're all thankful for that."

"And speaking of Mr. Bones," said Cornelius, "has he ever been invited back to the Hill Country to be on their Tribal Council?"

"I know that Lucinda Vulture asked him," said Winston, getting up and looking out the window. "I know that at first he didn't want to, but then he got a special invitation from Gaylord Cougar."

"I imagine Gaylord's anxious to mend fences after falling in line with Bruno so easily," decided the mink. "I know after the tragic encounter at the New Meetinghouse, he and his deputies disappeared pretty quickly."

"And isn't the autumn equinox tomorrow?" asked Mayor Beaver. "Isn't that when they meet?"

"Yes, it is. And I imagine Mr. Bones will be on his way early in the morning. I think I'd like to be in on that conversation," hooted the owl. "Now, I see that Hester Groundhog has refreshments laid out. I say we adjourn and head down to the table."

# CHAPTER FORTY-SEVEN

## BACK TO THE MIST

Since the night before the autumn equinox came on a Sunday, Needles Porcupine and Nosey Coon showed up at Billy Bones' cottage right on schedule. Billy was especially glad to see the two rascals, since he would have to face the Hill Country Tribal Council for the first time since his expulsion.

"How come you're goin' back? They weren't very nice to you," declared Needles.

"I guess I just can't refuse Lucinda Vulture and Maurice Rabbit," admitted Billy. "And besides, I can always leave if they get nasty again."

"Why don't you stop on the way and see Arnold Big Horn and ask if he'll spend next Sunday night with us. Maybe he'll come before Brigitte von Shepherd moves in and spoils all our fun," whined Nosey.

"Now you don't know that," laughed Billy. "She might be good at telling stories. She remembers a lot about the outside world."

"Yah, but she won't let us stay overnight," scowled the raccoon.

"Maybe not, but you can always visit during the day," said Billy thoughtfully.

"But I don't want that. It won't be the same," sighed Needles.

"Things change, Needles, so let's enjoy tonight and let the future take care of itself," smiled Billy.

"Then tell us a story about your battle with Brigitte's brother," begged Nosey. "Everybody's talkin' about it."

"But it's got a sad ending," said Billy, pulling up his chair.

"Yah, but it's a happy one too, 'cause you're alive, and that's the best part," squealed Needles."

The next morning, Billy grabbed a satchel he had packed and left in time to stop at Arnold Big Horn's lean-to. The ram laughed when the dog mentioned the rascals' request. "Sure I'll come, and tell them they can always stay with me on Sunday nights after Brigitte moves in."

After Billy's visit with Arnold, he just had time to stop at Maurice Rabbit's dugout and walk with him to the council meeting. "After today's session, I want to meet with you and Lucinda for a few minutes, if that's okay with you?" requested Billy.

"Does it have something to do with that satchel?" asked Maurice.

"Yep, but I'll explain later," said Billy, patting Maurice on the back.

When the two friends entered the sacred lodge, Billy noticed that his chair had been reset, and the councilors were already in their places, including Orville Bat who had apparently resigned his post in the North Woods.

"Come over and sit down, Mr. Bones," invited Gaylord Cougar, smiling sheepishly. "We already voted, and you've been unanimously reapproved. We hope you'll forgive our misjudgments and accept your seat back on the council."

The tone of the council meeting was much better than Billy had hoped for, and he realized that the cougar had come to the conclusion that Bruno had tried to use him for his own purposes. No one on the council spoke any more about the summer's tragic encounter, and Billy decided that was for the best. After the meeting, Billy met with Lucinda and Maurice.

"Inside this satchel I have the gun and holster that the sheriff gave me after our encounter with Bruno. Walter asked me to bring it back to you, Lucinda, since it came from the Sacred Chamber. He knows we can't destroy it but hopes we'll put it in a place where it will never be found again," explained Billy.

"If we put it back in the Sacred Chamber it's no longer completely safe since there are still two keys," decided Lucinda. "And who knows what the future will bring? Do either of you have an idea?"

"Yes, I do," spoke Billy, "but we need to go to Omar's cave. If you're up for it, we can do it right now."

"I take it you're thinking of putting it inside the mist," guessed Maurice. "But someday someone might still stumble over it—no matter where you place it."

"No, you're wrong," determined the shepherd dog. "But I'm afraid I'm the one that has to put it there."

When the three councilors got to Omar's cave, Billy went over to the boarded-up entrance that separated the cave from the mist. He tied the rope that lay close to the barrier around his waist and then tied the other end to one of the boards covering the entrance. Then he squeezed under the barrier, dragging the satchel along with him. "Maurice, if I pull on the rope several times, come and get me."

"But where are you takin' it?" wondered the rabbit loudly.

"Someplace where it'll never be found," the shepherd called back as he crawled straight into the depths of the mist. Once he got inside the cave where there was complete darkness he kept feeling in front of him. After some time he mumbled, "You don't suppose I've made a mistake!" Finally, however, he came to a place where the floor of the cave ended, and he reached down as far as he could. "Ah, this is the place!" he declared, as he took the six-gun and holster out of the satchel. "Well, so long and good riddance—you've caused enough trouble!" And without hesitating, the dog threw the weapon down into the pit and heard it bounce several times against the walls until it landed far below.

After accomplishing his task, Billy cautiously turned around and followed the rope back to the wooden barrier.

"You threw it into the pit, didn't you, Billy?" deduced Maurice. "It took me a while to figure out a place where no one would ever go."

"I hated to toss it in there, but since we couldn't destroy it, it's a place where no one can ever use it again."

When the three confidants stepped out of the cave, Lucinda turned to Billy. "I think I'll leave the two of you now. And Billy, thank you for bringing peace back to The Enchantment. You've accomplished it twice, both times at great peril to your own safety. Fortunately, this last time you were able to stay with us so we can delight in your company for years to come." With those final remarks, she touched Billy's forehead with her gnarled finger for only the fourth time and then spread her magnificent wings and flew south toward her home on the Twin Peaks.

# CHAPTER FORTY-EIGHT

## THE NEXT SUMMER

"Will you let me come back every summer as long as I live?" asked Billy Stuart III after spending the first week of his vacation with his grandfather, Will Stuart.

"Ah, before long you'll have other things you want to do, but until that time you're always welcome," said Will, still working at his desk.

"No, no, grandpa, I'll always want to come, especially now since Ringer has gotten older, and we can do a lot more things together.

"I'm just glad you're gettin' along now. And isn't it amazing how much Ringer looks like Bones?" said Will, getting up from his desk and easing into an armchair.

"Yeah, he's a wonderful dog, grandpa, but he's not Bones," responded Billy, reaching down and stroking the young dog's head. "I still remember how he used to sense things before they happened. Like that time when a storm was comin' up, and he knocked me down so I wouldn't get hit by that tree branch. I still don't know how he knew it was falling or that I might get hurt."

"Some dogs just have that extra sense," suggested the old man.

"I still say it's strange that he disappeared twice," said the boy. "Do you remember what Danny Red Feather's great uncle—you know, the old medicine man—told us about this passageway that opened up and swallowed animals close by? It's funny how Danny and I used to believe that."

"'Cause you wanted to think that Bones was still alive, that's why," answered Will. "But when he came back to us the first time after being gone for a year, we knew he couldn't have disappeared into such a make-believe place."

"It's fun though, to think he went to some wonderful place and that he's well and happy," decided the boy.

"Yeah, I suppose you're right," agreed Will. "But remember, like everything we really love, he'll always be with you as long as you keep him in your heart."

THE END OF BOOK FOUR
# THE GHOST OF CASTLE ROCK

THE END OF
# THE BILLY BONES SERIES

# RON OAKS

## AGE 6
## WITH GRANDFATHER'S DOG

# BONES

# ABOUT THE BOOK

*The Ghost of Castle Rock* is the fourth book in the series of *Billy Bones and* finishes the story. The books are outgrowths of bedtime stories that I told to my younger brother David and my daughter Laura when they were children. The hero of the stories is a shepherd dog, Bones, based on a remarkable dog that I played with on my grandfather's farm in Humbolt, South Dakota, when I was a boy.

The genesis for the fantasies really began when I stumbled across a number of abandoned trunks, plows, and other articles while hiking in Montana as a young man. I imagined that these deteriorating antiques embodied the hopes and dreams of settlers migrating west to the Oregon Territory. This memory gave birth to the idea that the power of the emotions embodied within these cherished treasures caused a great rift and ultimately a bridge to another world.

# ACKNOWLEDGMENTS

I began writing the *Billy Bones* series on June 30, 2003. Since then my four manuscripts of *Billy Bones* have gone through many revisions. Over those years I owe a debt of gratitude to relatives, friends, and students who have patiently given advice and encouragement. Next, I want to thank the very talented Howard Garrett who painted the front covers of my first three books and Sandy Rothberg who graciously agreed to be my photographer. I also want to acknowledge Louise Carlson and Anne Ostroff who edited and proofread my books. I will be forever grateful for their expertise and professionalism. Finally, I want to especially thank my wife Janet for her patience and support over the years and my daughter Laura who offered a number of suggestions in the writing of the four books, performed content editing, published the books, and generally reassured me along the way.

# ABOUT THE AUTHOR

**RON OAKS** was born in Aberdeen, South Dakota. He earned degree in speech and drama from Yankton College in Yankton, South Dakota; a degree in voice from the Peabody Conservatory in Baltimore, Maryland; and a master's degree in drama from Catholic University in Washington, D.C. Besides *The Ghost of Castle Rock,* Ron has written a musical comedy, a religious opera, a number of plays and poems, and the first three books of the fantasy series: *Beyond the Tall Grass, In the Shadow of the Lynx*, and *Return to the Golden Mist.*

Ron has directed or performed professionally in numerous operas, musicals, and plays from New York to Miami. He was the artistic director of the Garrison Playhouse in Baltimore County, Maryland, for 10 years and taught drama at Glenelg High School in Howard County, Maryland, for 16 years. More recently, Ron stage-directed seven operas for the Municipal Opera Company of Baltimore, Maryland, and numerous shows for the Woodbrook Players in Baltimore, Maryland. Ron was the bass-soloist with the Brown Memorial Presbyterian Church in Towson for many years and teaches voice in the Maryland and Washington, D.C. areas. Ron lives with his wife Janet in Central Maryland.

# THE HILL COUNTRY

# THE NORTH WOODS

1. The lodge
2. Arthur Elk's hut
3. Omar Mountain Goat's cave
4. The store
5. Maurice Rabbit's dugout
6. The Vulture Brothers' hut
7. Lucinda Vulture's hut
8. Deputy Eagle's office
9. Calhoun Coyote's chicken farm
10. Sandy Antelope dugout
11. Cornelius Van Mink's house
12. The Old Meetinghouse
13. Dr. Muskrat's office
14. City Hall
15. Thaddeus Turtle's cottage
16. Elmer Prairie Dog's store
17. Sheriff Lone Wolf's office
18. The boardinghouse
19. The New Meetinghouse
20. Arnold Big Horn's lean-to
21. The new deer's lean-to
22. Georgie Beaver's house
23. Clara Greyhound's cottage

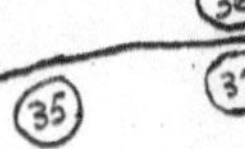


24. Victor Running Deer's lean-to
25. Nosey Coon's tree house
26. Needles Porcupine's hollow
27. Billy Bones' cottage
28. Justin Beaver's house
29. George P. Beaver's castle
30. Gloria Meadowlark's farm
31. Percival Gander's shop
32. The Fortress
33. The Peccary Brother's shed
34. Milton Brown Bear's cave
35. Farmer Jason Crow's farm
36. Winston Wise Owl's tree house
37. Hester Groundhog's tree house